TORMENTED SOUL

TORMENTED
SOUL

Dylann Rhea

DREAM
SEEKERS
Dream Seekers Press

Tormented Soul (Storm Trilogy, Book One)
Published by Dream Seekers Press

@2014, 2024 by Dylann Rhea
Cover design by: Dylann Rhea
Contributing editor: Marin Toni

Published 2024.
First edition Published 2014. Second edition 2024.

ISBN: 979-8-9899102-5-0

For
the one who believed.

PROLOGUE

Seattle, Washington
2014

Heavy rain poured against the asphalt as the witching hour grew near. Shrouded in darkness, the street was illuminated with only specks of light from the off-yellow glow of the streetlamp. The night was empty as a few stragglers scurried for shelter. A muffled rumble of thunder echoed in the distance as a young girl crossed the road. Her skin prickled with each passing breeze, and the fabric of her shirt was one with her skin - useless. Her body shivered and her boots squeaked as she made her way to the small Seattle police station. The glass door opened with ease and took the storm with it as it slowly shut behind her. Without the storm's grumbles, she could hear the inside of her own ear ringing.

Inside there was nothing but shuffling papers and worse lighting than there had been outside. Behind a large oak desk sat an older, stout man minding his own business behind a pair of glasses. Dark bags rested under his eyes. Even at a distance she could see them. Used and empty coffee cups cluttered most of his desk. She hovered in the doorway. Hesitant. Her disheveled appearance, her chopped hair, soaking clothes, along with everything else made her pause. She could leave, but…

"May I help you?" The officer asked suddenly, without looking up from the file on his desk. She froze, trapped in her own thoughts. His eyes only left the file in his hand when she didn't respond. A faint sparkle caught his attention first – a twinkle gleaming off the grayish light from the necklace she wore around her neck.

She took baby steps closer to the desk, closer to the light. An unease began curdling in her stomach. Her body quivered. The officer lowered his glasses when he realized her cheeks were streaked with tears. The expression on his face was a mixture of things. Twisted with suspicion and furrowed with concern. By the time she reached the desk, she realized just how exhausted she was. "Are you alright, Miss?" he asked her.

"Yes…" her doubtful voice shook partially because she wasn't sure herself. "I don't know."

"I'm Officer Marks." He kept his tone light, almost a whisper like how a grandfather would speak to a child. "Are you hurt? What's your name?"

"I'm not hurt," she answered quickly. She glanced down at her clothes, "It's not my blood."

"Can you tell me what happened? Is there someone else who needs help?" Despite Officer Marks and her whispering, the other lingering officers had their eyes and ears focused on the front desk.

"I woke up in an alley," she told him shakily. "A few blocks from here. I…I can't remember anything." Her hand slipped into the pocket of her sweatshirt. She pulled out a dagger. The dark gold handle was laced with more traces of fresh blood. An intricate design with twisted Celtic knots covered the sheath and hilt, forming a vicious golden dragon.

When the officer saw what the girl presented, his eyes widened with disbelief. He placed one hand on his gun holster with the other held out toward her, not aware of her motives.

"I've never seen this before in my life," she placed the weapon on the counter to appease the wary man. "I can't remember who I am."

CHAPTER 1

Three days earlier

"Working out is so overrated," Megan said before taking a bite of her Chunky Monkey ice cream. "I mean, these girls are way too skinny. Who wants to be a size four anyway?" She lounged alongside her best friend Kaden who mindlessly shoved another potato chip into her mouth. Her eyes began to droop at the electric light of the television. Seeing Kaden falling prey to the hour, Megan reached for her couch pillow and slapped her across the face with it. Instead of hitting her intended target, she sent several chips flying out of Kaden's hand and onto the floor. "Wake up! It's only ten!"

"I'm getting too old to stay up this late," Kaden replied, stretching off the couch to pick up the chips that had fallen.

"Too old?" Megan questioned. "These are supposed to be the best years of our lives…and stuff." With a burst of energy she grabbed Kaden's leg and began to rapidly shake her, "We are young! Heartache to heartache we band! Something, something, something with no promises!" she screeched incorrectly.

Kaden kicked her on her side, "Stop it, you're embarrassing me. It's a Friday night and where are we? Sitting in my living room watching reality television and eating bad food. I can feel my brain cells dying as we speak."

"So let's go out! We can go to a party," Megan took a deep, gasping breath, "Or a movie! What about a strip club?! I've always wanted to go to one." Her excitement over the most outrageous things could have been contagious if Kaden had been paying attention. She continued to ramble on about different things they could possibly do, but Kaden stopped listening after the mention of her worst nightmare: mini golf.

After high school, Kaden's world felt as if it had ended, not begun. She was nineteen and had no idea what living a life outside of her family looked like. College wasn't something she ever really dreamed about. She didn't have a collection of brochures and hadn't bothered visiting a campus far or near. In her mind, she was a ghost caught in reality.

While everyone else seemed to enjoy the freedom of being a teenager, Kaden's thoughts were always elsewhere. Most of the time she was just relieved to be out of the house. She kept her head down and her grades decent enough so that it wouldn't warrant any kind of disruption in her home life. And then there was Quinn, her younger sister.

Something unspoken happened as they grew up. A bond formed—one out of survival. When she got home, Quinn was her protection, and she was Quinn's. She helped her with homework and cooked her dinner. And when their mother was away, a calmness fell among the house. But when she would return…

Breaking Kaden's silent thoughts, Megan said, "Are you even listening to me?"

Kaden shot her a quick glance. "Of course I'm listening to you," she sighed. "How could anyone possibly not hear *your* voice?" she teased, knowing Megan was the loudest most outspoken person she had met. "We should go out, maybe tomorrow night. But I'm not going to a strip club. What about…" The only interesting event Kaden knew of was some jazz festival weekend at a pub downtown. She had seen a flier for it at the grocery store the day before. "What about O'Brien's?" she wondered. "They're doing that jazz weekend. I'm sure there will be a lot of strapping young men for you to toy with."

Megan's doe eyes beamed, "That's genius! We can pretend to be these incredibly intelligent scholars studying art history at the University of Seattle." She nodded her head while rubbing her hands together, devious methods at work behind her gaze. "Alright, my name will be…" She leaned back against the couch eyeing the room for assistance to come up with a fake identity, "Victoria Wrench."

"Victoria Wrench?" Kaden repeated. "*That's* what you're going with?" She followed Megan's line of sight to find a Victoria Secret bag that hung on the banister.

"Absolutely! It's sophisticated and sexy," she crossed her legs together on the couch to face Kaden. "Now, your name should be..." Again, Megan searched the room for help. "Torrey Jackson," she said, squinting at Kaden with an approving look. Kaden couldn't tell what corner of the room she summoned the name from.

"Alright then, it's settled. Tomorrow at six you can come over. But we should probably leave around seven thirty so we can get good seats," Kaden said.

"This is going to be so much fun!" Megan cheered, spilling more chips on the floor.

By eleven Megan was gone. Kaden was left to the silence of the house. A wave of relief washed over her as she piled the snacks from the living room into an armful. Carpet turned to linoleum and she managed to flip the switch on to the kitchen with her elbow.

Her heart sank to her stomach when she saw her mother slumped in a chair with a bottle of vodka resting on the table. Kaden's mother didn't seem to notice the lights turn on.

The kitchen was a perfect square–much like a cubicle– with decrepit appliances left over from the previous owners. With her mother seated in the chair in the corner, Kaden felt her skin crawl with claustrophobia. Under her breath her mother babbled to no one in particular in a slur that sounded like it could be from another planet. Whenever Kaden heard the grumblings of drunken talk, she knew to avoid any kind of communication at any cost. What would be the point? Her mother wouldn't be thinking straight and probably would just end up yelling about something random.

"Ugh, I just don't know anymore," her mother began to say as she sipped the last bit of her glass. Her dark brown hair was roughly pulled back into a messy ponytail. The dark circles under her eyes contrasted against her pale skin, making her look more raccoon than human.

The muscles in Kaden's body stiffened as she felt her mother's anger radiate off her body. With eyes boring into her back, she put the junk food away. She suddenly became the prey before the hawk dove in for the kill. She could have made her escape, left her mother to her sulking - but she noticed that no one had cleaned the dishes. The water was rancid with spoiled food but she didn't mind as long as she could wash them in peace. "You know," her mother began, "you always cried."

"What?" Kaden asked even though she didn't want to. After each plate she scrubbed clean, she then placed them in the drying rack with the hope she would escape before the conversation could continue.

"When you were a baby..." Her mother paused to collect her jumbled thoughts. "You cried all the time. It was annoying," she giggled to herself. Milliseconds passed before the giggle shifted into a light sob of tearless cries.

Then Quinn opened the front door.

"I'm back," Quinn announced, shaking off her

raincoat before placing it on the banister. Her wavy brown hair was soaked and frizzy. Kaden watched Quinn slip out of her mud-caked boots and her body relaxed, releasing all the tension she didn't realize she felt.

"Quinn! You're home!" Their mom practically sang. "How is Justin?"

"You mean Joe?" Quinn corrected. There was a hint of annoyance buried in her tone, which made Kaden smirk to herself.

"Yes, Joe. That's what I meant."

Quinn entered the kitchen with her arms crossed. She was only sixteen but she acted much more mature than anyone her age. She took the bottle of vodka from their mother, placing it back in the liquor cabinet where it came from. Kaden knew if their mother hadn't been in the room, she would have dumped it down the drain. "I'm going to go to bed now," their mother stood up grabbing onto any piece of furniture to help steady herself. To their surprise, she somehow managed to make her way up the stairs without falling.

"Has she been like this all night?" asked Quinn.

"I don't know," Kaden shrugged. "I was watching TV with Megan. She must have slipped in through the back door," she hoped to change the topic before getting a headache. Quinn helped her by drying the dishes she had finished washing.

Her mother found comfort in drinking and drinking and drinking. It left Kaden and Quinn dependent on one another. Despite the chaos, Kaden was glad they had one another to rely on. They knew exactly what the other was thinking with just a glance or a flick of an eyebrow. But when it came to looks, they were polar opposites. Quinn took after their mother to the point of being mistaken for her when they went out. She was a few inches shorter than Kaden with thick shoulder-length brown hair. Her hazel eyes matched the olive skin she had, which was a trait she received from their father. On the other hand, Kaden was the tallest of the family, though she herself was considered short at the height of five-foot-two. Her hair was a gorgeous bleach-blond that matched her gray eyes and fair skin.

The girls raised one another. With their mom out of commission most of their life and their dad gone, how could they not?

Their mother's depression weighed on both of them throughout their childhood. And their father spent his nights sitting on the couch watching endless amounts of television with whiskey in one hand and the remote in the other.

The relationship between their parents had always been rough, even before things got bad with their mom. When Kaden and Quinn were young, their parents always argued, mostly because of their moms' depression—which she developed after Kaden was born. She struggled to adjust to motherhood. A few years after that, her father thought it might help her if they had another kid, Quinn. Although at first their mother was better, she continued to struggle with 'inner demons', as their dad used to say. Once her postpartum depression turned into chronic depression, it took a toll not only on her parent's relationship, but their entire family dynamic.

Kaden often recalled one Easter when their mother remained locked in her bedroom with the blinds closed. While she sealed herself off from the world and the girls, their dad seemingly forgot the holiday altogether. He had sat on the couch like any other night, spacing out to what Kaden imagined was a better life. But it wasn't the day that bothered Kaden so much, but the night before. Every Easter was always when their mother tried to put toys out in the living room from the Easter Bunny. Since that year was clouded in sadness, Kaden searched the house for her old toys to give to Quinn. She placed them in the living room to make it look like the giant rabbit had visited while her father sat, watching her. The following morning, Quinn hadn't noticed her new gifts were old gifts. She simply smiled.

"How's Joe?" Kaden asked with relationships on her mind.

"He's good. We walked around the park which was nice until it started raining. I'm pretty sure tomorrow we're going to a movie."

"So are you guys going to get dinner near the theater? Megan and I were planning on going to O'Brien's for the jazz thing they're having."

"Really?" Quinn asked. She half turned to Kaden with a soft smile across her lips, "That sounds like fun. Maybe you'll meet someone." She raised her eyebrows up and down at her sister.

Kaden stifled a laugh, "I doubt it." As they finished up, a curious notion itched at the back of her mind. What if she did meet someone?

As Kaden drifted peacefully in the comfort of her own bed, pictures began to float through her mind. Her brain flashed vague images from her childhood until landing on her sixth birthday party, and then she fell asleep.

In her dream, it was a bright October day for Seattle. The air wasn't too cold yet so she wore her blue fall coat as she sat at the picnic table. The park was barren aside from a squeaky swing. The pink tablecloth that decorated the occasion blew in the wind. Her cake sat in front of her with six colored candles and each seat had a plate laid out for her guests, even though there were none.

The childless park was so unnatural, so eerie. The lonely slide, the empty monkey bars, and the deserted swings blowing in the wind. Even the park bench, where all the mothers sat chatting as their kids ran around playing, was lifeless.

"Happy Birthday," a tiny girl tapped on Kaden's shoulder. She jumped at the sound of the voice, half expecting it to be in her mind. The girl had her long black hair tied in a ponytail. Kaden recognized her immediately as her best friend from class.

"Thank you," she smiled. "Where is everyone?"

Megan shrugged her shoulders and took a seat at the table next to Kaden. "I have a present for you," she reached into her pocket and pulled out a stone, "It's my favorite."

Kaden held the tiny stone in her palm. It was small and shiny, black with deep red blotches. The six year old Kaden eyed the trinket. "I love it," she said, rubbing the smoothness of the stone underneath her little fingers.

"You won't," Megan said.

CHAPTER 11

The next morning Kaden was the second to wake up.

While Quinn showered upstairs, Kaden decided to head for the kitchen to make breakfast. She searched the empty fridge for anything edible but there wasn't much. The only thing that could be made into a meal were the two eggs that sat on the shelf with the last bit of orange juice. So she whisked the eggs together in a small metal bowl when she heard her mother come stomping down the stairs. Without realizing it, Kaden's spine stiffened.

"Morning," her mother said as she entered the kitchen. "What are you making?" Her tone was flat as she spoke, almost lifeless. It was a familiar tone, one in which she usually tried to steer clear of.

"We only have eggs, so I figured I would finish them off. I was planning on going to the store before I go out tonight," she answered, pouring the egg batter into the frying pan. Her mom double-checked the fridge anyway.

"You only made enough for yourself?" she questioned. The muscles in Kaden's jaw tightened.

"No," she replied. "I wasn't going to eat any." The anger growing inside of her boiled. "I don't like eggs, remember?" She sipped the last of the orange juice and placed her cup in the sink.

"You know, maybe if you had a job instead of sitting around doing nothing all day, we could afford to have our fridge filled," her mother roughly shut the fridge door. Out of the corner of her eye she could see that her mother's hands were on her hips. "If you were more like your sister we would be better off." Kaden refused to look at her mother when she compared her to her sister. The frying pan started smoking a bit, which meant that she had burnt the only breakfast in the house.

"I'm sorry?" questioned Kaden, although she wasn't close to being sorry. She had no desire to spend thousands of dollars on the most expensive piece of paper she would ever buy and didn't even guarantee her a job unlike Quinn. As if her life weren't frustrating enough trying to figure out what she wanted out of it, she had her mother nagging her constantly.

"You drank the last of the orange juice?" Her mother's voice made it sound like the most traumatic thing in the world.

"Yes," Kaden sharply replied. "We would have had enough for everyone, but you used it for your cocktails last night." She turned the stove off before slapping the burnt eggs onto a plate, then headed back upstairs where her mother wasn't.

"How dare you talk to me with that tone!? I work my butt off for you and your sister!" Her mother yelled after her. "Yeah! That's right, just walk away!"

When Kaden reached her room, she shut the door behind her and body slammed her bed, "Ugh." With a deep cleansing breath she rolled from her stomach to her back to stare up at the ceiling. She closed her eyes tightly hoping to prevent her headache from turning into a migraine. To soothe herself, she began to hum a random rhythm. The melody was like a story painting a vivid image in Kaden's mind. A place where she could be whoever she wanted to be. A place where no one could find her.

The image was erased when Quinn knocked on the door. "Hey," she said as she slipped through the door. She closed it behind her, "What's mom bitching about now?" Her hair was wrapped in a towel, but instead of her pajamas she had on jeans and a t-shirt.

"The usual," Kaden sighed. "How I'm a failure and everything is my fault." Quinn sat down next to Kaden with her legs folded over one another. "Oh," Kaden almost forgot. "There are some burnt eggs downstairs if you want some."

"Don't listen to her," Quinn said as if it was simple. "She just has her own problems she can't deal with."

"At least I can go out tonight." As much as Kaden disliked going out, it was better than staying in. "Sometimes I just wish I could leave. Take my birthday savings and go."

"You can," Quinn shrugged.

"I know," she admitted. "But I also can't? Does that make sense?" she wondered. Kaden sat up using her elbow to lean on, "It's like…like I've been programmed that I can't, you know? Do you think we'll ever really be able to leave her?"

Quinn pondered the question before answering, "Maybe… I don't know. I'm sure things will get better. Just watch, soon we will be able to do anything."

The daylight faded into a mid-afternoon glow of yellows and orange. The parking lot of the department store was just as vacant as it was inside. After rummaging through endless amounts of clothes, Kaden had only found three things she wanted to try on. "Quinn," she whispered zigzagging through the rows of racks. "Quinnnn," she called like a child bugging her mother. She found Quinn holding an armful of various sparkling shirts.

"What?" Quinn was fixated on the tag of a gold sparkly bra. When she was in shopping mode, Quinn blocked everyone and everything out.

"Are you almost ready to try your clothes on?"

Quinn quickly glanced away from her desired bra, "That's all you have?" Kaden looked at her pile and thought what she had was too much. "You're the one who's going out tonight." She decided to add the bra to her heaping pile of clothes.

"I hate shopping," Kaden shrugged. "I don't have the patience for this."

"Hold on," Quinn half sighed. "Let me just grab a few

more items." She quickly moved around the rack on the opposite side as Kaden followed behind her. As she waited, Kaden scanned the store as other shoppers actually shopped. A younger woman had a little girl in a stroller, an older lady tried on some jewelry, and a woman in the back inspected a dress for loose strands of fabric. Kaden tapped her foot, anxious to get the shopping over with, "Why did mom even agree to take us shopping? I thought she said we didn't have enough money for groceries?"

"She likes to shop when she's mad," Quinn lifted a sweater off the rack. "And sad," she added. "Besides, she's using her credit card. And you are in desperate need of something to wear tonight. Okay, I think I've got enough for now," she grabbed two more shirts off the rack. "Do you want to share a dressing room?"

"Yeah." The girls headed towards the cashier who seemed to be asleep though her eyes were open.

"How many?" she asked before they entered the changing rooms.

They spoke simultaneously.

"Three."

"Eleven."

The woman handed Kaden her number, but had to give Quinn a five and a six since they didn't have one past ten.

As they faced the opposite direction, they began to try on what they had picked out, "Guess what?" Quinn's voice was full of excitement.

"What?" Kaden wondered curiously.

"My favorite band is touring again," excitement

seeped through her words. "We should go see them!" The indie British band was under the radar, as Quinn liked to put it.

"Have you asked mom?" The words fell out of her mouth before she could realize the relevance of her question.

"She'll find out when we go," she turned to face the mirror to get a good look at herself. When Kaden looked over to see what Quinn had on, she realized they were both wearing the identical green button-down. "Damn it," Quinn slapped her arms to her side.

"We'll just share it. We're the same size anyway."

Once they were both done, Kaden exited the dressing room with a new dark blue strapless shirt that she didn't fully like, but Quinn convinced her otherwise. "Trust me. It will go great with some black jeans and boots." Their mother was waiting by the jewelry section, eyeing a silver pair of earrings. "Hey, we're done," Quinn told her as they approached her from behind.

Naturally Quinn began to check out the jewelry as well.

"Okay, you're not getting too much are you?" She saw Quinn with four shirts and a sparkly bra, but didn't question the purchase.

"I'm just getting this," Kaden waved the new top she picked out. "Did you find anything?"

"Just some shoes, and maybe these," she showed both girls a pair of heart shaped earrings. Kaden never really liked earrings; she didn't even know why she had her own ears pierced. She only had one pair of really expensive earrings she received from Megan's parents as a graduation present. They were white gold studs and cost too much money for her to accept, yet Megan's parents refused to take them back. "After all, you're like family," her parents had said.

"Those are pretty," Kaden complimented.

"I know." Their mother replied negatively. Quinn and Kaden widened their eyes at each other. *She always has to bite my head off,* Kaden complained in her thoughts. A small pair of trinity knot earrings caught Kaden's interest.

"What about these?" She held the small box up to her mom. Her mother stared at the box a little too long without saying anything, "Mom?"

She snapped out of her trance looking away from the box, "No, I like these. Let's pay, I want to get out of here."

"I love clothes," Quinn said as she practically skipped to the register.

"Everyone knows you love clothes, Quinn," Kaden teased her sister.

The blaring music seeping out of the speakers matched the frustration tightening Kaden's shoulder blades as she riffled through the contents of her closet. The dark blue top she had just bought complimented her light features perfectly and yet Kaden could not get rid of the feeling that there was something better she could wear. Her room appeared ransacked as piles of clothes she hadn't seen in years occupied her bed. It took a visit from Quinn to rationalize the outfit they had discussed in the car ride home from the store would be best. Black jeans, knee-high boots, and the new blue top. Her hair was pulled back with two bobby pins, one on the left and the other on the right. Kaden studied her reflection in the mirror behind her door for a few minutes. There was a distance between her and the image of her that appeared in the glass.

"Knock, knock," Megan said with a light tap on the door. Kaden's attention shifted off the mirror, "Are you decent?" Megan asked. She flung the door open before Kaden could respond. "Damn, you look hot." She let out a low whistle in Kaden's direction. Megan wore an extremely short miniskirt with a shirt that was a size too small and made her boobs pop out at the top.

"Your boobs were not that big when you left here yesterday," Kaden said as she sprayed herself with some perfume.

"I bought a water bra this morning," she explained with a hint of pride. "I bought you one too, but it doesn't look like you need it." Kaden glanced down at her boobs in confusion. "What do you think of my hair?" Megan spun in a circle for Kaden to get the full effect of her bouncy black locks. It was long, like Kaden's, but wavy with side bangs. Megan's hair was probably her proudest achievement.

"I think I'm extremely jealous," she honestly answered while she slipped on her black pea coat.

"I love the earrings you're wearing," Megan noted. "*Wherever* did you get them?"

"Like you don't know," Kaden threw a small black bag over her shoulder as Megan jumped in the air, her face glowing like a five-year-old.

"You will never believe what I got!" She fumbled

through her purse. Megan pulled two licenses out of her bag, "I got my brother to get us some fake IDs to match our fake names we made up yesterday." Her mouth was wide open waiting for Kaden to have the same overly excited reaction.

"But we have IDs," Kaden reminded her as she scanned the ridiculously flimsy piece of paper Megan handed her.

"Not the kind that can get us alcohol," her voice went up in pitch. "Besides, he owed me a favor after his little trip to California that my mom and dad don't know about. So-rules for the night: we flirt our butts off, but no hookups. And we are out of there if anyone gets too attached. I don't want a repeat of Halloween last year."

Kaden snorted at the reminder, "But Harold really thought you two had a 'connection'," she teased. She sucked in her lips to prevent herself from bursting out in laughter.

Megan glared at Kaden, "We don't talk about Harold. Ever."

Megan drove her parents' car from the outskirts of the city limits to where the jazz festival was being held deep in the city. By some miracle, they found a parking spot on the street not too far from O'Brien's. They were greeted by a line of shivering, dragon-breathed people waiting to get in for showtime. The girls took their spot at the end of the line, hoping they would make the cut of the people who actually got in and the people who waited for nothing. Most of the people in line were either young college students or older couples who already seemed to have a buzz going on.

The building was old with red brick and a huge, glowing green sign that read 'O'Brien's'. Kaden wondered why she thought this would be a good place to go to for their big night out. They were shivering and weren't guaranteed to get in. She peered around the people in front of her to see if she could tell if they would be one of the lucky ones who made the cut. As she was counting the tops of heads, a tall guy wearing a trinity cap with a cigarette dangling out of his mouth walked into her shoulder. "Sorry," she said out of habit. She watched him continue walking without noticing anything happened at all. She grimaced at the arrogance and turned to watch him continue to stride along. He wore a white buttoned down shirt that was tucked in. The sleeves were rolled up to his elbows with a black vest over top. As he walked in the opposite direction of the line, he turned the corner of the building, disappearing before Kaden could say anything else. "This is exactly why I hate social events," she grumbled under her breath. "People are so rude."

"I am freezing my ass off," Megan said through gritted teeth. She hugged herself to keep her arms as warm as possible with her knees bent.

"I told you to wear a coat," Kaden reminded her. "It looks like they're letting people in now."

Fortunately, they were one of the lucky ones who got into the cramped pub. The bar to the right seated six at best while the rest of the seating filled the small room. Two long wooden tables with benches stretched the length of the room where everyone was meant to fit in. On the back wall opposite the stage was a lonely string of colored Christmas lights that aided the dark and dim ambience. "Let's sit near the back," Kaden pointed to an empty space at the first table closer to the exit.

"Why?" Megan asked. "We would be able to see better from the front."

"Just in case we need to make a quick escape," Kaden whispered. Megan rolled her eyes, but took the seats anyway. Kaden sat leaning against the cold back wall with Megan next to her on her right side.

"You're an idiot," Megan said, "we look like two loners back here by ourselves." The two scoped the room as everyone began to find their ways to the seats they wanted with drinks already in hand.

"You know what," Kaden protested. "You're going to thank me for taking these seats." Megan glared at Kaden when two horridly ugly guys sat across from them.

Megan stared for a long moment, "Yes," she said. "Thank you so much." One of the guys had tattoos crawling up and down both arms, extending to his bulky neck where veins looked desperate for water. His shirt was tight on his body, leaving nothing to the imagination. The fabric followed his excessive muscles perfectly and exposed what Kaden hoped were piercings. His almond brown hair was spiked up with too much gel, but that didn't distract her from the stone cold expression resting on his face. His friend beside him, however, made the hairs on Kaden's arms stand on end. He wore a twisted smile—one of mischief and mayhem that sent a cold shiver down her spine. He was younger and scrawny compared to the other man, with a face that reminded her of a rat. His nose was small, the tip of it was red, and he had ears that seemed too big to be on his head. Both wore matching silver chains around their necks the end of which hung beneath their shirts.

"Great," Kaden muttered under her breath.

"Told you we shouldn't sit here," Megan raised her eyebrow.

"Congratulations," she replied, "would you like a medal?"

Megan caught a glimpse of the matching silver chains. "We have two gang members across from us," she leaned close to Kaden. "If I go missing," she added, "you know who did it." Megan eyed the men for a moment, but they weren't paying attention to either of the girls. She waved her hand for Kaden to disregard what she had just said, "Never mind. I forgot I have pepper spray in my purse." She spoke loudly and directly, staring at the guy who looked like a rat. Kaden felt all the blood in her body rush to her cheeks as she desperately searched for something, anything to look at.

"What was that love?" The scrawny one, who Kaden thought hadn't been paying attention, asked in an Irish accent. His voice was surprisingly low and neither one of them expected an accent. Nevertheless, both Megan and the guy were watching each other, almost silently daring one another to look away. Panic tumbled around in Kaden's gut. She let out a deep breath as she scanned the room. She noticed the bulky man was fixated on the stage. No one else surrounding them seemed to notice the tension building between Megan and the scrawny guy sitting in front of her.

Kaden wished Megan would have kept her thoughts to herself.

"I wasn't talking to you," Megan snuffed.

"The name's Riley," he said as he ran his fingers through his bleached hair. "Do you like magic, Victoria?" Megan furrowed her brow when she heard him say her fake name.

"How do you know my name?" Megan questioned. Kaden wondered the same thing. Neither one of them had taken out their fake identities.

"I know a trick or two," he replied. Riley pulled out Megan's I.D from his sleeve and slipped it across the table to her. At first she just stared at it, then grabbed it and analyzed it to ensure it was hers. She frantically opened her purse to check for her wallet, only to find it wasn't in there. "Can't go around without that, now can you, love?"

"Is that supposed to allure me? Who the fuck do you think you are?" Megan was fuming which normally would have shocked Kaden, because she always loved it when boys would flirt with her. But they weren't just boys. They were the psychotic murderer type.

"You're a fiery one," he said, "aren't you?" It was a question, but the way it slipped off his tongue was unnerving. "I could have fun with that." Riley's face twisted with delight, transforming from a creep to someone who studies serial killer documentaries. Kaden took Megan's arm before she could say or do anything else. She lifted her off the bench and pulled her towards the other table.

"Why are we moving?" Megan protested. "*They* should be the ones to leave."

"You didn't even want to sit there," she answered. "They could kill us." Kaden dragged Megan to an empty spot near the front.

As they settled into their new spot, a few people stepped in from the back door into the hallway that led to the stage. They carried their own instrument cases as they each stepped on stage one at a time. The tipsy audience applauded as the performers took their spots. First, an older man with a long gray beard sat to the far left holding a saxophone, followed by a young woman who went behind the drum set. A younger guy stood next to the drum set with a trumpet, and then the last person to come up was the bass player who stood to the far right. The stage lights brightened around them and the pub's dim lighting seemed to grow dimmer.

The group began to play and after every song the audience clapped. Some of the more obnoxious people whistled instead. The last song was a Richard Boulger tune, only played by the trumpet player. It was then that Kaden recognized him as the man who bumped into her outside the pub. Outside, she had missed what the guy looked like. But now, with the beaming white stage lights, she could see his face clearly. He had dark brown hair which was cut short, but spiked up a little in the front. Sweat from his forehead dripped down his smooth face. His leaf green eyes were focused on something at the back of the room. Kaden inconspicuously turned her body to see what the musician was drawn to. At her first glance she didn't notice anything special, but then her eyes followed the path back to where the almond haired man from before had been concentrating on the stage. Her eyes followed the path back to where Megan and Kaden's old seats were. She saw the tattooed man had a disgusted expression while Riley was practically jumping out of his seat. Riley's face was a mix of murderous and joyful. When he caught Kaden looking at him, her face turned the same bright red as before. She turned away from him, but not before he managed a wink. When she sharply turned back in her seat, Megan leaned in closer to her, "What's wrong?" she asked.

"Don't worry about it," Kaden replied, but Megan didn't listen. She turned around only to find Riley making gestures at the girls. Megan's fury got the best of her: so she retaliated with the middle finger. Kaden slapped her hand down before she could cause more damage, "Stop it. I really don't want to end up at the bottom of the Puget." Megan rolled her eyes as they both turned back to the finale.

"He's just a wannabe Backstreet Boy. I mean, seriously, what's with his hair?"

At the end of the show most of the attendees stumbled to the bar for more drinks. The girls sat there for a few minutes before they decided whether or not to leave.

"Maybe we should go," Kaden insisted. She took a quick glance around the room for the two men who had been taunting them all night. Well, mostly Riley, who creepily lingered behind the entire time. She spotted them in the cramped hallway near the back exit, and saw how much taller the tattooed man was compared to Riley. Riley stood in his companions' shadow, as if he were a school boy following a kid two grades above his. But they weren't the only ones in the hall. The trumpet player was there too. The tattooed man clenched the trumpet player's shirt in his hands, pressing him up against the wall. Megan followed Kaden's wide-eyed gaze, witnessing the same scene.

"We should definitely go," Megan agreed. "But next week, *I'm* picking where we will go. And we'll find some boys who don't look like they kill children for fun."

Once outside, the girls were greeted with a light drizzle and a cold breeze. "Shoot," Kaden said under her breath. "I forgot my coat inside. Let's go get it," she said as she took a step back toward the pub.

"You go," Megan replied, watching the massive crowd fumble out of the pub. "It's too crowded. Besides, I have my pepper spray. I'm good," she jiggled her purse for reassurance. "I'll meet you back at the car." Kaden nodded before reentering the pub. This was the one time she embraced her tininess, it was easy for her to swiftly swerve past people. She grabbed her coat quickly off the table, but before she left, Kaden shot a glance to where the men had been arguing. They were no longer there, but a woman waiting for the bathroom, to her relief. Without giving it a second thought she darted past people to get back outside to Megan's car.

Megan was well aware of how dangerous it was to be walking alone at that time of night. Especially since she had a miniskirt on that she should have gotten rid of two years ago. She used her dry hands to warm the upper part of her arms as she walked the few blocks back to her car. Her teeth chattered in the damp, chilly weather. Megan was far enough away from the pub–goers that she decided it was time to speed walk to the car and get to the warmth she craved. Speed walking didn't do much for her since she was just as short as Kaden. It was more like a bunch of quick steps, one after the other. But the blue beaten-up Ford was straight ahead of her and Megan let out a sigh of relief as she got closer.

"Hey, Victoria!" Warm breath hit her ear as the Irish voice whispered. Megan jumped to the side, practically falling, not realizing anyone was near her. She scrambled through her bag for her pepper spray. As she struggled to get it out, Riley spoke again, "Looking for this?" He flipped the small pepper spray high in the air then caught it.

"How did you…" Megan's voice quivered.

"Like I said before," Riley tossed the bottle into the air, "I know a trick or two." Once it reached its highest point, he snapped his fingers together making the bottle disappear into thin air.

Fear paralyzed Megan. She threw her purse at him in an attempt to run past him back to the crowded pub for help.

"Hel—" She began but was cut off by Riley's hand over her mouth.

"Now, now, love. Don't spoil all my fun," he whispered into her ear. Megan kicked every which way she knew how, but Riley only laughed in her ear, amused by her failed endeavor. Warm tears streamed down Megan's cheek, as she tried her best to call out for help. "Don't worry, I've got you, lass. We're going to have fun."

Chapter III

One year ago

Megan and Kaden sat on the ice cold metal of the bleachers of their high school football field. The air was crisp around them, on the brink of the first snowfall. Watching football games was one of the few activities they could do on a Friday night that they both enjoyed. Still, Kaden wished she had thought to bring a blanket for her seat. The warmth of the hot chocolate in her hands was comforting, and the crowd was rowdier than usual. Parents and teachers-but mostly students-who gathered around the snack shack, without paying much attention to the game.

Kaden glanced down from the top of the bleachers to the huddles of her classmates. There were two kinds: eager ones, glad to be out of the house and mess around, and the popular group. Both Kaden and Megan immensely hated the popular group. They drove fast in new cars and wore brand names and got expensive gifts. They traveled to far away places and partied in basements and never thought about much else other than themselves. It drove Kaden crazy. But she was envious of the freedom they had.

"Hey there!" Heather Godwin waved as she climbed to the top of the bleachers where Kaden and Megan purposely sat to avoid socially awkward situations. Unfortunately for them, Heather didn't make the connection.

"Hey," they sighed unenthusiastically in unison. Kaden prayed she was just being polite by greeting them and that she would leave them alone. Instead, she took the spot right next to Megan.

"It's been forever," she gleamed. "I feel like I haven't seen anyone this year, you know with *all* the extra stuff. I've been so busy with my college apps."

"Apps?" Megan repeated, unnerved by the shortening of the word applications for no reason.

"Yeah, you know, applications," she answered in an overly cheery manner. The Vice President of their class, hospital volunteer and annual church bake sale runner, Heather was a peer that Kaden and Megan tried to avoid. Heather was extremely smart, putting her in almost every honors class. She was the leader of the debate team, which most students only cared about because they were able to miss class for in-school debates. "So how have your college applications been going?"

"They're going," Megan said. She sipped her coco and nudged Kaden as if to say 'your turn'.

"I actually think I'm taking a gap year to figure out what I want to do." Kaden leaned past Megan to see Heather with her radiant smile that she was ninety percent sure never left her face.

"That's…cool," Heather said as she nodded her head in response, like it was such a brave thing to do. Though it was supposed to be a nice comment, there was an undertone to her words. Kaden imagined what she was really thinking: 'Really? That's so weird and not the norm'. "Well," she said as she cleared her throat. "*I'm* hoping to go to Stanford." A half smile curled her lip with a faint shrug, "UCLA is my backup school."

Megan shifted her body to face Kaden, "I want to punch her," she smiled through her teeth.

"Did you say something?" Heather asked over the roars of the cheering crowd.

"Just that we should get going," Megan stood up suddenly. Kaden stood then, giving her butt a relief from the bleachers. They slid past Heather into the aisle, "See you later."

"You're leaving so soon?" Heather innocently asked. Megan didn't bother to answer her.

"Yeah," Kaden said. "It's really cold out here. We'll see you in school." She waved goodbye politely, feigning a weak smile to Heather's overbearing one.

"I hate her," Megan said, throwing the last of her hot chocolate in the trash bin at the bottom of the bleachers.

"She means well," Kaden replied. "I don't get why people are so obsessed with college though. Obviously she's getting into wherever her heart desires. It's like she *needs* to be congratulated."

"I know," Megan agreed as they made their way up a steep hill to the parking lot. Megan bumped into Kaden lightly on purpose, making Kaden flail her arms in the air to avoid falling down the hill, which would have been utterly embarrassing seeing how the entire football team was but a few yards away.

"I will kill you," Kaden said in a southern accent. Megan gave her a weird face and they both burst out laughing.

"What's with the southern accent all of a sudden?" Megan asked through her laughter.

"You caught me off guard," Kaden said, defending herself. "It just came out that way." She managed to balance herself to finish the hike up the hill.

"This is why we're best friends," Megan laughed as she relieved a sigh.

"Everyone else in this city sucks," Kaden agreed. "Thank god I have you."

They ventured into the full parking lot in search of Megan's mom's car. It wasn't hard to find it, considering it was an old, beat-up Volkswagen. It stuck out like a sore thumb compared to all the brand new cars.

"No matter what happens," Megan began, "promise me we'll be best friends until we die." She unlocked the drivers' side and then leaned over to unlock the passenger side.

"We are going to become crazy cat women and do the most ridiculous things together. Trust me," Kaden reassured her. "Now let's go back to my house and make fun of people."

"Only if you have Chunky Monkey," Megan responded before starting the engine.

"I don't think I do," Kaden thought. "But we can stop and get some."

They made their way over to the nearest 7-Eleven to get some snack foods before going to Kaden's house. "We need peanut butter and Oreos, the ice cream, and some chips," Megan commanded as they swerved in and out of aisles looking for their goods.

"Do they have Twizzlers?" Kaden scanned the shelves top to bottom.

"I don't have enough money for that and all the other stuff. It'll have to be a sacrifice."

The lack of Twizzlers bummed Kaden out, "Okay, then we better hurry before I find some." Seconds later Megan came shuffling around the aisle with her arms filled with the snacks they decided on. "That was fast."

"I don't mess around when I'm hungry," she said as she laid their items on the counter. A travel magazine near the front caught Kaden's attention. The sharp green hills on the cover and ruined castle made her pull the magazine off the rack. There was something breathtaking about the Irish countryside. She flipped the pages to find cobblestone streets, pubs, and castles galore. But the green grass against the pale blue sky was captivating.

"Come on, let's hit the road," Megan interrupted with two plastic bags in her hands.

"Give me five minutes," she said. She lifted her head from the magazine for only a few seconds before being drawn back to the images. "I just want to glance at this."

"I'll wait in the car," Megan shrugged. In her wake the door's bell rang out. The boys in the back continued to play around with the machine, speaking loudly intentionally. The noise was too distracting for Kaden to pay attention, so she decided to forget about it and leave.

Outside, she saw the drivers' seat was empty. "Megan?" Kaden called looking around the parking lot. She walked around the car to find the bag of stuff they had just gotten, scattered on the ground. "Megan!?" Kaden began to panic.

"Boo!" Megan yelled from behind her.

"What the hell!? You gave me a heart attack!" She held her hand over her rapidly beating heart.

"Oh come on, it was just a joke," Megan teased.

"Don't ever do that again," Kaden warned. She made her way to the passenger side of the car. The relief she felt didn't drown out her heart still racing in her chest.

Megan started the car up when she paused. "I totally forgot," she said suddenly. "I'm so sorry."

Kaden shrugged her apology away, "Don't worry about it," she said. The unwanted panic eased behind her chest and her nerves began to settle back down to a normal level.

"Can you tell me the story again?" Megan asked. She tried to hide her guilt in her tone, but Kaden could hear it.

"Why?" Kaden wondered. It was a funny story, she figured, one she had told a hundred times, but it wasn't fond.

"Because it's funny," Megan said. Kaden's face

expressed how irritated she was. "Oh come on! I revel in your misery."

"Fine," she sighed. "But you have to promise that you'll never do that to me again."

"Promise," Megan held up the 'scouts honor' hand signal.

"One day my mom, Quinn, and I went to the grocery store," she began as Megan pulled out of the lot. She headed in the direction of Kaden's house. "It was before I had a cell phone, so I must have been eight and Quinn was six. The two of us went to get something while my mom went to grab some milk. After we got whatever it was we needed, I strolled back to where my mom *should have been*." Megan snorted, lowering the music because she knew the funny part of the story was coming. "I was panicking because I had no idea where she was, so I pushed the cart up and down every aisle twice and I still couldn't find her. And the entire time Quinn sat in the cart playing with the food and saying 'Can we get Goldfish? I want Goldfish. Where's the Goldfish?' over and over again. I kept telling her to shut up but she wouldn't listen. This stupid little kid's voice was on repeat asking for damn Goldfish but I was trying to find my mother," Kaden went on to Megan's amusement. "Anyway," she continued. "By the time I figured out I should go to the main desk, I let Quinn open a bag of Goldfish so she would shut up. And the whole time I found out later my mom left the store without us."

"Oh God," she wiped the corners of her eyes from tears. "That's my favorite story. Your mom is such a..."

"I'm glad you enjoy it," Kaden laughed along with her

despite how she felt about her mom abandoning her.

"Where was your mom?" Megan asked as she changed the song.

Kaden wracked her memory for the answer. "At the park I think, I can't remember."

"Well," Megan added in an upbeat tone, "at least you have a funny story to tell at dinner parties."

CHAPTER IV

When Kaden discovered the deserted car, her heart sank to her stomach, "Megan?" she called out, "This isn't funny." She listened for a snicker but there was nothing but the wail of an ambulance fading into the distance. There was nothing but asphalt and an abandoned car. "Come on," Kaden called out again to the darkness of the alleyways. "This isn't going to work," she swallowed the lie.

Panic began to reset in her muscles, tightening her chest. She dialed Megan's phone over and over again but only got her voicemail. *Maybe she went back to the bar*, Kaden hoped as she hustled back to the pub. With the night just beginning, people entered and exited the bar at a steady pace. As each person left, Kaden asked if they had seen a girl matching Megan's description. In between each person, she dialed Megan's phone hoping to catch something other than her voicemail. The more time that went by, the tighter Kaden's chest grew. She thought about calling Quinn, just to have someone to talk to, but the thought was lost among her worry. When she found Megan, she was going to kill her.

Rain began to trickle down on the pavement. The temperature dropped and wind started to sneak its way around the buildings to meet her cheeks. She ignored the chill that lingered in her veins as she walked around. *Breathe*, she told herself. The breath she exhaled came out as a frigid cloud of warmth. *This is Megan.* Megan. *She's fine.* She tried to soothe her racing mind, but the thoughts kept coming. She couldn't get past the feeling growing in her gut that something was very, very wrong.

"Megan!" She screamed into the night. Kaden made her way around the pub, to the back exit. *She probably went to the bathroom,* she told herself. *Maybe she got lost.* The excuses varied in her mind and some were ridiculous but it was enough to keep Kaden moving. Her vision started to blur with her watering eyes, "MEGAN!" She screamed one last time into the back alleyway. It was a dead end.

"You looking for someone, lass?" Kaden was startled to hear a voice from the darkness. It was an Irish accent. *Riley*, she grimaced at the thought. The alley was only lit by the exit sign above the back entrance. Through the darkness she couldn't be sure it was him. Steam mingled with smoke polluting the air and mixing with the darkness. She couldn't see the person walking toward her, but her fists clenched at her sides and the muscles in her jaw tightened. She heard his shoes hit small rain puddles. "You did this!" she seethed. "You know where she is!" As soon as the silhouette of the man's body appeared before her, Kaden forced all her body weight to slam him against the wall of the other building. "Where is she?" She swung her arm for a right hook across his jaw, but he grabbed her wrist just before she was about to hit his face. He grabbed hold of both her wrists, twirling her swiftly so she was backed up against the wall.

"Do you make it a habit of punching strangers?" he asked as she struggled to gain control of her wrists again.

"Let me go!" she demanded. "I'm going to report you to the police!" Kaden kicked his shins in hopes that it would injure him in some way, but it was like kicking a wall. It hurt her more than it did him.

"Report me for what?" he wondered. "Would you stop struggling? It's quite annoying." The little amount of time she had spent with Riley, she knew his voice was threatening in every word he spoke. Whoever had her pinned, there was a softness in his voice that made her stop. His voice was calmer and didn't make the hairs on the back of her neck stand up. Once she stopped attacking his ankles, he let go of her wrists. Kaden moved past him and into the dim light, only to find that it was the trumpet player facing her. The same person who had been arguing with Riley and the tattooed man in the hall. He had remnants of blood spatter on the collar of his white shirt with a small cut on his forehead.

"Where's my friend?" Kaden asked him sharply. She made sure there was distance between them. A few strides and he could grab her and restrain her as he just had. But Kaden didn't care if it meant finding Megan.

"How the hell should I know?" He reached in his pocket for something. She slid back a bit farther away from him. "Relax," he said. "I'm just getting my cigarettes." The trumpet player pulled a single cigarette out, lighting it too quickly for Kaden to see the match or lighter. She watched him take a deep drag, releasing it out into the rest of the smog. He gestured to her to see if she wanted a drag. Kaden grimaced.

She was still dazed by the entire ordeal. "You fought with those men," her voice shook more than she intended. "They were taunting us, her, and now she's gone. I think they took her," she added. "You know them, right?" The trumpet player took another long drag of his cigarette. He studied her with suspicious eyes while she searched for answers in his. "Tell me," she begged. "Please. I already called the cops. You can tell them who the guys were. The cops can question them. See if they know where she is. You won't get in any trouble. I'll make sure of it. Just please tell me what you know."

"You called the cops," he sounded surprised. "Well," he chuckled, "that'll be interesting."

"Why?" she wondered. "Are you saying they can't help? Or are you saying—" She didn't want to verbalize what she was thinking, that Megan could already be hurt or violated or worse. Tears started to form in her eyes again, but she forced them away just as they appeared.

"Don't—" he said genuinely. He reached out to pat Kaden on the back, but she half stepped away warning him not to touch her. Though she was completely scared and overwhelmed, it wouldn't change the fact that she knew he knew something and she wanted to know what it was.

Red and blue lights flashed as a squad car slowly crept past the dark alley. Both Kaden and the trumpet player moved their heads in the direction the lights were coming from. Kaden walked toward the car, waving her hands to signal them to stop. "Over here!" she called. The spotlight the cops were aiming down the alley landed on her. As soon as the cops realized Kaden was the one who needed help, the car stopped and a tall officer stepped out of the passenger seat. "Officer, this man knows who may have taken my friend," Kaden pointed behind her as she approached the officer.

"You're the one who reported your friend missing? My name's Officer Hendricks," he replied. He wore a dark uniform with his raincoat over top.

"Yes, yes. We went to the pub and these guys were there, and one had a lot of tattoos, the one guy's name was Riley," she rambled then took the officer's arm to direct him to the trumpet player. "But this man knows them. He spoke to them after the show." She dragged him further into the alley. When they were near the back exit of the pub again Kaden came to a halt. No one was there, and the trumpet player was gone.

But he couldn't have gone anywhere, there was no way out, Kaden thought. *The alley had a dead end; he would have had to pass them to get out.* Kaden tugged at the back door to the pub but it didn't budge.

"Miss, have you been drinking tonight?" Officer

Hendricks asked un-amused. His partner was by his side with a notepad in hand ready to take notes.

"No. I haven't, I swear. He was the trumpet player." She searched every inch of the back area. No fire escapes he could have climbed, no broken windows to climb through. There was a dog lying next to the dumpster she hadn't noticed before.

Maybe he's hiding in the dumpster, she thought as she walked to the massive garbage can. Kaden lifted the heavy lid only to find nothing but a couple of bags of garbage. She stood there in confusion. The dog shifted its position next to her. Kaden's eye was drawn to a small fading light on the ground that turned out to be the trumpet player's cigarette. She bent down, grabbing it to show the officers as proof.

"See, this was his. If you ask the owner of the pub who he was then I'm sure we can track him down so he can tell you who the men were."

"Miss, are you under the influence of narcotics?" The female officer asked after the two officers exchanged impatient looks.

"What?" Kaden's voice rose up a pitch. "No, why would you ask that?" She realized she was still holding the cigarette so she flicked it away.

"Can we see some ID?" Hendricks asked. Kaden reached in her pocket for her wallet and then passed the officer her ID. Hendricks inspected it for a few minutes and passed it on to his fellow officer. "Miss, are you aware it's against the law to carry a fake identification?"

Kaden had completely forgotten about the stupid ID. She felt like an idiot for not giving him her actual ID. "No, wait— I mean— yes I am aware it's illegal to have a fake ID, but here," she handed him her real license. "My name's Kaden Storm." Her panic had her in a frenzy. The adrenaline and everything wrong made her come off as a lunatic crackhead.

"Well, Miss Storm, we'll be able to escort you home in our squad and we will be confiscating this identification," the female officer, whose name Kaden didn't catch, sounded as frustrated as a high school math teacher trying to teach vacant faces.

"Wait," she started. "So that's it? You're not going to look for my friend?" A fury burned deep inside her.

"Miss Storm," the other officer said. "Clearly you're under the influence of something. Now we can take you home or down to the police station for a drug test."

"I'm not on drugs! Her car is still here," furiously Kaden refused to believe the authorities she was taught about in grade school would not even acknowledge a missing girl.

The officers exchanged looks, "Is there any chance your friend could have gone home with someone?"

"No. She wouldn't do that without telling me," Kaden explained to Hendricks.

"We'll have to take you down to the station if you want to file a report," he answered. His partner turned away from them to speak into her walkie-talkie.

"I don't want to file a report; I want to look for her now. She could be dead by the time we get to the police station. The guy I was telling you about knows the men that have her."

"We can't do anything until a report has been properly filed and the person has been missing for at least twenty-four hours without any contact to her guardians."

"She could be dead in twenty-four hours!" Officer Hendricks took Kaden's elbow to guide her to the squad car.

"Come with us, Miss Storm, we'll get everything worked out at the station," the woman said.

"Please, you have to find her!" She yelled, squirming to get free. Hendricks's grip was too tight for her to pull out of.

The female cop was already by the driver's side, just as Hendricks opened the back door to the car. Kaden twisted as much as she could, but still had no luck as she was forced into the seat. The door was about to be shut when the dog from the alley came up behind the officer and bit his right leg.

"What the fu—" Hendricks screamed out, Kaden took the opportunity to dart past him. She ran as fast as she could down the street, past some buildings into another alley that would lead her away from the cops. The female cop chased Kaden for a while but must have slowed down because Kaden couldn't hear her panting anymore. What she did hear were the paws of the dog catching up to her. She ran faster. She couldn't risk getting attacked by a mad dog while being chased by the cops. But the dog galloped a good five feet past her. The big gray dog slid through a door that was ajar, and then proceeded to turn and bark uncontrollably at Kaden. *He was helping me*, she thought. *A dog is helping me.* Kaden followed the dog into the cold and dark building. She could wait here until the cops decided to give up looking for her.

The building was silent except for the occasional dripping sound of rain on the roof. Kaden peeked out of the door into the alley for any sign of life, but she heard nothing, no sign of anyone. She decided to stay inside for a few more minutes before leaving again. She still didn't know how she was going to find Megan or where she would go for help. A rustling noise came from behind some crates, but she dismissed it as being the dog. More noises formed from behind her, so she took a quick glance back but couldn't see anything unusual. She needed to keep her focus on the alley and how she was planning on finding Megan.

The blue and red lights of the cop car reflected off the window of the adjacent building. Kaden slowly backed up further into the building to ensure she wouldn't be seen. Once the flashing lights passed she slipped out into the night again. The dog nudged past her, trotting out of the alley and onto the street. She dialed her phone to call Quinn as she continued to search for Megan closer to town. "Hello?" Quinn sounded half-asleep when she picked up.

"I can't find Megan. I called the cops and they aren't going to do anything until she's been missing for twenty-four hours. There were these guys who I think may have had something to do with it, but I can't find the trumpet player to help me prove it and—" Kaden babbled into the speaker.

"Wait," Quinn said. "What are you talking about? Are you drunk?" she asked.

"Why does everyone keep asking me if I'm drunk?

No, I'm not on drugs either. And if you were paying attention, Megan is missing." Kaden peered down every alleyway as she spoke into the receiver.

"Are you sure she didn't just hook up with someone like last Halloween?"

"No she didn't, we agreed not to. And I'm freaking out," she whispered as she passed a couple holding hands. The darkness of the streets became brighter when Kaden reached an intersection with more businesses. She pushed the button that would get her across the street faster, "What do I do? I'm not just going to leave—" her thought was abruptly interrupted when she saw the trumpet player strutting down the other side of the street. "Quinn, I gotta go."

"What? Why?!" she heard before she cut her sister's voice off completely.

"Hey! Trumpet player person!" she shouted to the other side of the street. Kaden couldn't wait for the pedestrian sign to tell her to walk across; she dodged past moving cars to reach him as he turned the street corner. "Hey!" A car simultaneously honked their horn at her for jaywalking.

The trumpet player's attention was finally caught when he heard the pitter patter of boots following him. He turned around to face her, "And here I thought a crazy girl was calling after *another* trumpet player."

"How did you get out of the alley? The pub was closed, you couldn't have gone back in," she breathed deeply to catch her breath.

"Obviously I got out of the alley, I'm standing right

here." He held his hands in his pockets for warmth.

"I didn't ask *if* you got out of the alley, I asked *how* you got out of the alley. So? How did you get out of the alley?" She repeated her question which she thought was a simple one.

"I ran," he responded as he turned back around to walk forward.

She took a few quick steps ahead of him to step in front of him and block his way. "You couldn't have run past me and two officers without any of us noticing," she protested.

"Well, I did," he shrugged, "so if you'll excuse me." He pushed past her easily. Kaden turned and continued to follow him anyway.

"How do you know those men?" she asked. "Just tell me where I can find them so I can send the police to them. Your name won't even be involved."

"You know, some people would call this stalking," he slightly turned his head to face her.

"Well, excuse me for wanting to find my friend from psycho kidnappers who were last seen with *you*." The trumpet player picked up his pace, so Kaden did as well.

"You're really getting annoying," he told her, sharply turning another corner.

"What's really annoying is someone who refuses to cooperate. I can call the cops again," she warned him.

"Yes, because that worked out so well the first time. Just another tweaker runaway, this city has plenty of them."

"How do you know that?" Kaden wondered since she didn't see him in the alley.

"I have a dog-like sense of hearing," he said simply. Kaden scrunched her face and grabbed him by the elbow to stop him in his tracks.

"Wait," she held her hand up. "Are you trying to tell me that you are a dog?" *Great. He's insane and I am too,* she thought to herself.

"No," he sounded disgusted by the thought. "Are you?"

"Those men were there for you tonight, weren't they?" He didn't respond to the question but picked up his pace with Kaden barely keeping up on his heels. "I'm not leaving until you tell me what the hell is going on. Where is my friend?" He stopped abruptly in his steps, Kaden not aware he was going to stop, bumped into his back.

"Your friend is a lost cause," he said as if it were a fact. "If you were smart, you would go home and wait for the police to give you the bad news."

He started to walk away from her as she yelled after him, "You are a pathetic coward! You know where she is and what's going to happen to her but you won't do a damn thing about it!"

He turned to face her sharply with furrowed brows. "You know," he began with anger not so subtly drifting through his tone. "It's not nice to call people names. I am anything but a coward. If you want to go after the girl, you'll die."

Kaden planted her feet firmly where she stood. "It doesn't matter what it does to me," she told him. She stared into his harsh gaze and shook her head slightly. "I'm not going to stop. I have to at least try to find her."

He squinted as a hint of admiration swirled in his eyes, "Even if it kills you?" he wondered.

"Even if it kills me," she answered. "She's my family."

The trumpet player lifted his head slightly, "You'll die for her."

"Yes," she nodded.

He remained silent for a long moment. Kaden wasn't sure if she should say anything else as, what sounded to her like a frustrated sigh, escaped his mouth. "Alright," he finally agreed. He took a step closer to her, "But, a fair warning, this was your choice." He waited for a moment allowing her time to change her mind she imagined. But she didn't. She wouldn't. "Follow me," he nudged his head in the direction he was headed.

"So that's it?" Kaden asked. "You'll help me now? Just like that?"

"You called me a coward," he said. "I take offense to that. We'll just have to see who the real coward is as soon as you know everything."

"What's your name?" Kaden asked as the two continued to speed walk in and out of alleys to different streets. He seemed to know exactly where he was going, which frightened Kaden a bit since he was a complete stranger. With every one step he took, it was three for Kaden which made her lose her breath keeping up with him.

"Finley," he answered, taking a quick glance back at her.

"I'm Kaden," she replied although he didn't ask.

"I know," Finley said as he weaved his way to

wherever he was leading her. She looked over at him curiously, "I have very sensitive hearing," he added before she could ask how he knew her name.

"Right," Kaden said with uncertainty.

"We're here," is all he said back.

Kaden looked up at where 'here' was to find a diner that had seen better days. "Here?" she asked. Inside, she could see only two people and both were employees, not anyone remotely close to what Riley had looked like. "Are you serious? This is where Megan is?"

"No," he replied. "This is where food is, and I never joke about food. This way," Finley held the door open for her. She remained in her spot in disbelief for a moment before entering the diner. Standing in the doorway, she could see there was an older man who sat along the luncheonette talking to the waitress. And the cook was slouching behind the small window frame with a view into the kitchen. Finley slipped around Kaden to get into a booth not far from the door. She took the seat across from him and waited patiently for him to speak first. He flipped the pages of the menu several times, nonchalantly. Kaden stared at him. She wasn't exactly sure how this would help Megan. Finley took a toothpick from the table to chew on, "You're not going to eat?" he wondered.

"How is eating going to help find Megan?" she asked. If she was being honest, her stomach was in too many knots to eat anything.

Finley scrunched up his face like he forgot, "Who?"

"My friend, Megan." She replied with irritation. He nodded as if he remembered.

"So you're not eating then?"

"No," she said flatly. "But I am starting to think you're useless." Finley shot her a quick glance before he closed the menu. A red-haired waitress approached them.

"What can I get you two?" she asked in a way too cheery fashion for what time it was.

"We'll take two coffees and a short stack," Finley answered with no eye contact to the waitress. She jotted down the order and headed for the kitchen. Kaden continued to stare at him, mostly because she didn't fully know what the hell was going on.

"Staring is impolite," Finley remarked. He watched a rain drop drip down the window outside and Kaden watched him. When he realized she was not going to look away, he returned the same stare.

"Who are you?" was the first question she wanted the answer to. "How are you involved with those guys? Are you part of some gang—" he squished his face together as though it was the furthest thing from the truth, "or something?" she finished. She craved the answers to her questions; there would be no point in being with him if he wasn't useful.

"I can be anyone," he said simply. "You're going to have to be more specific." His eyes held her curious gaze. He didn't blink or flinch once. The waitress returned with their order, placed it down, and went back to flirt with the man she was talking to. Finley took his utensils and began to saw at his pancakes. He proceeded to stuff his mouth and smile at Kaden, "I do love pancakes."

Kaden slid his plate far enough away from him where

he couldn't reach it. Tired of his nonsense, she had half a mind to walk out of the diner and head back to Megan's car. Finley cocked an eyebrow, staring longingly at his short stack, "I'm not a *dog*."

"I didn't think so," she said. She slid the plate back over to him. He put his fork and knife down and leaned forward.

"You *really* want to know what happened to Miranda?" he questioned, slowly moving back against his seat awaiting her response.

"Megan," she corrected.

He shrugged, "Same difference." The muscles in her jaw began to tighten. She wanted to spill his coffee in his lap for wasting her time. She wanted to look down every street from the diner to the pub. She wanted to know her friend was okay.

"If you don't help me," she warned. "I'll just go around looking for her myself, even if it takes all night."

"Here's what's going to happen," he began. "I'm going to attempt to explain what happened to your friend. You're going to think I'm completely insane, and then, when you get past that part, I'll escort you to the last place I know those guys were located. See this coffee?" He pointed at the white mug before him and the darkness inside. Kaden stared down at the mug and looked back up at him. "Watch it."

She reluctantly glanced back down at the coffee. "I don't—" Kaden started.

"Just wait," he cut her off. Kaden waited for a moment. Before her eyes, she watched as the blackness shifted. From dark as night to milky hot chocolate. She blinked. It was hot chocolate. Kaden looked from the cup to him and back again. She pulled the cup toward her and the richness of chocolatey goodness hit her nostrils. She glanced at her own cup of coffee and the burnt scent that drifted out of the mug.

"Maybe I *am* on drugs," she muttered under her breath. Finley slid his mug back toward himself and returned his attention to his pancakes as if nothing happened. "Okay," Kaden breathed. "Someone slipped something into my water." But she didn't order a water, or a soda, or a beer, like Megan had wanted.

"You're not on drugs," he told her but then thought to himself for a minute. "Well, I don't think so anyway. What you do in your spare time is your business." He shoved more pancakes into his mouth.

"This has to be some kind of magician thing or an illusion, right?" Finley snorted loudly with amusement at her attempt at rationalization. "Are you a magician? Like, besides being a trumpet player you perform magic for kids parties?"

He rolled his eyes and dropped his fork and knife suddenly, "A magician?" he repeated with disgust. "Don't insult me," he grabbed a napkin from the dispenser at the end of the table. "Do all you humans know where magicians learned how to do half the shit they know?"

"Wait," she straightened up in her seat, "you humans? As in, you're…not? You seriously believe you're not human?"

"I don't *believe*," he said. "I know."

"Okay…" she began slowly sliding out of the booth. "I'm just going to go now. I think I'll have better luck by myself."

"Alright," he sighed, "I guess Marge isn't that important to you after all." He ate the last bit of pancake on his plate.

"First of all," she corrected, "it's Megan. Secondly, you're insane." She hovered next to the booth as she spoke to Finley.

"Your friend will be dead in a matter of days, the cops won't find her, and you need me if you want to save her. *You* wanted *my* help, remember?" Kaden's jaw locked again as she slowly plopped back down in her seat knowing he was right, even if he was insane.

"Fine," she surrendered. "What is your crackpot theory?" She wanted nothing more than to find Megan; the only thing preventing her from doing so was the fact that she had no idea where to begin.

"It's not a *theory*. I can't help you if you won't believe me," he told her.

"You expect me to believe that magic is real? How is that even—? How did you—? How?" The words fumbled out of her mouth.

"Love is magical and *that's* real," he drank some of his hot chocolate.

"But that's not the same as what you're talking about. You're talking about—"

"Changing my physical shape into anything or anyone," he cut her thought off. "Like a dog."

Kaden ran her hands through her hair to clutch her

skull which felt like it was going to explode. "So you're saying you're a shapeshifter?" She guessed against her better judgment. Finley slammed his head on the table, mumbling something under his breath.

"I can make anyone see something that isn't there, and with the snap of my fingers, I can teleport almost anywhere." He said, speaking to the floor. He lifted his head to face Kaden, "Nowadays your people call us 'faeries'," he used an exaggerated American accent of the word faeries while making a fancy hand gesture with a bow. "I prefer the term fae though. It provides a much more dramatic flair. However, fae is more of a general term for any supernatural creature."

"A fae?" She gently questioned. "So where's your magic fairy dust that takes us to a far away land?" Kaden mocked his insanity. Finley's face fell as he furrowed his eyebrows.

"This," he pointed to himself using his fork, "is not a fairytale. This is very real and extremely dangerous. Fortunately for you, I'm good with danger," he smirked. "Any questions thus far?"

"So, if this is *so* dangerous, why would you help me?" Kaden wondered.

"Good first question," Finley winked at her while giving her an okay hand signal. She loathed the sentiment.

"Normally," he began, "a fae is either Dark or Light. I used to be a part of the Light fae. Once I left, the Dark fae were very keen on getting me to join them. That's the price I have to pay for being amazing." He put one arm on the top of the booth seat while Kaden rolled her eyes at his cockiness. "I don't particularly approve of how the Dark fae spend their time. And since they took Mary—"

"Megan."

"Whatever," he brushed her off. "They were there tonight for me, not for your friend. Do you believe me now that I've explained the situation to you?"

"I'm still on the whole supernatural creatures are real part," she said honestly. "How could any of this be possible without the world knowing about it?"

"Some people have experience with the fae world. It just doesn't usually end well for them. Most of the survivors are institutionalized, some of them live on to write legends about what they've experienced."

"So, you're telling me that every mythical creature I've learned about is real?"

"No," he answered, which confused Kaden more than she already was, "I don't know what mythical creatures you've learned about in your life."

"These Dark faeries have Megan?" She wanted to verify she had the correct information.

"Yes."

"And they're going to torture her?" she winced at the thought of Megan being in pain.

"I don't know," he shrugged. "It depends on what they feel like doing for fun." He flicked a crumb off the table.

"How do they have fun?" Kaden swallowed the lump she had in her throat, not knowing if she actually wanted the answer.

Finley, intrigued by the question, sat up straight.

"Well, they tend to be very cruel with their punishment if one decides to mess with them. Inflicting pain on humans is one of their greatest pleasures. Occasionally they hold cage games, swap their babies with human babies, create illusions to disrupt the mind of mortals, umm....let's see what else..."

"What are cage games?" Kaden interrupted.

"They take humans and put them in cages, then take bets to see how long they last before they..." Finley stopped and didn't bother to finish the rest of his sentence.

"So why would they take Megan if they were there for you?" Kaden questioned. What she really wanted to know was why they didn't take him instead.

"I pissed them off. As I told you before, they wanted to take me to Doyle and, if you have ever met him, I'm sure you would do anything to make sure you didn't see him. I'm assuming since they didn't get me, they figured they had to return with something, or someone."

"Who is Doyle? Do you know what they will do to Megan?"

"Doyle," he said, " is their King. Sometimes referred to as The Cruel One. He's a bastard, too."

"And what about Megan?" she worried. "Do you think they will play the..." Kaden forgot the words Finley had just used.

"Cage games," he said for her. Finley watched Kaden, searching for the right phrasing. "The Dark fae are unpredictable, and they have fun in many different ways," he paused and shifted in his seat. "I don't know what they'll do for sure, but I know they prefer to play with their food before they eat."

Kaden felt as if she was going to vomit. "They're going to eat her?!" she gasped.

"Oh God no! Faeries don't eat people, are you insane? That's revolting." Finley was shocked by even the thought of a faerie eating a human. "Let's just say we should find her as soon as possible."

"Okay," she said, unaware of what she had found herself in. Kaden stood up from her seat, waiting for Finley to do the same.

"I haven't finished my hot coco yet," he said as he lifted his mug to his mouth while sticking his pinky up in the air. "Yum. Tasty."

Kaden took the mug from his hands, placing it back on the table. "Let's go."

"Let's go? Not but two minutes ago I told you fae were real and very dangerous and your response is 'let's go'."

"I don't totally trust you. But I know my friend is in trouble. And if what you said is true that means she is in more trouble than I thought, so yes. Let's go." Finley rolled his eyes as he slid out of the booth. "Aren't you going to pay?" Kaden asked as they headed for the exit.

"I wasn't planning on it." Finley reached in his front pockets which ended up being empty. Then he tried his back pockets making an 'a-huh' face. "Here we are." The wallet was small and black with the letter 'K' written on the side.

"Hey, that's mine," Kaden pointed out as she recognized it. She reached out to retrieve it from him, but her hand was blocked by Finley, who moved swiftly past her to the waitress.

"Here you go, miss," he handed the waitress a handful of cash, "keep the change." Kaden waited for him to return. "What?" he said in response to the expression on Kaden's face.

"I don't exactly have money lying around." She grabbed the wallet from his hands.

"You were the one who wanted to pay, it only seemed logical. Come on, let's get to it. I know where they should be and hopefully this will be an easy thing," he stepped out of the diner, making a sharp left.

"Where they *should* be?" she asked.

"Do you really think they stay in one place all the time? They're always moving around. I just happen to know where they were recently."

"What happens if they aren't there? Or if it doesn't turn out to be an 'easy thing'," she asked.

"Well," he said into the bitter air. "We'll deal with it then."

CHAPTER V

The two walked in silence. The soft sound of their footsteps against the sidewalk filled the void between them. The streets were cast in shadow, not bright enough for Kaden to really look at Finley. He was a person, walking on the sidewalk like she was. He seemed ordinary yet he claimed to be something else. Something other. She watched him out of the corner of her eye, weary that she may have found herself in a trap. Maybe Megan wasn't in danger at all, but Kaden was. Light and Dark fae were real— or perhaps none of it was real. It all seemed impossible. Kaden wondered if she should call Quinn again, but she ignored the thought.

"Where are we going?" she asked suddenly. She kept her voice low and even despite struggling with unease. She wanted to know everything and nothing at all. Where they were headed. How far it would be. Would Megan be there unharmed? Finley was leading her through paths she never would have thought to go down. Kaden was practically on his heels every step of the way, keeping an eye on him. She didn't want to get lost, especially in a part of Seattle she hadn't really been to before. Secretly, she wanted to be close to him in case someone tried to jump her; he was much taller than her and definitely looked fit enough to defend himself. She hoped he would defend her if something did actually happen. But could she trust him?

"A club," he finally replied after several minutes had passed. Finley avoided each puddle of rain by sidestepping them or by jumping over them altogether. Kaden tried to do the same, yet somehow she managed to step in the puddle anyway.

"That's a bit vague," she noted. When he didn't say anything in return, Kaden bit her lower lip. "How is this going to work?" she asked mid-puddle jump.

"What do you mean?" He glanced over at her quickly before returning his focus on where he was going.

"Obviously we can't just ask, so what do we do?"

"*We*," he started, "don't do anything. I am going to do everything." They turned down a narrow alley full of rotting garbage. Kaden couldn't decide if the stench bothered her more or Finley's comment.

"What is the point of me coming then?" Kaden asked. She knew she wouldn't be of much use, the only training she had was from a free week-long karate class she and Megan took one summer. The program was actually three weeks long but neither one of them could stand the aching pain they felt in their muscles afterward.

"Moral support," he reassured her.

"I may not be familiar with *faeries* or *fae* or whatever—but I'm not totally useless," she argued as she dodged a tiny mouse with food in its mouth.

Kaden most certainly wasn't going to let some stranger take control of the situation for many reasons; she didn't know this guy from a hole in the wall, which caused her to be cautious about the entire plan. Plus she wasn't about to put Megan's life in his hands.

Finley laughed loudly like she had told a hilarious joke, "Yes you are. *I* don't even know what to expect. How do you expect to be prepared for something you didn't know existed ten minutes ago? Besides, I'm trained and you're not, which means I will be doing all the heavy lifting in this business transaction."

"So this is a business transaction now?" her voice rose with anger at his sudden change in mood. "I thought you were doing this because you felt guilty for getting *my* friend mixed up in *your* business."

"Look," he stopped next to a pile of decaying garbage for a moment which Kaden really wished he hadn't done. "I will not be responsible for the loss of two human lives. We are stepping into dangerous territory, for anyone. I'm not saying you're incapable of helping, I'm saying for now you're incapable of helping. Until we figure out what's happening, I will be the one doing most of the work. These fae are capable of all sorts of things. Never underestimate that."

"You're right," she straightened her posture. "I don't

know what I'm doing and I need you if I want to find Megan. I know that much. But if there is something I can do to help in any way, I'm going to do it, regardless of what they're capable of. And if *you* try anything, anything at all that doesn't seem right to me…I will do everything in my power to take you down." When she finished her threatening speech, Finley gave her the strangest look. He was not offended by what she said, but impressed and almost delighted to continue on to the 'club' of which they were headed.

He half smiled with a respectful nod, "This way."

Blasting music reverberated off the brick walls of nearby buildings into Kaden's ear drum. Laughter mixed with drunken shouting poured out of the club Finley had said they were going to. From down the street the only details she could make out were bright pink and purple lights with a flickering green sign that read 'Gentlemen's Club'.

"A strip club?" Kaden questioned with a sigh. She exchanged a glance with Finley, "Dark fae hang out in strip clubs?"

"Sometimes," he said. "I wouldn't argue that it *is* the best kind of club. Would you?"

Stumbling men struggled to stand on two feet as they walked out onto the streets from the club. As they passed Kaden and Finley, she could smell bitter alcohol and sweet perfume following in their wake. Some of the men sparkled with glitter. "Are they fae?" she whispered, practically hanging on Finley's arm. A few of the men gawked at Kaden making her want to run and hide with their gaze.

"Why are they staring?" she asked.

Finley glanced down at her and continued to walk to the entrance. "They're not fae," he told her. "The better question is, have you seen what you're wearing?" Kaden immediately closed her jacket shut and hunched forward. "Who goes downtown wearing that? I'm surprised no one offered you money," Finley said. Kaden wasn't offended by the insinuation when she herself honestly didn't feel comfortable wearing it anyway.

They approached the bright red doors which never seemed to stay shut since men continuously came in and out of them. Kaden was unsure if the smoke that followed the men out was cigar smoke or smoke from a fog machine for one of the dance shows. The doors were open enough for her to see lights flashing various colors inside as various girls danced on stage around poles. Finley had one foot in the door when the oversized bouncer who stood outside put his arm out to prevent Kaden from entering.

"Men only," he huffed at her.

"But—I—" Kaden began as she gestured toward the doors. Finley quickly pulled back to Kaden's side.

Finley jumped in with, "This is the twenty-first century. If she wants to go see naked girls dance, then she is going to." He cocked a smile and took a step closer to the bouncer, "If you have a problem with a woman in your club well, it seems to me you'd be out of a job. Is there still a problem?" The muscles in the man's jaw tightened. He glanced between Kaden and Finley before letting them both in. Apparently, letting a woman in wasn't worth losing his job. Kaden felt her cheeks blush bright red as she slipped through the red doors. Finley didn't seem bothered.

The room was glowing as a half-dressed woman paraded around seeking men to lure into private rooms. Two topless women danced on stage with men throwing dollar bills at them. Some others in bikinis and tight outfits offered drinks to men in booths.

Finley spotted the bar where a dancer with a French maid outfit waited. Her long black hair fell to the middle of her back. Her face was perfectly painted in makeup and she appeared more bored than anything. Finley glided over to her side, "Stacy," he said as he slid his hand around her waist. "You just look absolutely stunning in that outfit." Kaden waited beside him as a man passed them with two women on each arm. "My friend and I would like to get a private room with you."

Taken off guard by Finley's request Kaden tugged his arm, "*We* would?"

"Yes," he said to her, removing her grip from his arm. "We would." The woman glared at Finley before taking his hand playfully to escort them to a back room.

Kaden wasn't sure what any of this had to do with getting Megan. "What are we doing?" she whispered to him.

"Trust me. I know what I'm doing." He assured her even though she didn't understand what was going on.

"And what exactly is that?" she bumped into a topless woman's shoulder, "S-sorry."

They were taken down a red colored hall with individual doors, bodyguards outside each one. The woman brought them into the furthest from the rest of the club. She allowed Finley and Kaden to enter the room first.

Inside, was a red love seat, a strip pole, with a few mood-setting lights. The French maid closed the door, locking it behind her which made Kaden uneasy. "What do you want, Finley?" she asked him. The three of them stood in the room, Stacy blocking the door while Finley and Kaden stood by the love seat.

"Just checking up on my favorite succubus," he took a seat on the couch and crossed his legs. "Kill anyone lately?" Kaden discreetly took a step away from Stacy. She didn't know what a succubus was and wasn't sure that she wanted to know if it involved killing people.

Stacy crossed her arms over her chest, "I told you I don't kill people anymore. Why do you think I work at a strip club?"

"I just thought you were following your lifelong dream of pole dancing," he fiddled to roll his sleeve further up his arm. Stacy, with her arms folded, strutted closer to the conversation. "Where is Riley and his gang of misfit fae? I thought they were holding up here?" he asked her. Stacy shifted her stare from Finley to Kaden and back again.

"Why should I tell you?" Stacy questioned.

Finley took a deep breath in while he rolled his eyes, and then let his breath out. "Because if you scratch my back," he paused. "I'll scratch yours." Stacy's attention was drawn to Finley's words with wide eyes and a tilt of her head.

Stacy pondered for a moment, "What are you offering?" Her interest was evident when she uncrossed her arms as she made her way closer to Finley.

"Let's say three minutes," his eyes drifted to the

ceiling to come up with a good deal. Kaden squinted with one eye, *three minutes of what?*

"Ten," she firmly countered. "If they find out *I* was the one who helped you, they'll kill me."

Finley took her point into consideration, "Five is my final offer. Take it or leave it." He leaned back against the couch and waited for her answer. *This has to be some weird sex thing,* Kaden thought.

"Done," she said, finalizing their agreement. "What do you want to know?"

"Riley and the others, where are they?"

"I don't know. They haven't been around for the past couple of days."

"What else do you know about what they're doing?" Kaden watched Stacy, who didn't seem to care much about her presence. Her focus was solely on Finley's questions. *Whatever Stacy wanted, she wanted it desperately.*

"Not much, just that they needed more space for the amount of Dark fae they have gathering."

"Gathering for what?" he leaned forward intently, listening, interested in the information.

"I don't know," she answered, "but that's everything I know. Now to your offer, is she staying or….." Stacy hesitated.

"She'll wait outside," he said. "Take the back exit and wait for me there." Kaden was resistant to leave Finley when he could easily ditch her. She also didn't feel too safe waiting alone outside in a supposed Dark fae hang out. "Trust me," he nodded his head slightly toward the exit. Before closing the door fully, she turned to give him a stern expression to warn him about the wrath he would face if he did anything to mess up finding Megan.

Kaden waited impatiently outside the strip club. She paced back and forth for five minutes and in between each one debated again if she should call Quinn or try Megan's cell phone again. After the five minutes Finley came merrily out of the back exit with smeared red lipstick surrounding his mouth. "Right then, let's go."

"That's it?" she asked. "You get a lap dance by some weird creature and we leave without Megan?" Kaden pressed as he skipped down the steps to her.

"One," Finally said. "It wasn't a lap dance. And two Stacy isn't a 'weird thing', she's a succubus." Kaden widened her eyes with no clue what that meant. "She feeds off of sexual energy through kissing. If she feeds too much, the person dies, hence the reason she works at a strip club. She gets to feed a little on many different men so no one dies."

"If that's how dangerous Dark fae are, I don't think it's something I can't handle."

"Stacy is what you might call a low level Dark fae. She doesn't exactly have special abilities like Dark faeries do." Finley cast a glance at Kaden and began to laugh uncontrollably.

"What's so funny?" Kaden pretended to smile as though she knew what was funny.

"She told me to bring you along for a private dance sometime."

Kaden was taken aback by this, "That's not funny."

"Yes, it is," Finley pointed at her as he continued to laugh. "Oh please, don't be so dramatic, sexuality is nothing to be ashamed of."

"Sexuality isn't my problem," she retorted. "I just don't see how we're supposed to find Megan now if Stacy doesn't know where they are." The validity of her point made Finley's smile slip to a frown. "So," she began, "now what?" She leaned against the stairs banister while Finley looked at his shoes.

She watched him ponder the question, "We should probably go to my flat." Before Kaden could process what he said, Finley turned and began waltzing down the street again.

Kaden's eyebrows furrowed as she rushed down the staircase after him. "Umm, no offense, but I thought we were spending the night *searching* for Megan. We've only been to one place which was a dead end."

"We can't search for Megan anymore because the only Dark fae lead I had was pretty much useless," he explained. "I can ask some Light fae, but unfortunately we'll have to wait for tomorrow."

"The entire point of me coming to you for help was so we could get her back tonight," the warmth of her breath formed smoke as she spoke to the back of his head. "Would you slow down?" Finley lightened his pace up just enough for her to be by his side.

"Correction, the reason you came to me was because you knew I knew something, which I did." They waited at a street corner for moving traffic, "You are the one hell-bent on finding her tonight which, let's be honest, was never realistic."

"Well I'm not just going to go back to a stranger's

apartment," she protested. "It's one thing that I'm trusting you to take me to various places where you could potentially kill me, but it's another to actually go to your apartment alone." The pedestrian crossing sign remained red, but Finley decided to cross the road anyway.

"It's your choice," he shouted over his shoulder while Kaden waited on the street corner. "But if it were my friend's life at risk, I would stay with the guy who knows what he's doing." She bit her lower lip before crossing the street behind him. He continued his thought though he wasn't sure she was still following him. "Besides, the cops have probably been to your house, which means you'd be too busy filing a missing person report to be looking for her."

"I should at least call them," Kaden pulled her phone out with her fingertips ready to dial Quinn again. Not to her surprise there were twenty text messages, among them several in all caps and a dozen voicemails.

"I wouldn't," Finley warned her with a sigh.

"Why not?" Her thumb hovered over the send button.

"Do you really expect your family to understand what you are doing? *You* barely know what's going on. How insane did it sound to you?" he reminded her. Kaden knew it would sound crazy because it had sounded crazy to her. Especially since she had no way of showing them solid proof. And after everything Quinn had been through with their mother, Kaden had to admit to herself it was a bad idea.

"How do I know you won't kill me in my sleep? Or

kidnap me for a slave trade?" she asked.

Finley stopped in his tracks abruptly, pondering the question. "You don't," he continued to walk forward.

"That's very reassuring," Kaden remarked. "How much longer are we going to be on the streets?"

"Why do you insist on asking so many questions?" She didn't respond to spite him. The two found themselves standing in front of a tall, broken down building. It was brick with an old heavy brown door, and some kind of answering system on the wall. Finley lifted a flower pot off the building's crooked stoop. "You keep your key under a flower pot?" she snorted. As soon as the question slipped through her lips she realized what he meant about asking too many questions.

"Judge all you want," he said. When he opened the main door the bottom of the frame caught against the uneven ground. Finley used his body to force it open the rest of the way. "After you," he made a hand gesture for her to go first. Kaden stood with her feet firmly planted in one spot. "...After you," Finley waved his hand once again for her to enter the building.

Before she could manage to get her feet to cross the threshold, she looked from Finley to the unknown space ahead of them. "How do I know you're really a fae? Any good magician could have done the things you did in the diner, and you *did* take me to a strip club where I didn't actually see any type of magic take place." Finley lifted his eyes to the sky and shook his head. "Just," she started, "humor me. I need hard visual proof here. Otherwise I'm just a gullible girl who went into a creepy guy's apartment and was found dead the next morning."

"Fine," Finley let the door shut, "what kind of proof do you want?"

Kaden thought for a moment. "You claim you were the dog from the alley, so turn back into it." He squinted his eyes as he stepped off the stoop of his building while he muttered under his breath.

She watched him walk into the alley next to the apartment building until he was satisfied with his placement. "Can you see me?" he asked with a hint of irritation rubbing off in his tone. "I'm only doing this once." Kaden made her way down the stoop towards him, a little closer before nodding her head. He raised his hand into the air and snapped his middle finger and thumb together. The transformation was simple. Like a blink of an eye. After the snap of his finger, Finley no longer stood in the alley. The same gray dog from the club took his place, seated on all fours. Kaden's wide-eyed expression remained frozen on her face. The dog let out a deep bark that snapped her out of her shock. She found herself mesmerized.

"Which way is your apartment?" she asked the dog.

On the main floor there were two doors, but a set of stairs led up to more levels, each with two apartments. "Third floor," he said. "Apartment 3B." Wailing cries of an infant somewhere in the building echoed. An argument of hushed threats and seething anger shifted the atmosphere. The thump of techno music vibrated off the walls and through the entire building. The array of characters living inside seemed so strange to Kaden who had only known her small house and her neighbors through hellos and goodbyes.

Finley's apartment door was a lime green with peeled paint revealing an awful blue it used to be underneath. Unlike the main door, it swung open with ease as he unlocked it with the key under the doormat. "You're not afraid of someone breaking in?" she wondered at his lack of security.

"If someone wanted me dead, they aren't going to knock," he replied simply.

Compared to the state the rest of the building was in, his apartment was surprisingly gorgeous. The dark lighting of the hallway gave way to bright fixtures with seemingly new modern furnishings. When Kaden first set foot in the apartment building she feared the worst, roaches, mice, or bedbugs. Stepping into the small entryway with marble flooring she was in awe. Every inch was clean. The gleaming light shone off glass and stainless steel. Right beside the entryway was a kitchen that included an island bar and cutting edge appliances. The kitchen flowed into the living area where a cushiony brown couch with a matching set of coffee and end tables rested. There was a fireplace across from the couch with a large gold framed mirror above it. The floors turned from marble to dark wood once she stepped foot beyond the entryway. Underneath the windows in the living room were low bookcases filled with old records and old books and old antique pieces that blended perfectly with everything else. Behind the living area, two steps up led to a curtained off bedroom with floor to ceiling windows. The elegance was captivating and surely the most luxurious place Kaden had ever been to.

She couldn't quite comprehend how the apartment felt and looked more like a loft than an apartment. Even the high ceilings gaped down at her.

The moment Finley shut the door behind him the madness of the building outside the door ceased to exist. Kaden watched him reach behind his neck to unclasp a necklace he wore which she hadn't noticed before. In the bright lighting she could see what it was. It was a Celtic cross. As he removed the necklace, she watched his ears morph from normal human ears into slightly pointed ones. At first Kaden thought she was imagining it since it was almost two in the morning, but when she blinked again they didn't change. He put the necklace along with his keys in a small dish that was on top of the shoe cabinet.

"What?" Finley asked once he saw Kaden's bewildered expression. "Do I have something on my face?" he wiped his cheek.

"Your ears?" she stared in amazement.

"What about them?" Finley was very nonchalant as he went into the kitchen to open the fridge.

"How did they change?" Kaden took a seat at the island bar and removed her jacket.

"The necklace," he took out a container of food from the fridge and smelled it. His face twisted from the scent, yet he put the container back in its place instead of throwing it out. "It's a talisman of a warrior's cross. It has a charm on it that protects our physical appearance. It's just a nice way of saying our ears really. But, some fae have wings or other different appearances which need to be concealed if they're living among humans. Some fae have different necklaces, sometimes rings." Finley had a mouthful of pizza and a can of soda in his hand as he kicked the door shut.

"Riley," she recalled, "and the guy he was with had a talisman too, right?"

"We all have them," he added through his chewing.

Kaden sat with that for a moment. How many fae had she encountered in the past? How would she ever tell? "How did you get all this nice stuff anyway?" She changed the topic as she studied the brick walls that had elaborate paintings hanging from them.

"I stole most of it." Kaden shot him a look. For a moment she thought he was joking, but he didn't laugh. Somehow she wasn't surprised.

"Well," she sighed. "At least you're honest."

"Faeries don't lie," Finley sounded surprised she didn't know. "We have to tell the truth. Some of us simply use riddles and rhymes. I find that a waste of time."

"Why don't you?" She hopped off the bar stool to check out more of his stuff. The old fireplace across from the couch seemed to be the only thing that didn't match. It had cracked white paint with pieces of wood missing from the frame. She picked at a piece of the corner and felt a huge chunk of the fireplace shift under her finger.

"I've lived with humans for roughly twenty years, give or take. I assimilated." Finley left the kitchen to go into a room to the left of the entryway shutting the door behind him.

"Wait," she slowly walked over to the bookcase. "How old are you?" She recognized some of the records he had stacked against each other in his bookcase, most of them were blues groups.

"Older than you think," he responded from the other room.

"Once again," she mumbled to herself, "vague." She pulled a vinyl from the shelf as the rushing water of a shower started running. When Kaden put the record back to its proper place, her eye was drawn to an old gold book with no title on the binding. It was heavier than she thought it would be and probably really expensive. Part of her wondered if he had stolen it. She flipped the book open to the first page, only to discover it wasn't a real book at all. It was a secret storage place, cut in the center for a good hiding place. "So," she called over her shoulder, "are there vampires?" She took a quick peek of what was inside of the gold book.

"Vampires?" he questioned back from the shower. "Vampires are merely a concept created by a perverted man with a blood fetish." Kaden's fingers traced a bunch of old letters written in two elegant scripts of handwriting.

"So then what else is there?" She desperately buried her desire to read one or two by closing the book and slipping it back into its home on the shelf.

"A lot," he replied. "Various types of faeries, mermaids, nymphs—"

"Mermaids?" she repeated back quickly. Her mind drifted, forgetting the letters for a moment and were replaced by the image of Ariel singing on top of a rock.

"Yes, have you not heard of them?" he said as the shower water stopped running.

"Of course I have, I just didn't know they were real. How do you know so much about this stuff if you used to live with the Light fae?" Kaden swerved to sit on the massive couch to prevent him from seeing her snoop. She flipped open a magazine that laid on the coffee table when Finley came out of the bathroom with only a plaid pair of pajama pants. She was taken aback by his bare chest and the soft indents of a six pack. His skin was still wet from his shower and Kaden looked away quickly.

"Well," he rubbed his damp hair with a towel. "When you are a part of this world, it makes sense to make yourself acquainted with the other fae. I keep a bestiary." Kaden closed the magazine waiting for him to elaborate on the unfamiliar word. "It's kind of like a journal of notes about other fae. What they do, how to kill them, etc." With every passing moment Kaden spent with Finley, more and more questions filled her brain. With the questions came fears. Fear if Megan was okay, if *she* would be okay, and how she would find her. The questions and worry collided in her mind. For a moment, the adrenaline of the night eased and Kaden was met with heavy eyelids.

"So tomorrow," she yawned, "we're going to look for the Dark fae's lair?" Kaden leaned back into the couch's comfort. When she first arrived she was nervous to be wearing her shoes in the apartment, but she found herself grabbing a fluffy pillow to put on top of her lap as she folded her legs.

"It's not a liar, more like a…" Finley searched for the

right word, "hideaway." He went back into the kitchen for another snack. Kaden wondered if fae have to eat more than humans do. "And we need to find a Dark fae," he added. "I'll be able to get an answer out of whoever it is. Shouldn't take that long." His head was in the fridge shuffling things around. "We should be able to have your friend back tomorrow night, depending on..." Finley put the stuff he picked out on the counter when he saw that Kaden had fallen asleep on the couch, "where they have her," he finished to himself.

CHAPTER VI

Kaden's eyes fluttered open to the stillness of the morning. There was a moment, watching the sun's morning rays cascade through the window where last night was nothing but a bad dream. A moment where she and Megan drove home and nothing more happened. But the moment was brushed away once her eyes adjusted to the space around and she didn't recognize it. She lifted her head off the pillow and found her jacket laying over her for a blanket which she didn't recall doing. The crisp richness of freshly brewed coffee invited her to wake up as morning birds, the few that there were, sang outside. A beautiful morning, but Kaden's skin was on fire, like a thousand fire ants invisible to her crawling everywhere. She spent the night in comfort when Megan was alone. She stood from the couch abruptly in search of the coffee maker. As she poured herself the largest mug she could find in the cabinet, she bit back the anxiety growing inside of her. Kaden's mouth was filled with hazelnut and caffeine when she spotted a plate of freshly made eggs and bacon that sat waiting on the island. She held the warmth of the mug close to her chest as she inspected the apartment for any sign of Finley. To her dismay she only found a quiet apartment staring back at her. Her stomach gurgled loudly and she wasn't sure if it was from hunger or worry. She snaked a piece of bacon off the plate with hopes to hush her insides.

A cool morning breeze whispered against her skin, drawing her attention to an open window above the bookshelf. She followed the draft to find the smell of cigarette smoke hit her face before she stuck her head out the window. Finley sat on the fire escape with his legs swinging in the air through the railing. He had a cigarette dangling out of his mouth as he watched passing cars. Kaden placed her mug on the bookcase before climbing out to join him, almost knocking her mug over in the process. "Morning," Kaden said.

"Afternoon actually," he corrected.

"I slept that late? Why didn't you wake me?" she asked.

"You needed rest," he said through his cigarette smoke. "I can't worry that you're too tired to defend yourself."

Kaden leaned against the railing watching people walk past down below. They were going to work or school or home. Yesterday, she would have been one of them. "What are they going to do to her?" she wondered mostly to herself.

Out of the corner of her eye she watched as Finley sucked in another drag of his vice. His hair was a mess, as if he himself had just woken up. He wore a black T-shirt with blue jeans and a pair of red converse that stood out against the dark colors. Everything about him seemed normal except his ears. In the daylight, his soft features and youthfulness reminded her of anyone else her age.

"Thanks for the bacon," she said. Kaden waved the piece she had in the air.

"What?" his concentration seemed to be elsewhere. "Oh. Right. You can tell that to the lady who made it in the floor below us."

"You're not wearing your necklace," she pointed out. He flicked his cigarette allowing the burnt ashes to fall three stories down.

"Nope," he said, still not paying much attention to her.

"How come?" Kaden took a seat next to him; in hopes maybe if she was next to him, he would have to engage in conversation.

"Because I live here. I'm not going to hide who I am in my own home. And besides," he took a long drag from his cigarette, "no one can see me from up here." Kaden leaned over the railing to look down at the street.

"I thought you were supposed to wear the necklace whenever you're outside? Isn't there always a possibility someone could see you?" Finley shifted his attention from watching the road to looking at Kaden. His eyes seemed sad when they met Kaden's.

"You know, you don't always have to do everything people tell you. If you want to do something, do it. Don't be afraid to be who you are, I say," he went back to watching the street. "If I could," he paused, "I would never wear the necklace. But it's not just my life it would be affecting. Could you imagine if they found out the truth?"

"Anyone who's ever told me to do what I want, never truly means it," she said watching him.

"Well they're stupid," he said flatly, making Kaden laugh so hard she nearly snorted. Finley smiled at her amusement with the cigarette still hanging out of his mouth.

"Well, let's head out. We should start in the park since it's early, then we'll make our way to some other places if need be," Finley flicked the cigarette down to the sidewalk before standing to his feet.

"Which park?" she asked as they made their way back through the window. Kaden pulled her coat on while Finley quickly reached for something underneath the coffee table and held it by his side so she couldn't get a good look at it. He shoved it into a jacket pocket before putting the coat on. Kaden grabbed another piece of bacon off the plate.

"Discovery Park.," he said. As Finley slipped his silver talisman over his neck she witnessed his ears turn from their normal shape into human ones. With the T-shirt he wore, she could actually see the necklace with greater detail. Around the arms of the cross and the body of it was a circle with an intertwined Celtic pattern. "If we hurry we should be able to catch the bus," Finley held the door open for Kaden. She had forgotten what a terrible building Finley lived in and was reminded by the overwhelming smell of dirty diapers.

"I thought you could be anywhere you wanted to be with the snap of your fingers?" Kaden mocked his cockiness from the night before.

"No."

"No?"

"How the hell would I be able to teleport somewhere I've never been before? That just doesn't make any sense."

"I'm not exactly familiar with faerie 101," Kaden added in her defense.

"Besides, we can't teleport there when there could be potential witnesses. If there was an empty building, then maybe. But this is broad daylight. Anything can happen."

Most of the seats on the bus were occupied by commuters. The bus took off just as quickly as it stopped, leaving little room to navigate around. In the far back, where the air seemed far more stuffy there was one open seat next to an elderly woman with hoards of plastic bags with her. Within seconds, Finley darted for the spot without so much as losing his balance. He politely waved to the woman as a sly smile slid across his face. "I always thought plastic bags were very fashionable," he commented. The woman maintained a poker face while Kaden desperately attempted to cling onto the bar above their seats for balance. "Lovely day we're having isn't it?" Finley noted, but the woman beside him stared blankly.

"I don't think she can hear you," Kaden guessed. Finley pouted before he proceeded to poke the woman on the arm several times until she turned to him.

"HELLO!" he shouted, drawing the attention of the entire bus to himself.

"May I help you?" she asked loudly, inching away from him with her plastic bags.

"My name's Finley." He held out his hand for the woman to shake. "Nice to make your acquaintance." She looked at his hand confused and then pushed her way, along with her bags, past Finley to the front of the bus. Finley slid over to the window seat and patted the seat next to him, "Got you a seat." Kaden sat, not sure if she should be happy to sit or embarrassed by how she got it. The light rays from the sun shimmered against Finley's necklace, catching her eyes.

"So, the talisman has a charm on it, right?" Kaden asked as she munched on the bacon she had stuffed in her pocket.

"Yes," he held his finger over his mouth, attempting to get her to lower her voice.

"Why can't you cast a charm or something to find Megan?"

"Charms can only be cast by witches or an elder faerie, and those people aren't exactly easy to come by. They don't like flaunting what they can do. Most fae keep to themselves or live hidden away from people. Dark fae like to live in cities because there are more people they can mess with."

"If the Light fae live somewhere else, then why do you live in the city?" Kaden asked.

Finley didn't answer at first; instead he fiddled with his

necklace. "It's complicated."

"It's complicated. That's all I get? How do I know *you're* not a Dark fae and this is all just some sick part of *your* fun?"

"Technically you don't know for sure. But you'll just have to find out if you want to see your friend again." After a comment like that, Kaden felt fear grow larger inside of her, but when she looked at his green eyes, she saw they weren't threatening. "We should probably give the fae talk a rest, too many people around." Finley shifted in his seat to view the scenery they passed on their way to Discovery Park.

The calming harmony of chirping birds eased Kaden's mind for the briefest moment. After an hour-long commute to the edge of the city with Finley hogging most of the foot space, Kaden embraced the pureness of nature which was a pleasant change in scenery from the city. Gray clouds blocked the once shining sun with a slight trickle of rain. The canopy of trees was darkened by the missing light. As the two headed down a nature path they passed some joggers who ran accompanied by their dogs, parents who guided their young children, and occasionally one person who sought to explore the path by themselves. Most of the park's guests aimed for the shore line or Scheuerman Creek, but Finley and Kaden followed a different path. Kaden envied the people enjoying what was a nice day and there were quite a few of them. It made her wonder why a Dark fae would come to a park over a strip club. Despite the gloomy weather it was open and lacked a disconcerting factor. The strip club was more obvious, however the park was an easy place to take someone without anyone knowing.

As soon as Kaden and Finley were separated from regular park goers, Finley veered off the path into the dense woods. The lanky tree trunks were dark from the rain they'd gotten in the past few days; their leaves dripped raindrops softly to the ground. "Go on," Finley looked back at Kaden who'd always seemed to be one step behind him.

"Go on what?" she lifted her eyes from focusing on where she was stepping to return his glance.

"I'm sure you have questions. You *always* have questions," as he spoke he climbed on top of a boulder instead of walking around it. Kaden couldn't deny her curiosity about everything that had to do with his world. She wanted to know how each step they seemed to take would get her closer to rescuing Megan. She wanted to know who or what they were going to speak to, and she wanted to know more about Finley himself.

"Okay," she took a moment to gather her thoughts for which question she was most curious about. "What Dark fae are we searching for in the woods?" She dodged fallen tree branches as they stepped further and further away from people.

"We aren't exactly looking for a Dark fae. We are looking for someone much harder to come by."

Kaden waited for him to explain what that someone was, but he never did. *He always says I have too many questions, but he never explains himself.* So she continued to press for more answers. "Who is this someone?"

"A gnome," Finley said casually. The path they had come from was now lost in the distance along with anyone who was visiting the park.

"Like a garden gnome?" Kaden knew that was probably a stupid guess, but that was the only type of gnome she was aware of. Of course Finley shook his head in utter annoyance.

"It ceases to amaze me how little people really know about the fae world." He jumped into a puddle of watery mud. "Do you know what the term 'gnome' actually means?" Kaden shook her head even though he wouldn't be able to see her. As she was about to answer he said, "Know."

"I was just about to say I have no idea."

"What?" he asked, "No. I wasn't answering for you, I was telling you. It means know as in 'I know the answer'. Gnomes know a lot about almost everything. They are one of the wisest fae. They mostly live in holes in the ground in parks or woods, sometimes they travel into the city, but it's not likely. They're basically the gossip girls of the fae world. If we find the one I'm thinking of, he should know exactly where to find the Dark faeries who took Megan."

"How do we find him?" She asked when Finley held his arm out to prevent her from walking any further. His concentration was on the ground at a hole that was about a foot wide.

"That's how," Finley pointed at it. He circled the hole as he inspected its darkness that seemed to go on forever. "Is anyone home?" he yelled into the abyss.

"Is that really how you get a gnome to appear?"

Kaden wondered with the utmost seriousness.

"No, but I didn't want to be rude when I do this," he plucked a medium sized rock from nearby and dropped it down the hole.

"So it's like the rabbit hole from *Alice in Wonderland*," she commented. Finley stared at her with his eyebrows furrowed.

"Like I said," he paused, "not a kid's movie."

They were interrupted by a rustling noise that rose up from the hole. A spout of dirt was the first thing Kaden saw, then a tiny, pale brown head with two, large brown eyes that peered around the wood floor before coming out of its home. When the creature hopped out of its hole, it stood at about two feet tall with a round belly and only a cloth hanging around its waist. Its nose was large and rounded much like its belly. The gnome had normal humanlike hands beside the fact that they were an unusual pale brown. Its feet didn't have toes, but melded into one point.

The creature shook its fist in the air at the two giants before it while speaking gibberish. "What!?" it said with a grumpy English accent and waddled over to Finley. "You! You have a lot of nerve showing your face around here." The gnome grabbed a fat stick off the ground and slapped Finley on the leg with it. "Take that, you wanker!" The gnome continued smashing Finley with the stick, but Finley just looked down at the tiny thing.

"Hello again, Theodore." Finley grabbed Theodore off the ground, holding him arms-length away like a small child. Theodore tried to wiggle his way free but had no luck. "It's been a while," Finley said as a sly smile slid across his face. The gnome kicked his feet as fast as he could, "Listen, I need a favor."

"A favor? Favor?!" Theodore laughed in his face. "You want a favor! I'll show you a favor," he turned his head quickly and bit Finley's hand. Instinctively Finley released the creature from the pain. When the gnome fell, he rolled to get himself back on his feet before darting for his hole.

"Kaden, grab him!" Finley yelled. Kaden scooped up the tiny man, hugging him like a teddy bear so he wouldn't get away. "Well don't suffocate the poor guy," Finley said. The gnome barely moved in Kaden's arms, so she loosened her grip.

"What in the bloody hell do you want, Finley?" Theodore gasped for air, "Last time I checked, you owe *me* a favor."

"Don't worry, I come bearing gifts," Finley reached in his pocket, revealing a shiny gold coin.

"What am I, a leprechaun?" Theodore wailed in disgust.

"This is a gold coin I borrowed. It will bring good luck to whoever has it." The gnome stopped wiggling in Kaden's arms.

"Let me see it," Theodore said. Finley nodded, indicating Kaden to release the gnome. She placed him on the ground and he waddled to the coin. The creature looked at the coin from back to front and over again. Then he sank his teeth into the gold to verify its authenticity and smashed it twice against a tree. Theodore side-eyed Finley, "What do you want?" he asked as he shoved it in the hem of his cloth.

"Where can I find the Dark faeries?" Finley crouched down to eye level with the gnome who eyed Kaden up and down.

"What's with the mortal?" he bobbed his head at Kaden.

"That's my business," Finley answered. "Now, the Dark faeries, where are they?"

"I don't know, they keep moving around the city," Theodore moved in closer. "Last time I heard anything about them, they were at some *ladies club*," the gnome added a wink at the end of his sentence.

"What about around here?" Kaden asked abruptly. "Have you seen any?"

The gnome walked around Kaden with his chest puffed out, "As a matter a fact, there have been. Couple of 'em have been coming here for the past weeks. They've been taking young girls, girls who won't be missed, from the park. That's about all I know." He raised his hands as if he were truly out of any more information. Finley stood from crouching and turned to walk back from which they came. Kaden watched as the creature turned towards its hole. He was a curious thing and yet had more information than the thing she met the night before.

"Wait a minute," Theodore shouted suddenly. Finley stopped dead in his tracks. The gnome spun around in circles while feeling his body for something. He opened the hem of his cloth and looked down unsatisfied, "You took my coin!"

"I did no such thing," Finley said. Theodore held up an angry fist at him.

"You faeries are so cocky with your tricks. Hand it over." He held out his bare palm.

"I did not take your coin," Finley said slowly again.

"Then she did!" Theodore pointed at Kaden with one hand on his hip.

"I don't have it," Kaden stuttered with surprise. "I swear. Finley, just give him his coin," she slapped Finley's arm.

"You listen here you wanker—" Before Theodore could finish his sentence, Finley turned and kicked him like a football player kicking a field goal. He flew through the air shouting several curses until he landed with a thump a good distance away. Once Theodore was on the ground again he didn't move for a few minutes.

"You killed him!" She yelled in a whispered tone as if people could hear what they were saying. Her fear was quickly erased when Theodore rustled in the pile of leaves he landed in. He began to get back on his feet when Finley took Kaden's elbow, directing her back to the path.

"What did you do that for? He helped us." She thought about how much he really hadn't told them anything useful. "Kind of."

"He called me a wanker," Finley replied with an are-you-joking look, "Twice. I find it very rude."

"But you took his coin," she picked up her pace, wary of the vengeful gnome which sounded like it could be a terrible horror movie.

"Correction. I took MY coin," he said, flipping the coin in the air with a grin on his face.

"Now we just have to wander around the park looking

for a Dark fae," Kaden said with a sigh of exasperation.

"It should be simple," he said.

"What?" she asked. Kaden grabbed him by the elbow to stop him from moving so quickly, "You're not serious."

"We have to keep moving unless you want that gnome catching up to us," he said. "You and him may share short legs, but he knows the woods."

Kaden let him go and they both hurried their pace trekking through the woods.

"Do you want to find Megan or not? Theodore did say they were taking girls from the park. And this is the easiest way, unless you would rather spend another day or two searching for another fae, but your friend would probably be dead by then." Kaden hated the idea with a fiery passion, but she wanted to find Megan more than anything.

"How does this work?" Kaden asked, crossing her arms over her chest.

"Just walk around the park," he replied. "It might take a while. Avoid people. It will be easier for the faerie to take you without anyone noticing."

"And where will you be?" Kaden's voice began to waver.

"Fret not," he began as they neared the path again. "For I will be around." She watched Finley leisurely walk back toward the way they had arrived without a care in the world.

"Around?" she repeated to the back of his head. "That's really comforting," she called after him. He simply waved goodbye with the back of his hand. Kaden relieved a deep breath she didn't realize she had been holding as Finley faded into nothing more than a dot leaving her on her own.

CHAPTER VII

Wandering down path after everlasting path in circles, up inclines and descending down hills, she wandered. When she first parted from Finley, Kaden's steps were anxious. A feeling of dread mixed with the urgency of finding Megan moved her forward until the day flourished into early evening. Her pace slowed as did the people who passed her by. Joggers disappeared with the daylight as did families and friends. With each step and each hour that faded Kaden found herself more and more isolated. The damp dirt beneath her feet became her companion as distant chatter turned to only the ambiance of nature. As time passed, there was a hidden appeal, a faint thought that drifted through her mind. She could run away. She could leave everything behind her. Kaden didn't want to leave Quinn or Megan. They were her only form of comfort. But everything else about her life, her home seemed so pointless in the depths of the trees. Perhaps the endless trees and crooked paths lead her to a spiral in her mind.

The only sounds that interfered with her conflicting thoughts were coming from her feet against crunching fallen leaves and the hum of chirping birds from above her. Kaden watched her feet take each step, hoping to come off as alone. Technically she was except Finley was somewhere. Either that or she actually was alone and Finley abandoned her. No one was in sight; she was completely alone. Not just alone on the path but also in life itself. She couldn't tell her family about this uncanny world she found herself in and her only friend was M.I.A. The only person, besides Megan, who Kaden was really close to was Quinn. But she had no physical proof of this strange world other than Finley who probably wouldn't provide any. And if he did, it was Kaden's job to protect her little sister and that would just put her in danger. Then there was Megan, the only one who would have believed her without proof, but she was the whole reason Kaden knew anything about any of it.

Kaden stopped at a fork in the path with a sign standing in the center. One arrow pointed to the left and read 'Parking Lot' while the other arrow to the right read 'Gloomy Woods'. Underneath the path trail there was a small cautionary sign that warned of a bumpy path ahead. Kaden was unenthusiastic about the trial's title and the cautionary sign made it so much more difficult for her to choose the path which was designed for more advanced hikers.

"Well," she breathed. "Of course I'll be taking the

creepy path. Why wouldn't I?" Kaden tried to amuse herself as a distraction from her impending encounter with a Dark fae.

The path was much more difficult to follow than the other trails she had been walking prior. After spending enough time for the sun to begin its descent behind the horizon, Kaden wondered how she hadn't managed to come across the path before. Protruding from the ground, the tree roots covered most of the faded trail along with bigger, slippery rocks. "Just remember this is for Megan," she whispered to herself as she cautiously stepped past rocks and roots. To make things trickier, the path was uphill for the most part with muddy surfaces. She swallowed the lump in her throat and brushed away her gut feeling that things were bound to go wrong quickly.

Kaden lifted a foot to avoid a tree root when the root itself rose out of the ground to purposefully trip her. She fell forward, hitting the ground hard and rolling off the path completely into the murky woods. After she finished rolling she ended face up with a view of the tree tops. For a moment the tree tops were spinning above her as if she were still rolling. A ripple of pain ached at the back of her head. She felt the back of her head for any signs of blood, but only discovered a bump. As she slowly sat up, Kaden found her jeans ripped open at the knees which were bleeding and scraped. Her palms were covered in sticky blood as well, combined with some dirt and small leaves. Kaden moved some of the debris off her right hand to find a gash that must have been made from a sharp rock when she fell. As she stood she brushed leaves off of her clothes,

"Great," she grumbled to herself. "Just great." She used trees to keep her balanced as she headed back up to the path when a girl, not much older than Kaden, came running down the path heading for the parking lot. Although the girl had ear buds in her ears, she noticed Kaden immediately and stopped her jog. The jogger was not hard to miss. She wore a red jogger's outfit with shoulder length black hair. She pulled the headphones out of her ears as she came closer to Kaden.

"Oh my God, are you okay?" she grabbed Kaden's hand tightly to help her up the last bit of hill.

"Yeah, I'm just…" Kaden's vision faded as blurry spots filled her eyes. The girl wrapped her arm around Kaden's hip to prevent her from falling over.

"You cut your head pretty badly, maybe you should sit," the girl put Kaden's right arm around her neck to help her walk. Kaden felt her head with her free hand and sure enough she felt a profound wound on her forehead. "I think you should go to the hospital. You might have a concussion. The parking lot isn't that far. I can give you a ride."

"No, it's okay, I came here with—" Kaden started when she caught a glimpse of a silver necklace under the girl's red workout jacket. *Do not freak out,* Kaden thought to calm herself. "Actually, my friend is just down the path. He's waiting for me." Kaden removed her arm from behind the girl's neck, but the girl clung onto Kaden's hip, pulling her closer. She clasped her hand over Kaden's mouth as she practically dragged her off the path back into the woods. Kaden's scream was muffled but it wouldn't have done any good seeing that no one was around. *Where the hell is Finley?* Kaden jabbed the girl in the ribs with her elbow. The girl staggered back, then Kaden slammed her heel into the girls' foot. The jogger let out a small grunt but the pain Kaden tried to cause seemed to only incite the girl more.

"You little bitch! The more you struggle, the more fun this is going to be," the girl hissed through a twisted smile. Kaden tried to pry the girl's hand off her mouth by clawing at it. Kaden's mind was rapidly thinking of a way for her to get loose before she was taken too. She threw all of her weight to the side to make both of them tumble to the ground. The Dark fae released Kaden in the process of falling over so Kaden crawled to grab a bulky branch off the ground for a weapon. As they both stood up, Kaden swung the branch as hard as she could into the jogger's gut, propelling her back down. Kaden sprinted down the path toward civilization seeing that Finley was nowhere to be found. She took a quick look back to make sure the Dark fae was still down. When Kaden looked, there was no one on the ground which made her skin crawl. Her feet were running before her mind had processed the scene.

When Kaden whipped her head to face forward, her eyes were greeted by the jogger. The Dark fae slammed Kaden back to the ground without so much as touching her. The jogger stood above her with a wry smile on her face, "You're going to be fun." She took one step closer to grab Kaden when Finley came up behind the jogger and slammed her in the back of the head with what looked like a pipe. The jogger collapsed to the ground like a sack of potatoes.

"Well done," Finley lifted the pipe to his shoulder.

"What the hell took you so long?" Kaden gasped, still on the cold ground with several bloody cuts. Finley pulled out a pair of handcuffs which he proceeded to put around the unconscious Dark fae's wrists.

"I had to get some supplies," he said as he picked the girl up in his arms. "These handcuffs come in handy, and I don't just mean for capturing a faerie." Finley gave Kaden a wink just as she stood up. "We should get back to my flat before someone sees me carrying a limp body," Finley gestured for Kaden to come over to him. His voice was even as he spoke until he noticed all the cuts Kaden had received from the fae, "Are you alright?" For the first time Kaden saw a flash of concern wash over Finley's face. What was more surprising was that it was for her. "Take my arm," he said. "We'll get you cleaned up soon." Everything felt like a foggy haze. Kaden gently put her hand on Finley's shoulder. He barely flicked his fingers together when all of a sudden Kaden felt like someone large shoved her from behind. The scenery changed from the gloomy woods to Finley's apartment in the blink of an eye.

"I'm going to clean myself up," Kaden weakly said, making her way to the bathroom. As she shuffled to the bathroom she held on to any kind of furniture so she wouldn't fall over.

She closed the door behind her, relieving a sigh and standing in place to give herself a moment. The afternoon had seemed so long and yet everything happened so quickly. Inside her head was pounding and she was covered in muck. Kaden started the shower so she could wash the dirt and mud off her sensitive skin and prevent her cuts from getting infected. She tossed her clothes to the tile floor, indulging herself in the steamy sanctuary. The water trickled down her, calming her nerves. The shower almost made time freeze. She felt her heart beating slowly but still strong. Her blood blended with the clean water giving it a tint of crimson as it fell to the drain. Once all the dirt and debris was off, she wrapped a warm blue towel around her body. She searched the medicine cabinet for bandages and some peroxide to clean her wounds. Gauze covered her hand, two band aids concealed her knees, and a small strip closed up the wound on her forehead. The last thing she did was take two aspirins before opening the door to ask Finley to borrow a shirt. When Kaden opened the door, the couch had been moved up against the bookshelf by the windows. The coffee table was in the small hall and in its place was a chair with the jogger seated in it. Her hands were bound behind the chair in the hand cuffs, with chains wrapped around her body. To her surprise, Kaden didn't even have to ask for a shirt. A nice blue plaid shirt lay on the floor just outside the bathroom door. She snatched it up before closing the door behind her.

With a new shirt that was oversized for her and her dirty, torn up jeans, Kaden opened the bathroom door to find Finley leaned against the fireplace eyeing the jogger. As soon as Finley realized Kaden was done, he came over to her before she could enter the living room. He took her arm to gently guide her back into the bathroom.

"How's your head?" he asked as he brushed her hair out of her face to reveal the cut. His touch was smooth against her forehead and it was then that Kaden noticed how perfect he was. He was almost completely flawless. All of his features were soft. His skin had no marks or cuts of any sort, even the small cut he had when she first saw him in the alley was gone.

"I'll live," she answered honestly although she had an excruciating migraine. And she probably had some kind of concussion. "What happened to your cut?" Finley pulled his hand away from her forehead as he furrowed his eyebrows. "The one you had from the alley."

"It healed. Very few things can harm faeries." He crossed his arms over his chest, "I think it might be best if you stay in here for now."

"I'm fine," she lied. "Really."

"It's not a good idea," Finley said flatly. "It's not safe. Faeries are tricky. Especially if they get into your head, which they will since you're vulnerable."

"How is it not safe?" she asked, sneaking a peek into the living room. "She's tied down."

Finley sighed lightly, "She's tied down with iron chains, which means she can't get out, but that doesn't mean she won't try," he replied.

"Iron chains?"

"Iron is one of the few things that are lethal to faeries." Finley glanced over his shoulder to make sure she was still tied down then looked back to Kaden.

"So the pipe you hit her with over the head with was—"

"Iron as well," he finished. "Stay in this room. You can listen, but I don't want her to see you." Kaden rolled her eyes with frustration, but accepted his bargain.

Finley set out for the living room while Kaden pushed her limits by standing at the edge of her boundaries. She watched as Finley shaked the jogger roughly to wake her from unconsciousness, "Shea," he said with a totally new voice. It was stern and angry unlike his usual calm and collected voice. "It's been awhile," Finley then spoke as if it was evident she was an old friend.

"Bite me, Finley," she spat at the floor. Finley clenched a hand full of her hair in his fist to force her to look at him.

"Alright, let's just cut to it then." He released his grip roughly and Shea kept her head up after that. "Where are you taking the girls?"

"To our safe haven," she laughed with enjoyment.

"Which is where?" Finley pressed as he paced back and forth in front of her.

"A place," she told him. "Where's your friend? I know she's here somewhere."

Finley glared at her, "Around. What is the address of the place you're taking the girls?"

"I would be honored to be the one to escort you there. Doyle would be so pleased to finally have you join us. She's here," Shea said with a hint of playfulness. "Isn't she?" Shea seemed to be studying Finley as much as Finley studied her. Even Kaden noticed a slight tightness set in his jaw. "She is," she said. Shea squirmed against the iron chains but it was no use. Finley quickly grabbed her hair again, but this time held some kind of a blade against her neck.

"Don't move," he firmly warned. Shea laughed

obnoxiously before relaxing her position.

"Did I hit a nerve? What are you going to do?" She teased. Finley swallowed hard before bringing the blade up to Shea's eye.

"I am going to kill you if you do not answer all of my questions to my liking," he stated. Kaden watched as Shea's body grew tense at the proximity of the blade to her pupil. "Where are you taking the girls?"

"Go ahead," she seethed. "Kill me! Doyle will kill me anyway if I answer you!" Shea struggled under Finley's grip. Finley slashed Shea's cheek with the blade, causing her to hiss from the pain. As the blade broke through her skin, it made a burning noise, leaving a deep gash on her face.

"Where?" he slashed her other cheek this time with more force.

Shea huffed and puffed through the torment. "She's near a berth where she learns her earthly lesson before her final judgment."

"Where!?" Finley stabbed the knife through Shea's right hand. The knife came out of the other side of her hand, which caused Shea to throw her head back as she screamed in agony. For a moment Kaden's mind couldn't comprehend what her eyes were seeing. She turned her gaze away, her fingers rubbed her right palm as she squeezed her eyes shut before returning them back to Shea's pain.

"The light of our world is where she learns her earthly lesson next to nothing," she clenched her teeth together. Finley twisted the blade in her hand. "Ahh forgotten repository that lies upon a prickle ditch is where you may find the girls," she cried. Finley pulled the knife out of her hand. Shea took a deep slow breath to ease her pain. He pulled away from her to attempt to decipher her clues.

Kaden shuffled barefoot, closer to the scene. "There was a girl who was taken last night by Riley," she said. She felt her jaw clench tighter as she spoke, "Will she be there?"

Shea tried to twist to face her, but couldn't find the strength, "The question you ask is above me."

Her nostrils flared. That wasn't good enough of an answer for her. "Has Riley talked about her?" she pressed as her hands turned to fists by her side.

"Indeed."

Then Finley asked the question Kaden was too afraid to ask herself. "Is she alive?"

A crooked smile slipped across Shea's face. "She won't be." She laughed as though she knew it would be her last. Kaden watched as Finley took the dagger and plunged it through the girl's heart. Her maniacal laughter was cut short, turning to a gasp before leaving the room silent. All that was left was the pitter patter of raindrops against the window. In one moment, every inch of life left inside Kaden drained. Replaced by a hollow sorrow, her eyes began to fill with tears she couldn't help creating. Even her heart stopped for a moment.

All her life she felt alone and now that she actually was alone, she felt dead. Without looking to see what Finley's expression was, she climbed out the window onto the fire escape. She leaned against the railing to breathe the cool air into her lungs. The oversized shirt she wore came in handy as she wiped snot and tears that she couldn't control. She felt the weight of another body climb out of the window. Finley mimicked her stance. He didn't look at her, but looked down to the sidewalk as she did. If she had looked at him, she knew she would cry even more.

"We're not going to find her alive are we, Finn?" she whispered the words she prayed weren't true.

Finley shifted his stare to watch Kaden's face for a moment before answering, "We're going to get her. We just need a little help."

"How?" she almost whimpered. "We have no idea where she is."

"Yes we do. We have clues. All we need to do is solve them. I know someone who can help. For now, stay here in the apartment. I'll go see what I can find out." Finley stood up and went back inside to get something before climbing back out to Kaden. When he came back out he had the dagger, cleaned in his hands. "It's an iron blade," he explained. "It can hurt any faerie, Light or Dark. Even me." He handed it to her. The handle had gold intertwined patterns that matched the sheath. The bottom of the handle formed a dragon with emerald eyes. It was heavy in Kaden's hands, but was a perfect fit for her. "Just in case you need to protect yourself." Kaden examined it. The blade felt paper thin. Kaden ran a finger over it. Despite its dangerous effect on fae, or anyone, it was actually quite beautiful craftsmanship.

"Thanks," she softly said as she gripped it tightly. In the corner of her eye she saw Finley wince. "What?"

"Faeries hate being told 'thank you'," his voice was soothing, "it's a sign of one forgetting the good deed done. Instead we prefer something that guarantees remembrance."

Kaden half smiled to herself, amused by all the little quirky things about fae, "Of course." She unclasped one of her earrings, the ones Megan's family had given her, sliding it into Finley's palm. "It's the best I've got." Finley smiled at it in his hand as he examined the tiny piece of jewelry.

"Unfortunately," he sighed. "I have to get the dead body out of my apartment before it ruins my hardwood floor." He made his way into the building leaving Kaden to her thoughts.

She observed from outside as Finley disposed of the jogger's body. When Finley first transported her to his apartment, she hadn't really digested what he actually did. Watching him through the window she saw as he put one hand on Shea's limp body and within a blink, he was gone. There was no magic smoke, just a split second of they were there, and then they were gone. As soon as Finley was gone, Kaden re-entered the apartment. She tried to push the couch back without help, but it was a failed attempt. Kaden tried to analyze the furniture for a moment before she tried again. She leaned her hand against the edge of the fireplace which felt like it shifted under her hand. When she quickly pulled her hand away she found nothing wrong with it. She decided to move the coffee table back to the center of the room, seeing that it was probably the lightest thing.

"I could have done that," Finley's voice came from behind Kaden.

Startled, she jumped to the side with her hand over her heart. "Jesus. Are you trying to give me a heart attack?"

"Allow me," he snapped his fingers together. Slowly the furniture slid across the room back to its natural position.

"I wish I had one of those Staples' buttons right about now," Kaden said. Finley appeared baffled at the joke.

"Because it says 'that was easy'," Kaden tried to help him understand, but it didn't work. "Never mind."

He shot a glance at a clock that hung on the wall, "It's almost six. I'm going out to ask around about Shea's clues." Finley grabbed a leather jacket off the hall coat rack.

"What do I do?" Kaden asked. Finley thought about her question while he grabbed an apple from a fruit bowl on the island.

"It's probably best if you stay here. I don't know how long this will take." He opened the front door halfway, "If trouble finds its way to you just call me."

"I don't have your number." She pulled her cell phone out of her pants pocket.

"Just call my name out loud. I'll hear you."

"Hear me? How?"

"I don't have pointed ears for nothing," he said as he closed the door behind him.

CHAPTER VIII

Megan awoke to a ceiling stained with greenish black mold staring back at her. Her skin prickled with goosebumps from the emptiness that surrounded her. She used her elbows to attempt to sit up only to be met with throbbing waves of pain pulsing through her skull. Half way up, Megan found herself dressed in a pale blue hospital gown. The room before her was vast with industrial windows and peeling paint. Under her was a bed not suitable for a hospital, but perhaps, a ruined jail cell. The throbbing in her skull only grew worse as she sat up further. She tried to remember if she had drank or if someone could have split something unholy into her water, but her mind was blank with details. And the room surrounding her was very real.

Megan looked beside the bed and found a small table

doctors used in surgery. It was filled with shiny new instruments. Needles and scalpels that showed her reflection back at her.

Her heart pounded against her ribs. The air in her lungs became frantic, and she wanted to scream but her throat was frozen.

Footsteps echoed down the hall outside her room. She went against all her feelings and jumped off the bed. There was no door for her to close so she went for the broken window. She was three stories up, too far to jump.

As the footsteps grew louder, she took the scalpel off the table and hid it behind her. Megan stood with her back against the wall next to the door frame to catch the person off guard. Her breath quickened with anticipation, her palms grew sweaty, and she squeezed her eyes tightly just as the person was about to enter the room.

The footsteps stopped. There was nothing. Not even the feeling of a presence hovering outside the door frame.

Against all her better judgment, she slowly stepped out into the door frame, scalpel first.

There was no one in the hallway. Only broken flipped wheelchairs with cobwebs, ripped up papers, broken glass, and one or two old hospital beds. She hesitated before she fully exited her room. *Someone was there just a minute ago,* Megan thought. *They couldn't have just disappeared.* A crooked sign on the wall told her she was in 'Eastern State Hospital', an asylum she had heard about across the state. But Megan knew that the hospital was open, not closed down. The place she found herself in looked like it had been closed down for years, decades even.

She cautiously stepped with her bare feet against debris, to the room across the hall. She prepared herself to find the mysterious walker, but instead found a girl. She was lying on a hospital bed just like Megan had been except her hair had been shaved and she wore no clothes. The girl was unconscious, breathing lightly like she was asleep or dreaming.

Megan rushed over to the girl to shake her awake, "Hey," she whispered in a harsh tone. As she shook the girl, she glanced over her shoulder every once in a while to make sure no one was coming. The girl didn't wake even after Megan slapped her so hard she left a red handprint on her cheek, "Wake up. You have to wake up." With no luck waking the girl, she decided she needed to find a way out. She would have to come back for her once she was safe.

She scurried back to the hall which was still quiet with the occasional rat scampering around. She hurried down the hall making sure to glance in each room for a way out only instead of exits she found girls. All asleep or unconscious, she wasn't sure.

She found a set of broken stairs that seemed to be her only way of getting out of the hospital. Before she allowed her whole weight to rest on each step she tested them by only using half her weight. With each step closer to her exit, Megan glanced behind her to make sure the mysterious footsteps didn't follow.

As she took the last step to the second level she waited a moment to listen to her surroundings. A faint cheering in the distance appeared to come from below. Megan was utterly confused by the overwhelming amount of cheers and screams. She hesitated to continue.

"I guess I underestimated your willpower," Riley's voice came from the top of the third level stairs.

She looked up, surprised by the sudden voice. "You're a sick son of a bitch!" She spat at him and darted for the steps, nearly tripping down them. Megan didn't hear his footsteps chasing after her, but she didn't care. She just ran as fast as she could. Until she hit a body so hard it sent her falling back on the hard floor.

"Now, now," Riley said. "No need to run." Megan used her heels to kick herself away from the man who took her. A twisted being who appeared to have captured all the girls. With each inch she got away from him, he stepped closer toward her until she was trapped by a wall. "Relax," he said. Riley squatted down until he was eye level with Megan, "It will all be over soon." He reached out to her and rubbed his thumb against her cheek. Megan squirmed at his touch, but she forced herself to stab his hand with the scalpel. She expected to find blood or for him to wince, but he didn't seem to care.

"What the hell?" her voice trembled.

"Sorry, lass," he smirked. His grin was filled with crooked teeth, "It may feel real, but it's all a part of the game. Believe me or not, but this isn't the first time you're awake."

"What?" Water began to fill her vision. "You're lying!" she yelled in his face.

"Afraid not," he ran his fingers through her hair gently. "The only thing real here is you and me and those crippling girls fading just as fast as you are. I do admit," he added with a slight chuckle, "you are a lot of fun." Riley gripped Megan's beautiful hair tightly and she let out a whimper. She tried to stab him again with the weapon although it was no use. Before she could fight back, he smashed her head against the brick wall, knocking her out completely.

CHAPTER IX

Kaden collapsed onto the couch. She stared up at the ceiling where intricate patterns stared back at her. The endless white stirred a restless energy around inside of her as she was left behind to feed further into her worried thoughts. She sat up abruptly taking the knife into her hand and placing it delicately on the coffee table in front of her. The golden handle spun in circles as Kaden twirled its handle. A sigh escaped her lungs and her gaze began to wander around the room. Her eyes stopped as soon as they hit the golden book she had peered into the night before. "I shouldn't," she told herself. Her stomach interrupted her curiosity as a loud growl announced its presence to the room. When she remembered she had only eaten two small bits of bacon, Kaden went into the kitchen to find something to eat. She poured herself a bowl of Lucky

Charms, which she found to be ironic standing in the kitchen of a faerie. The falsely flavored marshmallows couldn't break the appeal of reading some of the letters from the book. Kaden took a big spoonful of cereal as she stared at the gold sitting on the shelf. Her chewing grew louder as she paced the kitchen floor, eyes still locked on the book. "Just one peek can't hurt," she said to herself, nearly darting to the bookcase.

The book, which wasn't really a book, almost matched the design of the knife Finley had given her. She carried it back to the couch with her and placed it on her lap. *Okay, whatever I read in here, I cannot let Finley know I read it.* Part of her felt guilty, but the curiosity to read them was overwhelmingly strong. When she opened the book, she saw the same letters she had seen before. Most of them were written by Finley in elegant cursive handwriting. Kaden decided to only read some from the top and then maybe some from the bottom so she wouldn't feel as bad. The first one read:

Dearest Linette,

You have such grace and beauty. I cannot fathom how it is you who fancies me over others. Life is empty without you. You are my greatest self, my light, my sun, my moon. You are the single most important thing in my life. My heart. It is with this passion that, one day, you and I will run far away together. We shall wed and travel anywhere you wish. I will give you the world; for you have already given me mine. I will never stop thinking of you. Every breath I take is another that brings us closer to our happy ending.

Your Finley

Her eyes traced the words over and over again. With

the beauty of the language and the handwriting coming from someone so strange. The words were romantic and charming. Love filled the page, something she had never known. Kaden had never been in love with someone herself, but to read it first hand, not in a novel, was so unfamiliar to her.

Though she knew it was wrong to continue to read, she did anyway. Each letter was more riveting than the last. As each one became more personal with their secret relationship, Kaden felt like she was reading a Shakespearian play. She intended on only reading a couple, however the letters were too captivating for her to stop. *Who was Linette? Why haven't I met her yet?* Kaden wondered as she read. She finally came to the last letter and was surprised to see it wasn't written by Finley, but by the mysterious Linette.

My darling Finley,

Mother grows weaker each day. I fear with each breath she takes, it will be her last. I love you more than I have ever loved anyone, and I will never love anyone as much as I love you. My heart breaks to be writing this letter to you. I beg of you, do not think ill of my decision, for I have already come to hate myself. With Mother ill, it falls to me to take care of the family. I'm afraid there is no happy ending for us after all. Mother wishes for me to wed another, for the sake of the family, in a few short days. I only ask one thing of you. I would be forever grateful to have you by my side as I take over for Mother. I need you in my life, in some way. I'm afraid we mustn't write anymore, this box is a gift to you for all that you have given me. Your letters fill me with the greatest love. I cannot bear to read them anymore, for they make my heart ache for you. I beg your forgiveness, my love, my Finley.

Forever yours, Linette.

Kaden felt her heart slow in pace as the words she read filled her with sorrow. After reading the letters, she couldn't imagine the heartache that must have followed. All for family. She sat against the couch briefly as she digested all that she had read. "How could she betray him like that?" she said to herself. As she piled the letters back together, she noticed a small photo at the bottom of the box. It was an old black and white photo of a family; the father stood broad shouldered with a stern face in the back while the mother smiled lightly with an elegant grace about her. A young man stood centered in front of them with the same expression and likeness of the father. Finley was placed closer to what Kaden assumed was his mother with an identical smile. A small girl, about six years old, sat on the floor, a grin spread across her tiny face. On the back of the photo read 'Father, Mother, Thierry, Finley, and Eva 1934 Departure Day' in Finley's handwriting.

The photo reminded Kaden of her own family, which she realized she still hadn't contacted about her whereabouts. So she put the photo and the letters back in their proper place before she pulled her phone out to check her messages. There were hundreds of missed calls and just as many text messages, most of which were left by her sister. Kaden listened to one voice mail from her sister that was frantic and barely intelligible. She knew it would be hard to explain what she was doing, but she had to tell her something. As much as she knew seeing them was a horrible idea, she also knew her sister would drive herself crazy if she didn't actually see Kaden with her own two eyes.

She cared too much about her family to just leave them hanging any longer and with Finley gone for a little while, it seemed like the perfect time to go home quickly. He would have advised against her plan but he wasn't there and she probably wouldn't have listened to him. Kaden snatched the knife from the table, put on her coat, and locked the door behind her with the hidden key. When she got outside she headed toward her house, looking for a cab as she walked.

Kaden's house was dark. There were no porch lights or lights on in the house, as if no one was home. She prepared herself for the worst by taking a deep breath before entering the house. As difficult as explaining herself was really going to be, she knew she had to get it over with if she wanted to save Megan without worrying about her family.

The front door was unlocked which concerned her seeing that anyone or *thing* could get into the house. The first floor was completely dead with no one around, "Hello?!" Kaden called out. Within seconds footsteps tumbled down the stairs as if whoever was coming down was about to fall.

"Kaden!" Quinn squealed as she nearly tripped over herself. She flung her arms around Kaden's neck to greet her with a bear hug. "Where have you been? I was so worried, and then the cops came asking about you and said that something happened to Megan! Her parents keep calling, asking if we've heard from either of you. What happened? Is Megan okay? Are you—"

"Slow down, Quinn," she held her sister's shoulders with her hands. "I can explain everything, you're just going to have to trust me when I do. And I'm fine. I'm sorry I didn't call." As Kaden spoke to Quinn, their mother quietly came down the stairs to join them. "Megan went missing last night, so I spent the night and today looking for her. I still don't know where she is."

"How dare you not call," her mother seethed. "Who do you think you are? Your father? You think you can just leave and not tell anyone? I had to take off of work for this? For some rescue mission you think you're on?" Kaden expected her family to be worried, but comparing her to her father twisted an anger inside of her she didn't realize she had been holding. Their father was a selfish man who abandoned his family. Kaden was anything but that.

Quinn silently stood by her sister's side as their mom scolded her. "I'm really sorry I didn't call," she said honestly. "I know I should have, but I was looking for—"

"Yeah," she cut her off abruptly. "Megan. You said that already. But Megan is not your responsibility."

"Yes she is," Kaden took a step closer to her mother who stood with her arms crossed on the bottom step. "It was my idea to go to the pub last night. And she's my best friend. If something happens to her, it happens to me too." Her mother stood, towering over her with a silent resentment.

"If you do this again," she said, "don't bother coming home." She turned her back as if she had been waiting for an excuse to say the words for a long time. Her mother stomped upstairs, proceeding to slam her bedroom door shut behind her.

Kaden and Quinn waited in silence for a brief moment before either of them said anything. Quinn tugged on Kaden's arm, "Come on, you must be hungry." Quinn flipped the kitchen light on before she pulled a chair out for Kaden to sit in. She opened cabinets, pulling various ingredients out onto the counter. Kaden half stood up to help, "No, you sit. I'll make you something. I just have to figure out what." She started to boil a pot of water for some pasta, "Okay, now tell me what the hell happened?"

Kaden sat up straight in her seat while Quinn took the seat across from her, "It's really hard to explain."

"Try me," Quinn said, half her lip curled up in a smile. Kaden sighed, trying to figure out where or how to start. "Kaden, you're my sister and I love you, just tell me what happened."

"Let me start by saying you are going to think I'm crazy." Quinn waited patiently for Kaden to continue. "Megan and I were at the pub when this guy, Riley, gave us some trouble. Megan and I got separated for only like ten minutes outside. So I called the cops and searched the pub before it closed but I couldn't find her anywhere. I met this other guy who kind of is the reason for Megan getting taken. We've been looking for her together," she paused to see if Quinn had anything to ask. "He was a trumpet player at the pub. His name is Finley."

"Despite the fact that you are working with some creepy guy you just met, I don't see how that's something to make me think you're crazy."

"No, you're not going to believe me about the next

part," Kaden hesitated. She searched for the right words to explain that a fae world exists. It was hard enough for *her* to swallow let alone her sister who hadn't seen the things she had seen.

"Yes I will," she insisted. "Trust me." Quinn took Kaden's hand and gave it a light squeeze for reassurance. "I'm sure I've heard worse."

"No," Kaden warned her. "You really haven't." She knew the conversation probably wouldn't end well, but she needed someone to talk to about it, other than Finley who barely knew her. "No matter what I say, promise me you trust me."

"I promise. Pinky swear." The girls hooked their pinkies together like they did when they were little kids.

"The trumpet player…" Kaden eased into the truth.

"Finley," her sister finished proud that she remembered.

"Is not human," she winced a little, ready for her sister to burst out laughing.

"…What do you mean?" Quinn asked. She pulled her hand away from Kaden's to sit up.

"He turned into…a dog."

"A dog?" she repeated.

"Yes. A dog. But that's not all he can do. He can teleport, steal things when no one sees, and he has pointed ears. Well, he does when he takes off his enchanted necklace," she explained. Quinn sat upright, her eyes wide boring into Kaden's. "Say something," Kaden urged.

"So," Quinn sat back in her chair. "The trumpet player is a wizard?"

"That's what I thought at first too!" Kaden got overly excited that her sister had thought the same thing as she did and that she was willing to believe her. "But no, he's a faerie. Well, he uses the term fae," she corrected.

Quinn sucked in a deep breath, "Megan…" she began, "got taken by faeries…so you're getting help from a faerie to find Megan?"

"Yes!" Kaden breathed a breath of relief as if she had been holding onto it for far too long.

"Okay," Quinn said with a nod.

"Okay?" she questioned. "Just like that? Even I needed proof."

"Yes, okay. It's weird, but I trust you." Kaden pulled her sister in for a tight hug. She held her and didn't want to let her go. With Quinn on her side Kaden wouldn't have to worry as much.

"You have no idea how much this means to me," she admitted. A tickle appeared at the end of her nose as if she was just about to cry. "I have to go upstairs and grab some clothes," she said to stop herself from shedding a tear. "Can I borrow your boots?"

"Yeah, they're in my closet. Are you sure you should be doing this? Maybe you should leave this up to the cops or, you know….Finley." Kaden was already headed for the stairs while Quinn expressed her concerns.

"I told you," she called over her shoulder. "The cops won't know how to help. Finley said it can only be us." She opened the door to her room and grabbed her old backpack from under her bed.

"Finley, the trumpet player," Quinn said doubtfully.

"I trust him. He's gotten me closer to getting Megan. Can you believe the cops accused me of being on drugs? I mean they didn't even care that Megan was gone." Kaden shoved anything and everything she could find into her backpack.

"Look at your head, your hands," her sister pointed out. Kaden had completely forgotten about her injuries before Quinn mentioned them again. "This is dangerous. Maybe you should stay here. At least for a while." Quinn stood leaning against the doorway watching Kaden ransack her room.

"Megan is my best friend," she argued. "I'm not going to forget her. I thought you would know that," Kaden threw her closet door open and dug for shoes. "Can you get your boots for me?"

"Sure," she said as she left the room to go to her own. Kaden took mostly dark colored jeans, shirts, and a black jacket. She had never been a part of a rescue mission but thought dark colors would be the best for sneaking around.

Everything she needed was packed, so she went to Quinn's room to see what was taking so long with the boots. The door was ajar and Kaden heard her sister speaking to someone so she hovered outside the door.

"She's having some kind of breakdown," Quinn said into her phone. "She made up this whole story about fae kidnapping Megan. She's having some kind of post traumatic stress thing. She came home with cuts, Joe. I'm afraid she's going to hurt herself. Should I call someone?" Overhearing her sister speak that way about her felt as though a knife entered her heart. Her body grew hollow and numb. Her eyes began to water up as she pushed the door open so her sister knew she was there. "Kaden, how long have you been standing there?" Her sister hung up the phone quickly with a guilty face.

"You think I made this up?" She asked, holding back heartbroken tears.

"No, of course not. I think that maybe, after what happened, the other night with Megan..." Quinn stepped forward to comfort her.

Kaden took a step away from Quinn. "I'm telling you the truth," anger began to flow through her.

"Look, Mom went through the same thing when we were younger. Remember she would say how you weren't—"

"You think....I'm like Mom?" Kaden wiped her runny nose with her sleeve. "I can prove it, he gave me this knife." She pulled the dagger from her coat pocket to show Quinn.

Quinn's expression shifted from concern to utter fear at the sight of Kaden holding a knife. "Kaden," she paused as she lifted her hands up slowly. "Put down the knife. I believe you, just put it down. We can go find Megan together. Just put. It. Down."

Kaden felt wild and untamed as her fury grew. *How could Quinn possibly think I would hurt myself? How could she not trust me? After everything we've been through together.* "You think I'm going to hurt myself? Look at this!" she waved the dagger at Quinn, desperate for her to see the truth. "It's an antique, how could I have gotten this?!"

"Kaden, please. You're sick, I can help you." Kaden furrowed her eyebrows, confused and unwilling to believe her own sister would say such a thing.

"He told me if I called his name he would show up. Then you'll see I'm not crazy. Finley!" Kaden called out into the room, hoping to prove to her sister that she wasn't crazy. Nothing happened. "Finley!" She yelled louder looking around the room for him to appear.

"What is going on?!" Her mother barked before she saw the scene between the two girls. She blocked the doorway, staring at the knife Kaden held. Quinn took another step closer to Kaden as Kaden looked from their mother to Quinn, then to the knife.

"See, he's not real, Kaden. Now, put the knife down." Kaden knew she had to leave before they called the cops and sent her to the same hospital their mother had gone to. She shoved her mom out of her way, which to her surprise her mother didn't stand her ground. Kaden made it down the stairs, out the front door, and down the street while her sister yelled for her to stop. As she heard her sister's voice, it only encouraged Kaden to run faster and further away. Her vision blurred with tears of rage or sorrow, she didn't know. She ran four blocks before coming to a full stop, leaning and panting against an old telephone pole.

He was right. They didn't believe me, she thought. She let herself cry an ugly cry knowing her sister, the one she trusted more than anyone in the world, thought she was insane. "I'm not crazy," she sobbed, "I'm not crazy."

CHAPTER X

Ten years ago

 Her room was coated in stillness. At her feet, against the bedpost lined perfectly to her liking were Kaden's stuffed animals from lion to bear to everything in between. A ballerina night light glowed in the far corner, illuminating her music box and a few other trinkets she had on her dresser. The light from the hall switched on and crept through her door which she always left half open in case a monster tried to eat her. The hour was late, far past her bedtime, but the muffled arguments kept her from sleeping. She tossed and turned for what felt like forever as the light sound of a disagreement turned into sharp tones and bitterness.

"Do you hear yourself!?" her father's husky voice echoed into her room.

"I'm telling you, George, you have to believe me." Her mother sounded unsteady as the two shuffled around their bedroom across the hall.

"Ann, you have to take your medication," he insisted. "This is getting ridiculous." Several dresser drawers slammed shut which didn't soothe Kaden's insomnia.

"We aren't safe!" Her mother pleaded. There was a real certainty in her voice Kaden recognized. "They're going to come back," she continued, "and when they do, they could kill us."

Kaden watched as a short shadow grew larger in the hall as it came closer to her room. Quinn poked her head around the door to see if her older sister was awake. She wore her princess nightgown and carried her stuffed rabbit in her arms. "Kaden?" she whispered into the dark room. "Are you awake?" Kaden tossed to the side to face the door.

"Yeah," she answered as her little sister opened the door further, brightening up the room. Quinn tiptoed inside, closing the door shut behind her.

"I can't sleep," Quinn stood next to her bed waiting for her to come up with a solution to her problem. Kaden flipped her blanket down so Quinn could get in. She snuggled in next to Kaden and faced away from the door, to avoid the distant echoes of the fight. "When are they going to stop fighting?"

"I don't know," Kaden admitted. "Now go to sleep." As Quinn tried to fall asleep, Kaden listened to the argument that was taking place in the other room.

"Kaden will never be mine," she overheard her mother say. Kaden's eyes began to water, "I'm telling you," she continued. "I'm not sick. I don't need medicine."

"If you won't take your pills," her father said, "then tomorrow I'm taking you to the hospital like last time."

The covers of Kaden's bedspread covered her face as she pushed herself further under them. "I don't need them," her mom cried. There was pain in her mother's tone, a longing to be heard, but Kaden bit back her own tears from falling.

"I can't do this anymore! Every time I take you to the hospital you take your meds and you're fine. Then you come home and you're fine. A week later it's like you never went to the hospital!" her father's tone rose. Kaden wondered if they realized how loud they were being, if maybe she was supposed to do something about it. "'I'm fine' you say. 'I don't need my meds'. Well you do! I can't do this anymore. I'm done." More drawers began to rustle angrily.

"I'm not crazy George! What are you doing?" her mother asked frantically. "You can't take me back to the hospital now. Quinn's asleep."

"I'm not taking you anywhere," his footsteps moved quickly in their room.

"You're leaving?" Her mother asked, but he didn't answer. Their bedroom door opened which made Kaden shrink further into her bed so her parents didn't see she was awake. Her father didn't stop to check on the girls. He didn't stop to say goodbye. He just ran down the steps and left. Their mother did not try to stop him. She didn't run after him.

The house was finally silent. Her mother turned off the hall light and shut her door. The arguing stopped.

Quinn's light snoring rose and fell beside her. A faded noise made its way to Kaden. It was her mother crying in her bedroom. "I'm not crazy."

CHAPTER XI

Pine needles blanketed the forest floor under the glistening full moonlight. The fresh mountain air filled Finley's lungs as it had done in his past. Night and nature surrounded him. The soft melody of life cradled him as if he was home once more. He closed his eyes, taking in every ounce of it. "Cadell," he said into the night. Finley opened his eyes once more and began to stroll past enormous trees. "I require your help," he said, "old friend." He paused in between a small gap of trees, waiting. Seeking the help of a Light fae was frowned upon once a faerie was no longer among their ranks. For some, reaching out was forbidden. For Finley, it was painful.

"It has been quite some time," a voice said out of the darkness. Finley turned in the direction the voice came from. Among the shadows, Cadell appeared with his staff in hand, the top of which formed a moon. Behind him, an owl appeared on a low branch with wide eyes of wisdom.

"Just when I thought your overly coherent voice of reason had dissipated from my mind for good," Finley smiled lightly, but Cadell remained apathetic.

"What," he began. His voice was hypnotically soothing among the nightscape. "May I ask, are you in need of?" He used his elegantly carved wooden staff to step further into the moonlight.

"I find myself in a bit of a bind," Finley answered. The owl's yellow eyes followed him with each step toward Cadell he took, both watchful and threatening. "I've been seeking answers. None of the fae I've questioned seem to know them."

"I see," he said plainly. The glimmering light revealed the two twisted horns he had on top of his forehead. He was the only faerie Finley knew of that had ram-like horns.

"I fear the Dark fae are up to something more than their usual antics," he admitted through a sigh. His breath clouded the cold night in front of him. "More girls continue to get captured with each passing year."

"The Queen is familiar with the Dark fae's doings," Cadell noted.

"You know?" Finley asked to his surprise. He studied Cadell. Cadell's face had never given anything away. Standing in the middle of the forest under the moon was no different. "Tell me," he began, "what you have foreseen." As the question was asked, Finley watched as Cadell inhaled deeply, sealing the deep forest green of his eyes away. When Cadell exhaled, his eyes flew open, purely white.

"I see darkness on the horizon," his voice shifted to something lower, deeper than his normal one. "Whether it is the Dark faeries or not, I cannot tell. Blood will be shed and lives lost forever." Suddenly, Cadell closed his eyes, turning them green once more.

Finley pondered his words carefully. A deep sense that Megan was already dead riddled him with an unusual anger for someone he never met. He buried the feeling away, "A fae spoke of an 'earthly lesson'," he continued. "Does that mean anything to you?"

"Earthly lessons are associated with many things," Cadell said. He glanced over towards his owl companion, "Some believe it to be the judgment before death. It's symbolic of the number nine, the end of an era, but also the beginning of a new one."

"The light of our world," Finley whispered to himself. His thoughts began turning over in his mind again, "It could mean the source...is where she learns her earthly lesson next to nothing." He bowed his head and closed his eyes tightly so he could envision the clues.

"What is nine next to nothing?" Cadell pressed, guiding Finley toward the answers he was looking for.

"Ninety?" Finley questioned. "It couldn't be that simple?"

"Perhaps there is nothing simple about it," Cadell replied.

Finley raised his head, "She's near berth ninety. Or pier ninety." Suddenly, among Finley's thoughts a faint voice echoed in his ear. *Kaden,* he thought looking to the night sky as if that was where her voice had come from. He heard the panic in her tone. Pain mixed with sadness, but sensed there was no danger.

"Who is it that calls you?" the Seer wondered.

"It's not urgent," he answered, turning his attention from the sky back to Cadell.

"Certainly whoever it is," he began, "needs you."

"No," Finley decided. "She didn't listen to me, and now she wants me to rescue her from her own undoing. She needs this information more."

Cadell tilted his head gently to the side, "Why do you aid this girl?" he asked, curiosity slipping off his tongue. "If Doyle is involved, why would you risk a quarrel with him alone?" Finley didn't answer as Kaden's soft voice continued to call to him. "I fear you have grown lonely in your time away from the Court. Promise me, friend," Cadell added, "do not do something you will regret."

"I should return to her," Finley said. Cadell respectfully bowed his head, "Until next time." Finley teleported out of the forest, leaving Cadell behind, and went back to the streets of Seattle to Kaden.

Feeling alone and more lost than ever, Kaden meandered the long trek from her home to Finley's apartment. Dried tear trails stained her face. The mistrust Quinn expressed crushed her worse than any other pain Kaden had felt in her lifetime. It was a betrayal. And a brutal one. *Why didn't Finley show up?* Kaden found herself wondering. *He said he would. If he had, Quinn wouldn't have thought... No. I'm not. It's all his fault. He didn't show up. He was supposed to be there.* The soles of her feet barely lifted off the sidewalk as she tried to figure out what she was feeling. Was she angrier at Finley for not showing up, or Quinn for not believing her?

Finley's voice broke through her rambling thoughts, "What happened to *you*?" She glanced up to find him sitting on a random stoop to an apartment building a few feet ahead of Kaden. Her face was paler than usual. Her eyes bloodshot from crying, only half focused on the world around her with her backpack slung over her shoulder. She stopped abruptly in her tracks. She felt her rage rush to her face. His voice, his clothes, his arrogant smirk. He lifted himself off the stoop and walked toward her.

"What happened to *me*?"she asked him. The anger in her tone was not slight. "How about what happened to *you*? You said you would be there if I called you!" She threw her bag at him in hopes it would hurt him, but was made more furious when he caught it. "You lied."

"No I didn't," his voice was nonchalant like what she experienced was nothing. "I said if trouble finds *you* I would come."

"How would you even know I wasn't in trouble!? You didn't show up," Kaden fumed. She noticed his attitude shift once he came to realize how upset she was. "I'm so tired of all these double meanings you tell people. If you think being accused of being crazy by your sister isn't 'in trouble' then you're just...just an ass," Kaden pushed past him in the direction of his apartment. Finley remained silent but she felt him following right behind her, "I wasn't planning on telling Quinn everything, I just wanted her to trust me enough to let me save Megan. How the hell do you expect someone to believe you when you don't have hard proof? Especially since my mother..." Kaden bit her tongue, "All you had to do was show up! I could have been killed by Dark fae or Theodore for all you know!"

"I knew you weren't in any real trouble," Finley quietly started from behind her. Kaden quickly spun around to slap Finley across the face.

"How could you possibly..." She froze as she came to realize Finley *had* known where she was the whole time. Before she had thought he was clueless to where she was, but now she knew that wasn't the case. "You knew where I was didn't you?" Finley didn't answer. "You knew I wanted to show my sister," she said slowly. "So you didn't show up."

"Yes," he answered truthfully. "You don't want her to believe you. If she did, she could get hurt too. Do you really want that for her?" he tried to defend his actions but Kaden wouldn't have it.

"What I wanted," she paused, "was for my sister to not think I am crazy. I wanted to tell her the truth so if something happened to me she knew I did it to save Megan. So she wouldn't think I ran off and left her by herself! That's what I wanted! So don't assume you know what I want." Kaden turned sharply, walking back to Finley's place. The air was heavy with tension as neither one of them spoke another word.

Despite Kaden's curiosity about what Finley had discovered about the clues Shea had provided, she kept her comments to herself. She was fixated on her sisters' reaction. *When I do get Megan back, how am I supposed to explain everything to Quinn? How will she believe me without Finley as proof? How will she treat me now that she thinks I'm insane?*

"Do you hear that?" Finley broke the silence between them. He came to a halt, grabbing Kaden's arm to stop her alongside him. Finley surveyed the area where they stood. He looked behind them, in front of them, and across the street. He slightly tilted his head to the side as he listened to an unknown noise.

"Hear what?" Kaden tried to find the sound Finley was referring to, but all she heard were cars off in the distance.

"Nothing," he brushed the noise off as nothing and released Kaden's arm so they could continue to his apartment. With only two blocks to go, they passed parked cars, an alley, and more lifeless stoops. Kaden's feet screamed to her in pain. The boots she wore were not meant for long distances. She took a moment to lean on a stoop banister to readjust one, hoping it would relieve some of her pain. Finley scanned the dead street as he waited for her to finish messing around with her boots. He carried the backpack Kaden had thrown at him by slinging it over one shoulder. "We should hurry," he didn't sound afraid, but there was something about his voice that came off as skeptical.

"Give me a minute," Kaden said impatiently as she struggled to pull her boot off.

"You don't hear that?" Finley asked, squinting at her.

"No...but apparently you hear something." She slipped her boot back on accepting that she would have to endure the pain of her feet since they were close to Finley's anyway. "Alright, let's go," she started walking again, only Finley didn't follow. Kaden turned to see why he wasn't moving. "Hello? Earth to Finley," she waved her hand in an attempt to draw his attention, but he seemed to be focused on something else. Finley's gaze was set on a narrow alleyway they passed. Kaden back-tracked the few feet she had walked away from him. "Your apartment is this way," she pointed down the street. His eyes didn't move an inch off the alley. Kaden stood on her tiptoes in front of his dead stare to wave her hand directly in front of him. "Finley?" His body didn't respond. Kaden inspected the street for any sign of life, but no one was around. Finley began to back track toward the narrow alley. "Finley," Kaden called after him. When he didn't stop, she decided to follow him to see where he was going. He proceeded to enter the dim, cramped path that led out to another street. Kaden couldn't see what Finley was walking toward, but she had a feeling it wasn't good. She tugged on his arm for him to turn back, but he shrugged her off. "This is not a good idea," she hoped he would snap out of whatever trance he was in and come to his senses. As they approached the end of the alley, Kaden hung back a bit to insure she wasn't headed into a trap. She hid behind a gate that encased some kind of generator. At the center of the alley she saw a woman who seemed to have Finley mesmerized.

Her tall slim body wore a tight red dress that cut off at her thigh. Her lips were full and covered with red lipstick, matching her red waved hair. The woman seemed to be humming something Kaden couldn't hear.

The woman caressed Finley's cheek as she hummed her tuneless melody. She lured him behind the back of the building and he traced her every step. Finley slid Kaden's backpack onto the cement ground. Even though she wasn't familiar with how to use a knife as a weapon, Kaden pulled out the dagger Finley had given her. She'd never hurt anyone before and certainly never killed anyone.

The mysterious woman guided Finley to an unknown location which Kaden figured was her best opportunity to stop them. Waiting any longer to do something would probably end very badly for her. She ran up behind the woman, knife held tightly against the woman's throat. To Kaden's surprise the woman didn't fight back at all, she didn't flinch or show any concern that she was being threatened. Kaden wasn't fully aware of what would come next, even holding a knife against someone's throat made her squirm. She didn't want to kill the woman who seemed to compel Finley, but how was she supposed to get him un-compelled? "What did you do to him?" Kaden pressed the knife against her fair skin as she demanded an answer.

The woman smiled to herself which frightened Kaden. "I wasn't aware Finley was…occupied. This should be interesting." Kaden attempted to mimic Finley when he slightly cut the jogger's neck so she nicked the woman's neck. When the knife was used on Shea it had made a burning sound. But on this woman, the cut did nothing. Within an instant, Finley grasped Kaden's coat by the collar and tossed her backward into a pile of garbage.

"What the hell are you doing?" She yelled at Finley as he approached her. He plucked her from the garbage and threw her body at the wall. As Kaden's back hit the solid brick, she was sent once more to the ground where she stayed in pain. She gripped the knife in her hand in anticipation that Finley would come back for another attack. Still memorized, Finley did exactly as Kaden predicted by lifting her to her feet and pushing her body against the wall. "Finley, stop!" she pleaded. When he didn't stop, Kaden was forced to use his own knife against him. She sliced a part of his cheek in hopes that he would back off, but Finley didn't flinch. The knife caused his skin to burn a little around his fresh wound, but didn't seem to care. He caught her wrist, just as she was about to slash again, and twisted it making her release the dagger. "Ah!" Finley smashed her head against the brick wall , causing Kaden's vision to blur. She fell but Finley wasn't finished with her. He wrapped his hands around her neck and squeezed as hard as he could, cutting off Kaden's air supply. His face was emotionless in Kaden's eyes as he tightened his grip. She clawed at Finley's grasp as he lifted her off the ground. Her face turned bright red and her feet dangled in the air.

"Enough!" the woman called from behind them. Finley instantaneously let go of Kaden's neck. As he released her, she once more fell to the ground and gasped to catch her breath. Finley went right back to the woman's side and she put her hand on his shoulder before glaring at Kaden. Finley's stare was only on the woman as if she was his master now. She gave Kaden one last glance before the two of them shimmered away. It wasn't like when Finley blinked to where he wanted to go, it was more like they faded into the wind.

As soon as Kaden caught her breath, she picked up the dagger and her backpack, at a loss for what came next. The only plausible plan she could come up with was to find the bestiary Finley told her about. She could figure out who, or what, had taken him and seek out help. And she knew exactly who to go to.

Chapter XII

"Hello?" Kaden's voice echoed down the dark groundhog like hole. With her head being the victim of non stop throbbing she managed to make her way back to Discovery Park. She navigated the park as best as she could remember, but the night did not do her any favors. As she leaned over Theodroe's home, into the abyss of nothingness, she wondered if she should stick her hand inside. She worried he would bite it. "Hellooooooooo?" she pulled out a small flashlight from her backpack and shined it down into the darkness.

"What do you think you're doing?" Theodore spoke from behind a large tree a few feet away. Kaden pointed the light at him. His eyes squeezed shut quickly from its brightness, "Do you mind?" He raised his twig sized arm to block the light to cover his eyes. "I can't see anything," he grumbled. Kaden lowered the light to the ground, half kneeling to be at a closer eye level when she spoke to him.

"I need your help," she said softly. She flipped her barren wallet open, "I have some– money." When she saw that it only contained two dollar bills and her emergency credit card she realized she had very little to offer the small creature. "I can get more later," she added quickly.

"And what, exactly, would *I* do with money? Walk into a store to buy garden supplies?" He waddled his tiny body past Kaden to get to his hole, "Besides, you and your pretty faced faerie boyfriend can kiss my—"

"I understand your anger," she cut in. "But I wasn't the one to trick you, he was. And I need him to help me, so really you would be doing me a favor, not him." Kaden tried to persuade him as he selected a few creepy crawlies out from under some rocks.

"Not. My. Problem," he crunched down on some kind of beetle and the bug's guts squirted out of Theodore's mouth.

"What do you want?" Kaden wondered. As she waited for him to answer, she thought back to the strip club and the creature Finley had referred to as a succubus. "I'll get you the coin back," she offered. Theodore froze in his tiny tracks.

"I'm interested," he turned to face her. "But that's not enough for me to bite."

"How about..." she began to say, but nothing intriguing came to her. Kaden spit out the first words she could think of, "I'll owe you a favor."

"A favor!" Theodore clapped his hands together with

excitement. He seemed to be more interested in the favor than the lucky coin. "What kind of favor?"

"Anything you want, but you have to help me get Finley."

Theodore squinted one eye for a moment, "How do I know this isn't a trick? Or that you'll own up to your offer?" He asked valid questions and Kaden pondered how she *would* be able to prove it.

"Well, I'm not a faerie so I don't try to trick people," she offered. "I can give you my word."

"Well," he mimicked Kaden's accent, "I hate to break it to you, sweetheart, but your word means nothing to me. How about you shake on it?" She wasn't sure how exactly a hand shake would prove anything either, but she held her hand out to prove she meant what she said. His hand was about the size of a preschooler's compared to hers. Theodore grabbed her by the forearm and tilted Kaden's arm slightly to the side. She noticed a green light illuminating the veins of her forearm. In a panic, Kaden attempted to tug her arm loose, but Theodore gripped her arm tighter.

"What the hell?" The light dissipated and he released her arm.

"Just a little insurance," he told her with a grin stretching across his face. Kaden rubbed her thumb over her arm as she inspected it for anything different, but she found nothing.

"What does it do?" she asked him.

"You'll find out if you don't hold up to your bargain. Now," he puffed out his chest. "What exactly happened to the pretty boy?"

"I don't know," she replied, still skeptical. "One minute we were walking down the street to his apartment, and the next he just snapped into a..." Kaden scrambled her brain for the correct word. "A trance...Almost like a zombie. And he mentioned something about hearing a noise, but there was nothing there. Then he went to some woman..."

"Hmmm. A woman, you say?" Theodore glanced away from her into the distance. "Women are magical creatures enough. Sounds a lot like a siren," he exhaled deeply.

"You mean like from the Odyssey?" she asked. Unwanted flashbacks of high school reminded her of the never ending Greek tragedy from Sophomore year.

"Yes," he raised a brow, "but they don't usually stray away from the sea."

"Why would a siren come after Finley?" Kaden wondered with hopes Theodore would have an answer.

"What exactly have you and Finley been up to?" he asked her. Kaden wasn't sure if she should tell him the truth, yet she needed him to get Finley.

"Finley went to find out something about the Dark fae, but I don't know exactly what he was doing or where he went," she explained.

"See," he said with aggravation. "This is what happens. You start asking questions about things they shouldn't be asking about, then everyone wonders 'why are they asking questions?' One thing leads to another and the word gets out that a former Light fae is interested in Dark fae business."

Kaden paused. "So can you help me?"

"Well I have to now," his frustration was not something he hid well. "I have a friend in another park who told me about a siren in the area. See, gnomes are reserved, but we know a thing or two about the way the world works. The only thing is, I know it's difficult to believe, but I don't have fighting experience nor do I know how to kill a siren."

"I think I know where we can find something that can help us. Finley told me he had a bestiary in his apartment. We can get the supplies we need and maybe it will tell us how to kill her."

"First you want my help," he began, "now you want me to go into the city? Me?" he looked at his own body up and down with wide eyes. "I think I'll draw some attention to myself. I do parks and gardens missy."

"Don't worry, you can climb into my backpack," Kaden opened the flap for him to jump in.

Theodore looked at her with disgust, "What am I, a dog?"

She shook the bag, "Do you have any better ideas? I have a cab waiting for me by the park entrance. Now hurry up."

"There's not enough room for me," he protested.

"Okay," she found it difficult to hide her own growing frustration. "How about this. You can get into the bag yourself or I can throw you in it." He lifted his chin in the air and marched over to her bag.

"This is humiliating."

"My Mom is going to kill me when she gets my credit

card bill," she whispered once Theodore was securely in her bag over her shoulder.

"You mean *if* you survive, because if you die you won't have anything to worry about." Theodore spoke out of the top of her bag. The warmth of his breath sent a chill down her spine as it hit her ear.

"Thank you, Theodore."

He reached out and patted her shoulder, "Always here to help."

Kaden retrieved the hidden key to Finley's apartment from under the flower pot in a small dirt garden alongside the stoop to the building. The garden was practically dead with a shriveled up tomato plant and wilting flowers. She swung the building's door open before rushing to the third floor to release Theodore from her bag.

When she closed Finley's door behind her, she instantaneously flipped her backpack open with Theodore spilling out onto the floor. He sprawled his body on the floor as he gasped for air, "Finally! Fresh air!" His eyes studied his new surroundings and forced him to sit up in excitement. "So this is how the other half lives? Why am I not surprised, faeries and their need for luxurious things?"

"So I take it you don't exactly like faeries?" Kaden removed the stuff out of her bag and onto the kitchen counter.

"They're a bunch of pretentious snobs if you ask me," Theodore struggled to climb onto the oversized couch. "Gnomes like simple things," he explained. "We take great pleasure in aiding Mother Nature's beauty. Not this poppycock." He jumped merrily up and down to test the couch's bounciness.

"Finley's bestiary is somewhere in this apartment. Why don't you look in his bedroom and I'll take the living room," she suggested as she headed for the bookcase first. Theodore let out a slight groan before jumping off the mountainous couch, then walking over to Finley's bedroom.

Kaden pulled each book out of the bookshelf to ensure there was nothing hidden behind any of them. He had copies of all the classic books, from Shakespeare's Romeo and Juliet to the more modern Catcher in the Rye along with his gold book, but nothing that stood out to be useful for her now. "Find anything over there?" Kaden asked over her shoulder to Theodore who wasn't making any noise. When he didn't respond she twisted her body in his direction, "Theodore?" Kaden walked over to the bedroom to make sure he hadn't injured himself on any of the larger furniture. Theodore laid on Finley's bed, legs crossed over one another with a playboy magazine opened to one of its extended photos. "Theodore! What are you doing?"

"I found it under the mattress," Theodore tilted his head to the side as he scanned the picture. "Did I not say women are magical creatures?"

"Put that away," she tugged the magazine out of his hands and threw it across the room. "This is very serious Theodore, we need that bestiary. We have a deal. Now hold up to your end of the bargain. Keep looking."

He scrunched his face together, "Alright, alright. But

wherever it is, it's not going to be out in the open. That book is very dangerous." Kaden pulled each dresser drawer open, tossing all Finley's clothing onto the floor.

"How dangerous can it be?" She found a few daggers with different markings carved into them buried at the bottom of his clothes.

"Think about it," Theodore's voice became muffled when he crawled under the bed. "It's a book filled with various creatures. Not only does it have information about what they can do, but it has information on how they can be killed. Bestiaries usually are handed down from generation to generation."

"Which means…."

"Which means," he used his elbows to move himself around the floor as he knocked on different wood panels. "There has to be a lot of creatures in that book, starting from a very long time ago. Something as sacred as that needs to be hidden very well. And as much as I hate to admit it, Finley is not an idiot. It's not going to be in a brown box with his clothes. And don't tell him I said that!"

Kaden stopped looking through his dresser to think for a moment. "So where do you think it could be?"

"In a loose floor panel maybe?" He glued his ear to the floor and knocked on each piece. "Maybe behind the walls somewhere?" Kaden's memory flashed back to when she first arrived at Finley's apartment. She had leaned against the fireplace and it shifted under her weight. After all, the fireplace was the only old looking thing in there anyway.

"What about behind the fireplace?" she asked.

Theodore lifted his head away from the floor quickly as the wheels in his mind processed the theory.

"Let's find out," he responded.

The two of them analyzed the fireplace. They both took turns pulling at it at various angles. "I know that this piece moved," Kaden pointed to the top right frame of the fireplace. "But it's not budging now."

"Perhaps if we break it open," Theodore tapped Kaden's dagger which was hanging off of her belt. She removed it from its sheath, plunging it into the wooden frame. She forced it to move deeper into the fireplace, which made the wood crack apart. The corner of the frame was sent flying as Kaden had reached the opening. "Yahtzee," Theodore said quietly to himself which confused Kaden.

"How do you know what Yahtzee is but not what a dresser is?"

"Does it matter?" he responded. Kaden reached into the dust and cobwebs of the hole. "Is it in there? I can't see."

"Hang on," she said, clutching on to what felt like a leather-bound book. She pulled it out and dusted it off, revealing a dark brown cover engraved with a Celtic knot and filled with old, tinted yellow paper. Kaden untied a string that held its contents shut, "Hopefully sirens will be in here." When she flipped to the first page a small wave of doubt hit her as she saw most of the information was not written in a language she recognized.

"Let me see it!" Theodore jumped in the air to see what Kaden had been frowning at.

"I can't read it, I don't even know what language this is."

"Let. Me. See." Theodore bounced up and down and tugged at Kaden's shirt. She handed him the journal not expecting any good results from a gnome who lived out in the woods away from humanity.

"Well that's because it's written in Gaeilge," Theodore told her.

"You know it?"she asked with surprise.

"Don't act so shocked. Despite my good looks, I'm very old and like to read. Now let's see here," he flipped rapidly from page to page. "And what do you know, Sirens." He turned the book for Kaden to see, but to her it was just a bunch of jumbled scribbles.

"Does it say how to kill them?" she asked him.

"Shh. It says, 'A Siren can take human form, read minds, and make anyone fall under her spell with her malevolent melody. She fears mirrors, for it reveals her true appearance: gray faded skin, hollowed eyes, and the skin around her mouth and jaw is usually torn off....'" He began to mutter the rest to himself. "Ah! Here," he pointed one finger in the air. "...to kill a Siren one must retrieve a bronze dagger dipped in the blood of someone under her spell'."

"Well that doesn't seem too bad," she said optimistically.

"Wait," Theodore held a finger in the air to pause Kaden's hope. "There is a warning, 'Anyone under her spell is under her control and is forced to do anything she asks. The longer she has them, the worse it is'."

"So, here is a good question, how many men does she have under her spell?"

"And that will not be answered until we find her," he slammed the book shut, sending a cloud of dust into her face. "Could be a lot, or none."

"You said your friend knew where she would be?" Kaden tied her hair back into a tight ponytail and put her dagger back in its sheath.

"Well he told me about one a while ago," Theodore shrugged.

"How long is 'a while ago'?" Kaden asked.

"That's not important. We need a bronze dagger." He waddled to Finley's room to check if any of the other blades he had hidden were bronze. Kaden shoved the bestiary in her backpack, "None of these are bronze, of course."

"What if we use a bronze pipe from the sink? Do you think it'll work?"

Theodore shrugged his shoulders, "I don't see why not."

"Good," she breathed. "I think I saw a wad of cash in one of Finley's drawers. Can you grab it while I disassemble his kitchen sink?" They both headed in different directions, Theodore to the bedroom and Kaden to the kitchen.

"What do we need the cash for?" Theodore asked. Kaden used a wrench she found under the sink to unhinge a bolt off the main pipe.

"For the cab ride to the park to see your friend," she twisted the bolt off one end and began to work on the other.

"I am not going in that wreckage thing again," he

spat. "You want me to bring you to my friend, we take my way." Theodore hovered over Kaden's shoulder while she removed the pipe completely.

"And what, exactly, would your way entail?" She shoved the money and pipe into her bag. "Maybe we should bring a mirror," she whispered to herself, not fully listening to Theodore.

"We go by tunnel," he firmly said.

"Eh, I don't think he has a mirror beside the one on the bathroom wall."

"Hello!?" he waved both hands in front of Kaden's thought filled face.

"What?" she wondered.

"We are going by tunnel." Kaden froze. She hadn't realized Theodore wasn't joking. She didn't even know that traveling through some magical tunnel was an option.

"How? If you haven't noticed, I'm too big for one of your tunnels. Besides, don't you need dirt for that?"

Theodore nodded with pride, "The garden on the stoop," he said. "Don't think I didn't notice that monstrosity. Unfortunately, it is dead, but I can still make a tunnel there. And trust me, it'll work."

"So instead of taking a cab, you want to make a dirt tunnel in the stoop's garden where we would be visible to other people?"

"Precisely."

"No," she argued. "Even I know that's stupid and I'm not a fae."

"Hear me out," Theodore followed behind Kaden. "It will only take a half a second. I just need to create the hole and it will suck us to our destination."

"A hole that sucks people into a tunnel and spits them out in another location should be no concern to the other neighbors."

"It will disappear as soon as we get in, and the best part is the garden will be filled with life again," Theodore said with a smile, hoping to convince her to go with his plan.

"What if someone sees us? Then what?"

"It's relatively late, maybe no one will see us."

"*Maybe* no one will see us?" she repeated his own words back to him.

"You are the one who wants to save the pretty boy, taking a cab would just take longer." Despite the recklessness of his plan, Theodore did have a point. The longer Finley was under the siren's mind control, the harder it would be to get him out of it.

"Do you think you can do it without anyone seeing you?" Theodore paused for a brief moment, pondering her question.

"…Yes," he hesitated.

"That's not a very convincing answer," she told him.

"Yes!"

Kaden rolled her eyes, "But you go in the backpack until we get outside."

Kaden checked the street before allowing Theodore to step out of the backpack and into the open. She found only the faint glow of televisions and light from the surrounding apartment buildings. The street was as silent as she had ever seen it. She breathed a sigh of relief, but also reluctance. "Okay," she whispered. "The coast is clear for now. Hurry up." Theodore ripped open the bag and climbed onto the withered garden.

"Such an embarrassment this garden is." He shook his head disapprovingly.

"Theodore, not the time," she harshly whispered. Kaden kept her eyes locked on the surrounding area while Theodore walked in circles on the dirt. "Anytime now."

"Oh shush." Theodore tapped his foot twice on the circle he had traced in the dirt. The dirt caved into the ground almost like a vacuum was sucking the dirt back into the ground. As soon as the dirt was cleared, it left a hole identical to the one Theodore lived in.

"Are you sure this will close up once we get in?" Kaden asked as reluctance grew.

"I'm sure. Come on now." Theodore jumped into the hole without warning. He was pulled into the void quickly and gone within an instant. Kaden hated that it seemed to be one of those times where she wished Megan was there to push her in, because she didn't feel she could voluntarily jump in. However, the echo of a door opening from inside the building changed her mind completely. Kaden closed her eyes tightly as she held her breath and hoped she was making the right decision by jumping into the unknown void.

CHAPTER XIII

The tunnel Theodroe was insistent they use, accelerated Kaden through a whirlwind of earth. The pressure of the air and the velocity at which she was forced reminded her of a body slide she had only been brave enough to experience once. She swerved left then right. She was lifted high only to be sent soaring back down again. Her body rolled with the curves against her control. While a scream caught in her throat, Theodore's giddy laughter echoed from ahead of her. "See," Theodore's voice bounced off the dirt walls of the tunnel. "I told you this would be faster than a car. And you don't have to pay!" The wind tunnel forced her body to the left sharply, a quick right and then a downward spiral, "Wheeee!" Her stomach lurched with the motion and she could feel the little bit of food she had consumed begin to make a reappearance.

With one last jolt of air, Kaden was spit out of the tunnel and on flat land again. She stared up at the ever shifting night sky above her, "I think I'm going to vomit." Her motionless body laid on the grass as the tunnel filled itself with dirt concealing it had ever existed.

"You'll get used to it," Theodore leaned over Kaden's face with a wide grin.

"Get used to it? I'm never doing that again," she sat up halfway, but her vision whirled around her. "Next time we take a cab," she insisted. "Where are we anyway?"

"Smith Cove Park."

"How did you know no one would see us once we landed here?" She carefully rose to her feet as she scanned the park. It was vacant with a lifeless swing set near the waterfront and a walking path that ran alongside it.

"I didn't, but you forgot to ask so I didn't say anything."

"Someone could have seen us!" Kaden's voice carried a little bit further than she intended it to.

"But they didn't, and that's what matters. Now, my dear friend should be around here somewhere. Look for a hole, but don't trip over it."

"How does your friend know where the siren is exactly?" She kicked some dirt around with the thought that it was concealed by some magic. Although she wouldn't be able to tell if it was.

"Well, sirens typically live near water. This is the closest park near the waterfront and my friend lives here so he hears things."

"Do gnomes just gossip all the time?"

"For your information," he began, "we maintain nature's beauty among mostly gardens. We can't help but overhear things, don't act so innocent. I'm sure you gossip every now and again. Everyone does. Most people aren't willing to admit it."

Theodore spotted a small hole behind a shrub and waved Kaden over, "Over here." Kaden followed him as instructed to his friend's hole. "Clyde, my boy!" he yelled with one of his hands cupped around his mouth for an echo effect.

"Not so loud, we don't want to draw attention," she warned. Theodore shot her a look before a tiny bald head popped out of the hole. Its eyes peered around before cautiously revealing himself to the world. Clyde looked almost identical to Theodore except that he had less wrinkles around his eyes.

"Theodore!" Clyde shouted merrily in an American accent versus Theodore's English one. He tackled Theodore in a bear hug as the two jumped up and down like two best friends who hadn't seen each other for a while. "How long has it been?"

"Too long," they released each other from the hug but still held on to one another's shoulders.

"Wait," Kaden interrupted the gnomes' reunion. "I thought you spoke to your friend recently." Clyde, just noticing Kaden for the first time, backed up closer to his hole with a fearful expression.

"Don't be afraid Clyde, this one's with me," Theodore reassured him. "I said my friend had seen a siren. I never said how long ago it was. What's it been Clyde? One…two decades?"

"*Decades*?" she repeated.

"Three actually," Clyde replied as he cowered a little more towards his hole.

"Theodore, did it ever occur to you that this information could be outdated?" The irritation in her voice was made very evident.

"What information?" Clyde asked Theodore.

"About the siren you told me about," Theodore said. Clyde tilted his head to the side as he searched his memories for what Theodore was referring to.

"You mean at my three hundredth birthday party?" Clyde asked him.

"Yes! That's right, when Fiona had too much ale, remember that?"

"Of course, and the time we…" Clyde's eyes widened as he spoke of the fond memory.

"Back to the siren, guys," Kaden broke off Clyde's thought.

"What about her?" This time Clyde asked directly to Kaden.

"We need to find her," Theodore told him. "I made a deal to help this young lady retrieve another fae for a favor." Theodore raised his eyebrows when he mentioned the part about the favor.

"A favor, eh? You made a good deal, Theodore," Clyde nudged Theodore with his elbow. "Well, she's still around, I can tell you that much. She resides near the docks. I think she might have a boat there now."

"Do you remember what she looks like?" Kaden

asked him.

"Well, I've only seen her from afar- otherwise she could sire me. Let's see," Clyde crossed his arms and tapped his foot. "All I can recall is that she had long red hair. Quite the looker if I do say so myself. No wonder she collects so many men."

"Does that sound like the same siren Finley went with?" Theodore looked up at Kaden as he asked her.

"The woman he left with had red hair, so it must be, right?"

"Did you say Finley? As in the faerie?" Clyde's voice almost sounded shocked.

"Yes, the *faerie*," Theodore mocked. "And it's definitely the same siren. They only stay along the shoreline and don't usually like being near other sirens. Too much competition." Theodore answered both their questions as he silently tried to come up with a plan of action.

"How do you know Finley?" Kaden asked the shy gnome.

"Who *doesn't* know him?" Clyde asked her back. "No offense, Theodore, but I doubt I will be of any further assistance."

"Yes, you are quite right. Thank you, my friend." Theodore dismissed him to return back to his home.

"Don't forget," Clyde added before leaving. "You're both susceptible to her melodies."

"Yes, thank you, Clyde," Theodore said.

"Man, woman, or fae," he continued.

"Yes, yes. We know," Theodore added impatiently.

"Here, I have something that might help," Clyde

disappeared in his hole. He returned with two pairs of ear plugs, "These might come in handy."

Theodore seemed shocked by the token as Clyde handed a pair to him and a pair to Kaden. "Where did you get these from?"

"An elderly couple who brought their grandchildren left them on the picnic table. Good luck," Clyde dropped down his hole, leaving Theodore and Kaden to their endeavor.

"The dock isn't that far away," Kaden told Theodore. "I can see it from here." The garden creature peeked his head out of her backpack while she walked down the path along the waterfront. "Do you really think she has a boat?"

"I don't know," he admitted with skepticism. "Clyde is a smart fellow, but I don't think he was right about the boat. My guess is that maybe she's somewhere under the dock."

"I guess we'll just have to find out when we get there."

A moment or two passed of silence before Theodore's talkative nature kicked in. "So, what are you doing with a faerie boy anyway?"

Kaden used Finley's technique of vague answers for once, "It's a private matter."

"I'm risking my life to save Finley and all I get is, 'it's a private matter'." Theodore flipped the flap of the backpack open more to speak directly into Kaden's ear which made her feel uncomfortable.

"I already owe you a favor," she argued. "Whatever

that entails." Kaden glanced over her shoulder to meet the earthly brown gaze of Theodore staring back at her. "*And* I'm getting the coin back for you, which, by the way, probably doesn't work since Finley got taken. Telling you what I'm doing with Finley isn't a part of our deal."

"Point taken," Theodore said. Kaden felt him watching her through the small opening of the bag. "How about this then? What is a mortal girl doing in the fae world? Don't mortal's go to school or something?" Kaden rolled her eyes, though Theodore couldn't see her reaction.

"Are you ever going to drop this topic?" she asked him.

"Probably not," he honestly answered.

"This mortal girl doesn't go to school, or have a job for that matter."

"Why not?"

"Because…" she pondered his question that should have been easy to answer. "I don't know."

"Surely you have to know," he pressed for a better answer that Kaden wasn't sure she knew.

"I guess because I couldn't find happiness there." The honesty in her answer surprised her. She had never truly thought about why she didn't find normal life all that appealing.

"That's a perfect reason if you ask me," Theodore said. Kaden turned her head toward Theodroe's voice. His words were different from what she expected. Most of the time, she was met with an unnerving pause, including from her own mother. "The whole point of life is to be happy," he said simply. "That's all that matters." She fell silent as

Theodore continued to speak, "I love gardening, seeing a seed transform into a lush flower. Most fae don't care for plants or flowers, but gnomes do very much. Just because the other fae don't understand the pleasure of seeing that, doesn't mean I'm going to stop doing it." Kaden was in awe of Theodore's words, no one had ever explained it so nicely. "I'm growing on you aren't I?"

"Maybe just a little," she turned her head to look at him in her bag. "Thank you for understanding."

He grinned, "No problem. It's what I do...so about what you're doing with Finley."

Kaden released an exaggerated sigh, "Alright," she gave in. "He's helping me find someone."

"Ah, and who might that be?"

"A friend," she told him. She sensed he was about to ask another question so she cut him off before he could. "Do you know who Linette is?" She remembered the girl's name from the letters she found in Finley's apartment.

The pier was only a short distance away but Kaden had her own itching questions she wanted answered. "Maybe..." Theodore began. "It depends on why you're working with Finley." Kaden bit the inside of her mouth, frustrated because she really wanted to know who the mysterious Linette was.

"Let's just say my friend got caught in between the Dark faeries and they may or may not have sent a siren after Finley."

"If your friend was taken by the Unseelie Court," Theodore said, "I'm not too sure you'll *want* to find her."

"Unseelie Court?" she asked, unfamiliar with the

term.

"Yes, Unseelie Court. Has Finley told you *anything* about the fae world?"

"Not really," she admitted. "I only know a few things."

"Idiot! Absolute idiot that Finley is. How does he expect you to survive if you know nothing? Alright, I'm going to explain this as best as I can so pay attention. When it comes to the faeries there are two Courts. First, the Seelie Court, which your genius Finley hails from. Some fae call it the Blessed Court but they're morons too. They can be tricky but they don't cause harm to people. Are you with me so far?"

"Yes," she felt herself more intrigued in the fae world than ever.

"Now, the Unseelie Court are the Dark faeries you seem so keen on finding which forces me to question your intelligence. I like to call them the Unholy Court though; the name is more accurate to what they are willing to do."

"So why would you say I might not want to get my friend back?" A large lump formed in Kaden's throat at the thought of what the Unseelie Court could be doing to her.

"She won't be the same girl you knew, not when they're done with her. And to answer your question, Linette is a Light faerie, well known too. Her mother died some time ago, I think. It's hard to keep up with time. Why do you ask?"

"Curiosity," Kaden admitted as the overwhelming scent of raw fish welcomed her and Theodore to the pier. A large cruise ship, probably set to travel to Alaska, was anchored at terminal ninety one. On the opposite side of the pier were several fishing boats. Some were rusted and dingy while others were more clean cut. Next to pier ninety one was pier ninety, which consisted of two freighters with large cranes that aided in lifting heavy cargo onto the ships. "How do we know what boat she's on or that she's even on a boat?" A few people lingered about the docks for the late hour. Most of them were workers or on their own boats.

"Is it a good idea to be talking to me right now?" Theodore whispered. "I hear people out there."

"They won't notice," she told him. "And if they do, I'm sure they'll think I'm either insane or have a headset," she explained.

"What's a headset?"

"Doesn't matter. How are we supposed to find her?" After she asked her question, she realized it was more of her job to find the siren, seeing that Theodore was crammed at the bottom of the bag.

"If she's on a boat, it's probably a nice one. A yacht or something of the sort," Kaden felt Theodore's feet kick against her back to make room in her backpack.

"Could she be on the cruise ship?" She passed several fishermen looking men as she wandered.

"No," he answered, finally settling in one spot. "She'll have her own boat."

"Most of these other boats are fishermen's boats." She couldn't imagine someone like a siren living on a fisherman's boat. She came off as too prestigious to be found on a dingy, rusted boat.

"Keep looking! There has to be one that doesn't

match." Kaden took in a deep breath, passing the final entrance to the cruise ship. Only a few late-night workers straggled around the pier and their ships, nothing caught Kaden's attention to be of siren nature, whatever that would entail. "Can I peek out now?"

She observed the area quickly, "Only a little bit. There are still people around."

"Okay," he lifted a small corner of the top flap to get a visual of the pier. "Slowly spin in a circle so I can see." Kaden rolled her eyes because she knew she was going to look crazier than she felt. Despite her feeling, she did as instructed and slowly did a three sixty while a few sailors squinted at her odd behavior.

"See anything?" she asked as she came back to her forward walk.

"Yes, and I don't know how you didn't notice it. The boat at the very end of the pier." Kaden looked to the last boat. It was an older yacht that looked like it wasn't mobile. The paint on it was faded and it may have had two levels but Kaden couldn't tell.

"Are you sure?" she asked. "Wouldn't the siren have something a little more…" she began as she got closer to the boat, "luxurious?"

"Read the name of the boat," he whispered.

Kaden read the chipped blue words out loud, "Melodie de Mare? What does it mean?"

"It's Romanian for the melody of the sea."

"Great," she sighed. Kaden stopped a few feet away from the boat. She slid the bag off her shoulder and onto the pier in preparation of Theodore's exit. "So what's the plan?"

CHAPTER XIV

"Get the ear plugs Clyde gave us," instructed Theodore.

He gestured for Kaden to pull them out of her pants pocket as he kept a watchful eye on the boat. Kaden pulled them out of her back pocket and handed a pair off to him. The boat itself was an old yacht drifting with the shifting tide. Kaden and Theodore hunched not too far away from it behind a large crate of some sort.

"So what's the plan?" she asked Theodore. She pulled out the bronze pipe from her backpack.

"What?" Theodore asked louder than necessary. Kaden held a finger over her mouth to shush him and avoid giving the siren any warning they were there. "What?" he said more quietly and removed one ear plug.

"What," she repeated in a hushed tone, "is the plan?"

Theodore furrowed his brow at her, "Isn't it

obvious?" he said. "We sneak onto the boat and kill the siren."

Kaden squinted an eye, "What about the men protecting her?" she asked as if it weren't as obvious as he made it seem. "We don't know how many she has," she added.

Theodore stared at her for a moment too long. "Has anyone told you, you ask too many questions?" he said. "We don't know if she has any." Theodore puffed his chest out, "Now, is there anyone else on the pier?"

Kaden glanced over her shoulder at the piers' empty planks and drifting vessels. "Not this far down," she breathed. She was thankful, but also terrified. "Everyone is gone for the night."

A grin spread across Theodore's face, "Right then. Let's go." He stood up straighter, embracing his two foot tall stature and strutted towards the boat.

Kaden grabbed at his tiny arm before he could get too far, "We still don't have a plan," she whispered down to him. Theodore wiggled his way out of her loose grip. She followed behind him regardless.

"There are clearly no men outside," he snuffed. "So we'll look through the window first. Happy?" Kaden didn't respond to his aggravation.

A small gap separated the boat from the dock. A black abyss to the sound below. To Kaden's surprise, Theodore jumped first. He leaped through the air, barely catching onto the ladder on time. His weight shifted the boat to lean toward the pier a bit, but it wasn't enough to cause anyone who may have been inside to notice. All

Kaden needed to do was stretch one foot out to the rim of the ladder. She used one hand to grab another rim and pull herself onto the boat while the other hand held the bronze pipe.

As soon as she planted her feet firmly onto the deck, she plugged her ears. Kaden crouched down at the rear of the boat with the cabin's main door in perfect sight. Just as she was about to move to the side of the boat to see through the window, she realized Theodore was no longer by her side. She scanned the boat's deck, but he was gone. *Damn it,* she thought to herself. Kaden quickly shuffled to the side of the boat where the windows were. A thin bridge connected the front and rear of the boat. She pressed herself against the boat's frame and peered into a window.

The outside of the yacht was misleading. Inside the siren lounged on a leather sofa as two men fed her grapes and served her wine. Kaden slid back down out of the view of the window. She swallowed the lump forming in her throat. There were at least three people on board and hopefully Finley was somewhere to be found.

Kaden slowly, carefully, snuck another peek. The two men who served the siren had identical mindless facial expressions as Finley had when the siren took him. And if they were anything like Finely had been, Kaden decided it would be better if she pulled the dagger out of her belt in case she really did need protection. Though she hoped it wouldn't come to that.

She pulled the knife from her belt, only taking her eyes off of the siren and her love struck men for a moment. When she looked back up, the men were gone. The siren, with her long glistening red locks, lounged alone as she admired her nails. Kaden froze in her spot. Her eyes scanned the interior for any sign of the men when a strong set of arms snatched Kaden from the side. The bronze pipe fell from her grasp to the deck's floor, but she managed to hold onto her blade. She silently cursed Theodore for whatever game he was playing. Kaden twisted her arm to cut or somehow inflict pain to the man who held his grip tightly. The second man from inside took her backpack off her shoulder and threw it to the ground, then took her only free arm in his grip. She wiggled to get free and used her legs to kick the men as much as she could. The first man easily pulled the knife from her hand and dropped that to the deck floor as well.

Both men dragged her unwillingly into the main cabin where the siren was waiting. The woman, lounging lazily on the couch, watched as Kaden strumbled in. Her gaze seemed just as lifeless as her men, only she looked bored. She studied a chipped nail before glancing up at Kaden, "We meet again." Her gaze was just as piercing as her sharp features. "Why are you here my child?" Kaden attempted to pull out of the men's grip once more as the siren's muffled words barely hit Kaden's ear drum.

"Where's Finley?" Kaden snapped, hoping her words would prevent the siren from knowing she had plugged her ears.

"So that's what you're here for? The boy?" Kaden tried to focus on the siren's red lips to read them as she spoke but all she could make out was 'boy'. The siren noticed Kaden's concentration and she tilted her head to see small plugs in her ears. She chuckled to herself and gestured to the men who removed Kaden's only protection. "Clever girl," she said. "But not clever enough." The woman of the sea lifted herself off the couch seductively. Kaden averted her eyes away from her. She took Kaden's chin in her hand, lifting it enough to make Kaden look into the deep blues of her eyes. "You are an interesting thing," she smiled.

Kaden shifted her head quickly, removing herself out of the siren's grasp. "Who told you to take Finley?" she asked harshly.

"You are misplaced," the siren said. The sea swirled in her eyes as she stared into Kaden's gray ones. Kaden found herself staring back, as the tide flowed with a beauty she had never known. "Doyle," the siren replied. "He had a particular interest in retrieving Finley. The plan was to bring the boy to him tonight. But," she turned her back as she spoke. "As soon as I realized who he was, I just simply couldn't pass up the opportunity. Are you aware of what I do, child?" The siren turned back slowly to find Kaden's unknowing expression which gave her the answer that made her half smile. "Fae have a certain…appeal that normal humans don't," she began to explain as she poured herself a glass of red wine. "I love wine and grapes, assorted cheeses and fine dining."

"If you're going to kill me or control me, just do it," Kaden spat. "I'd rather not hear what you have to say."

"You have a sharp tongue," the siren said as amusement danced off her tongue. "You want to know what I love more than all of this? Souls." Kaden didn't quite understand what souls had to do with any of the other stuff.

"Every fae is different. Some are faeries, others are succubi, there are some mermaids alive, although, with the way humans pollute the oceans, I don't see how they will survive much longer. They all have their own agendas, their own abilities, but do you know what mine is? I can see souls like a human sees a light. The dullest souls are that of humans. They're easily lured, which to be honest, is quite boring. But fae souls... fae souls illuminate a brightness so powerful, so magnificent, they are hard to resist. The brighter the soul the harder they are to lure, and the more entertained I am."

Out of the corner of her eye, Kaden saw Finley come into the room from a door opposite the entry way. He moved next to the siren, his eyes only on her although the siren was fixated on Kaden. "The life you live is not one you choose, you seek more. And I shall give that to you," she said as if she was bestowing a gift. A sweet, haunting melody began to escape her throat. Kaden struggled against the men's grip, but it only made them tighten their grip around her arms. She pulled and twisted. But there was no use. The deadly lullaby floated into her ears and her mind and then her soul. Kaden stopped fighting as her body grew weightless as her mind melted into only thoughts of the siren. With the siren's instruction, the men released Kaden from their hold. She didn't move or fight, she simply listened to the siren as she rubbed Kaden's cheek with her thumb. "Bine ai venit acasa. Welcome home."

Before the siren stood four mindless servants. Their souls wiped to a blank slate of nothing but a void. Only concerned with their master, they waited for purpose. "What is your name child?" the siren's soft voice asked her new recruit.

"Kaden Storm." Her response was automatic and her attention bore deeply into the siren's presence.

"Well," the siren began as she sipped her wine. "I am curious. I have never come across something quite like you. I cannot see your true soul. Do you know why that is?"

"No," Kaden answered truthfully, without thinking of the word falling out of her mouth. Just as the siren was about to speak again, a loud thump from the boat's deck pulled her attention away.

She raised a brow at the two men who held Kaden captive, "Go." She commanded them and they instantaneously followed orders, stepping outside to find the intrusion.

While the siren, Finley, and Kaden waited inside, the two men searched the boat deck for any sign of life. Where Kaden's bag and other fallen weapons had once been left were nowhere to be found. The two mindless men stared out into the darkness, only to find moonlight beaming against blackened current. A high pitched squeak, like rusty metal moving against rusty metal echoed through the night. They exchanged confused looks before turning around to find a small, brown creature swinging towards them. Theodore laughed heartily as the horizontal pole, that he wasn't sure did anything, swung at the men, knocking them completely off the boat and into the depths of the icy ocean. The splashes outside the cabin made the siren gesture her head for Finley to see what was going on.

When Finley exited the cabin and leaned over the railing where he found the two other sires splashing frantically in the ocean. The mysterious threat made the muscles in Finley's body tighten. He studied the area carefully. He focused, scanning for the intruder. "Hey!" Theodore shouted at the top of his lungs from the second level inside the control panel room. "Come and get me you enormous brute!" He shook his rear end at Finley's face. Without putting any thought into his actions, Finley darted for the steps. At the top of the last step his foot caught on something invisible, sending him to the floor, but not before he was able to catch himself with his palms. Theodore waddled out, his chest heaving for air as he exerted himself. He smashed Finley's head with the bronze pipe Kaden had dropped. "Take that," he added joyfully as he used the gold dagger to slice Finley's cheek. As the wound bled, Theodore moved quickly to wipe the pipe against his cheek. Finley pulled Theodore's ankles which caused him to fall alongside Finley. Theodore continuously kicked Finley in the face as much as he could so he could get up and run to the siren. He managed to pull himself up, but he was not able to get down the stairs without passing Finley. The gnome waited for the faerie with great anticipation. Theodore held the pipe in his hand and grinned. Just as Theodore had suspected, Finley jolted toward Theodore. He ran as fast as his little legs could under Finley. Finley twisted his body quickly, catching the gnome just enough to kick him in the back. Theodore was sent flying down the steps to the main level of the boat. "Is that all you've got!" he yelled as he stood to his feet and headed for the cabin. Despite the fall, Theodore went into the cabin with a little bit of energy left in him. Kaden stood in the middle of the room prepared to kill anything that threatened the siren, who cowardly took cover in the separate room behind Kaden. "You've got to be joking," Theodore said, out of breath as he quickly analyzed the room.

Kaden lunged forward in an attempt to capture the gnome she couldn't recognize. Theodore dodged past her by ducking under a table which he proceeded to knock over. Luckily, the table not only fell on top of Kaden but managed to block the entrance. Theodore jumped for the latch on the door to where the siren was hiding, but he was too short to reach it. Finley stepped down into the room, barely absorbing the scene before him. He lifted the table off of Kaden and threw it at Theodore. He rolled out of the line of fire as it slammed against the bedroom door. Theodore used the opportunity to climb on the table as far as he could to slide the door open. The door cracked open just enough for him to slip his tiny body through it. Finley and Kaden frantically made their way to the gnome by throwing the table out of their way to get to the room and prevent any harm to their sire. Both Kaden and Finley clutched onto one of Theodore's arms and held him in the air. "Why have you come here gnome?" the siren asked him as he kicked his legs in the air.

"Doyle sent me," he said a little louder than necessary. "You were supposed to deliver Finley, and you didn't. He doesn't like it when people do not obey him." Still in his hand, he clutched the pipe.

"He is not my king to obey," she moved her face closer to his. "I have to say, I am disappointed in the lack of concern he has for my power. After all," she chuckled lightly, "he sent a gnome." She smiled at the thought of a gnome defeating her as she rubbed her thumb along his cheek just before she was about to hum her devious melody. Theodore bit Kaden's hand with his sharp teeth and she released her grip out of reflex. He then used all his weight to plunge the pipe directly into the siren's lungs. Although the pipe wasn't sharp, it magically pierced through her body. With a high pitched squawk the siren cringed back from the piercing pain that spread like a virus in her body. Her skin cracked, as if it were glass being smashed. The wound revealed her true form. A woman with porcelain skin and ruby lips shifted to hollowed out eyes with skin the color of death itself. Her mouth, which was once for her seduction, was covered with a flap of skin. All her beauty drained and shriveled away to nothing in an instant. She collapsed to the floor with the pipe wedged in between her lungs. The siren wailed as she watched her body turn into dust.

"Never underestimate a gnome," he told her ashes. Once the siren was dead, Finley and Kaden's eyes fluttered with life again. Both were confused as they looked at their surroundings, "Do you mind?" Theodore was hanging by one arm from Finley who still held him tightly. Finley dropped him with a loud thump to the floor without warning.

"How did we get here?" Finley asked Kaden while his eyes shot from her to Theodore then to the rest of the room. "And why is Theodore here?"

"You don't remember what happened?" She asked him back, but as she thought about it, she couldn't remember what happened either. "I can't remember anything after the siren sired me."

"That's because you didn't have control of your own thoughts or actions," Theodore's frustrated voice explained as he pulled out his ear plugs from his waxy ears.

"A siren?" Finley waited dumbfounded for someone to explain the entire story.

"That was your plan the entire time?" Kaden asked. Theodore proceeded to take a bow.

"As a matter of fact," he said. "It was."

"Would someone please explain to me how the hell all this happened?" Finley asked.

"What a shock the princess is confused, such a drama queen," Theodore mumbled to himself but both Kaden and Finley heard his comment and Kaden couldn't resist laughing a little.

Finley restrained himself from kicking Theodore yet again. Kaden broke the awkwardness by asking, "How did you know what the siren was saying to you?"

"When you've lived as long as I have," he began, "you learn a few tricks. Like reading lips for example. How else would I know what people were saying from my hole?"

Finley rubbed his beat red temple with his hand, "Did you hit me?" He first looked to Kaden who answered by shaking her head, then he angrily looked to Theodore.

"Guilty. And to be honest, I enjoyed it more than you think. Now," he opened his hand out. "Miss Kaden, as you promised."

"Right. Finley, give him your lucky coin," she told him. He furrowed his brow at her.

"Excuse me?" Finley asked as if he hadn't heard her the first time.

"The coin. Give it to him," she repeated her command once more. Theodore looked up at him with a wide grin like he won a game against his arch nemesis.

"Why would I do that?" Finley discretely flipped Theodore off so Kaden wouldn't see. Theodore replied by sticking his tongue out.

"I made a deal with him, one favor and the gold coin in exchange for his help. Now, Give. Him. The. Coin. I'm not going to ask again."

Finley sighed as he reached into his pocket, "Here," he clenched the coin in his hand as Theodore tugged for it. For a brief minute they fought over it, but it ended when Kaden coughed loudly.

"Well," Theodore said as he tossed the coin in the air and caught it. "This was exciting, but I will be off now."

"How will you get off the pier without being noticed?" Kaden asked while he walked past them to the exit.

"I'm old, I know how to get around without being seen."

"What about your favor? How will I know when you need me?" she called after him.

"Don't worry, you'll know. And don't forget about the poor fellows in the ocean!" he shouted back to them.

As soon as Theodore scurried off into the night, Kaden and Finley rescued the extremely dazed men out of the icy cold ocean and onto the pier. While the four of them made their way off the pier, the two shivered in a daze. "How did we get here?" One man with deep brown eyes asked.

The other man followed up with, "Who are you two? Have we met before?"

Finley and Kaden exchanged weary looks, "We haven't met before, but it's okay. You're safe." Kaden didn't exactly know what to say to two strangers who clearly had no idea or memory of anything.

"We already killed the siren, nothing to be afraid of," Finley told them. Both their faces turned drastically from scared to horrified.

"He's kidding," she said quickly after. "What was the last thing you remember?"

"We were on a boat for a Bachelor party. Someone must have spiked our drinks." The brown eyed man tried to make up an explanation for their missing memories. She moved away from them and toward Finley so they could walk separately and discuss what happened privately.

"I feel bad for them," she said.

"Why? We saved them," Finley pulled a pack of cigarettes out of his coat pocket.

"True, but they will never know what really happened. Imagine living a life without knowing the truth." Finley lifted his index finger to his cigarette. At the tip of his finger, a small flame formed to light his bad habit. He shrugged in response to what Kaden said and didn't seem to care that he used his magic in front of two traumatized men.

"That's it? A shrug? They are never going to be the same again," Kaden watched the city lights illuminate the midnight sky as they grew closer to the end of the pier.

"It's not my problem," he blew out some smoke. "The way I see it, those two will live. Who cares if they don't know what happened to them?" Kaden didn't say anything. She wondered what that kind of emptiness would feel like. A missing piece of time. Questions without answers. "So," Finley interrupted her thoughts. "You owe Theodore a favor?"

"Yeah," she shrugged. "I guess."

"You really shouldn't have done that," Finley said.

"I really didn't have another option at the time. I needed help."

"Favors aren't necessarily what you think they are," he took another puff of his cigarette. "It could be anything. It could be dangerous."

"Do you really think Theodore gets into much danger? He lives in a hole. Besides, I needed you back," she said before analyzing how that could sound. "For Megan, of course. Which reminds me, what did you find out?"

"I'll tell you when we get back to my apartment," he gestured his head to the two men who looked just as bad as they had while sired..

"Guys," Kaden said, they both looked at her. "Finley's going to call you a cab."

"I am?" he asked.

"And he'll pay for it."

"I what? With what money?" Kaden pulled a wad of cash that was rubber-banded together from her backpack which she had picked up off the boat deck before they left.

Finley immediately recognized the wad from his dresser, "That's my poker money!"

"It's not like you pay for anything anyway," she argued with him.

Finley imitated Kaden's voice, "It's not like you pay for anything anyway."

CHAPTER XV

"Well," Finley sighed as he glanced around what once was his pristinely glamoured apartment. "Someone made themselves right at home." He slid his coat off his shoulders and dropped it into the mess. The apartment hadn't seemed as messy to Kaden when she left with Theodore. Staring at the space under different, less stressful circumstances, she was proven wrong. The furnishings were thrown all over in places they didn't belong in. Half of Finley's books were sporadically decorating the floor. His clothes poured out of the dresser drawers and there was a newly leaking sink with a busted fireplace in the living room. As easy as it was for Kaden and Theodore to make such a mess, it was just as easy for Finley to mend. As he stepped through his apartment, without a word, each object he passed was returned to its rightful place. "What did you do to my fireplace?" he asked her. "That was an antique." He shot her a glance over his shoulder as he headed to the refrigerator.

"We needed your bestiary to figure out how to kill the siren," she told him simply. "What are you doing?" Kaden dropped her backpack on a bar stool and placed the dagger on the counter.

"What does it look like I'm doing?" The fridge muffled his voice. When he came out of it, he held a bag of shredded cheese in his mouth and two eggs in his hand. The cuts both Theodore and Kaden inflicted on Finley didn't seem as large as they once had. "You still have the bestiary, right?"

Kaden patted her bag where she kept the antique book. "You're already healing?" she asked him while he searched his cabinets for the proper cooking utensils. Before he answered her, he rubbed his finger over the cut on his cheek.

"Did Theodore use the iron blade I gave you?"

"Yeah," she nodded. "We both did."

"Then it will take a little longer to heal," he explained as he turned the stove top on.

"What would the difference be if we used a regular blade?" she wondered aloud as she snatched an apple from the fruit basket.

"It would have already healed completely by now," he cracked both eggs into the frying pan. "I told you there are very few things that can inflict pain or kill faeries. Which is a good topic to discuss. We need to really talk about what you think you're getting yourself into versus what you're actually getting yourself into."

"Are you kidding?" she scoffed. "I've seen a succubus, talked to a gnome, and helped kill a siren. I think I'm well aware of what I'm getting myself into."

"That's exactly my point," he said. "You think because you've experienced some of the fae world and survived this much it will be fine, but it won't. I've been around for a while. I was a warrior for the Light fae and a siren got to *me*. What do you think it's going to be like with the Dark faeries? They are much worse than the siren was. I might heal faster and have much more experience, but this is a risk even for me. Especially since we have no clue what is going on."

"We do know what's going on," Kaden argued. Her grip on the apple in her hand grew tighter. "They have Megan," she said flatly. A thought that killed her inside. A thought that made her want to die knowing what could be happening to her. Kaden put the apple on the counter in front of her, noting her nail marks she carved into it. "And," she began, " they have been kidnapping other girls."

"But we don't know *what* they're doing to them," he replied. "Or how many of them are there. You do realize if there are too many it's going to be an issue, right?" Finley focused his attention on the eggs in the frying pan.

Kaden swallowed hard before she changed the subject, "So what did you find out?"

He glanced over at her quickly before replying. "I went to a few Dark fae I have connections with first," he explained. "But no one knew anything. One of them probably ran back to the boss to gain his favor. But, do you remember what Shea said?"

"Not really," she lied. The only part of what Shea had said that stuck with her was the part about Megan and how she was going to end up. Thinking about it again, made Kaden squirm in her own skin.

"What Shea said was all true," Finley told her. "In nonsense, but true. She spoke in circles, which was what made it difficult to figure out. First," he started as the bottom of the eggs began to burn. "She mentioned them being near a berth. The word choice is what is important. A berth is another way of saying a port," he flipped the eggs with a spatula and sprinkled some cheese on top.

"Okay," Kaden said. "So they're at a port, there's a bunch of them here."

"Shea also mentioned 'earthly lesson' twice. I'm almost certain the first time she mentioned it, it was about the judgment before death." The words rang in Kaden's ears and cut into her gut. Death was final. Death you couldn't come back from. Blood rushed from her face making her paler than usual. "But," Finley continued, not realizing the effect any of his words were causing. "The second time she mentioned it, she said it was next to nothing. Now, the earthly lesson also happens to represent the number nine, so what is nine next to nothing?"

"Ninety," Kaden answered like it was just yesterday she was sitting in high school math class. It took a second for her to connect the dots but as soon as she did she couldn't help feeling a mix of pride and agitation. "So you're saying she's at pier ninety where we just came from and we're sitting here while you make eggs?"

"Would you shut up and listen?" Finley didn't bother

to put the overly cooked eggs onto a plate before indulging in them. "She said she was near a berth, which means she was in the area. My best guess is a warehouse. It's the only logical place near the pier that no one would notice something like that. The last significant words she said were 'prickle ditch'. Which leaves the question: why those words?"

"Double meaning," Kaden answered.

"Exactly and there just so happens to be a street by the name of Thorndyke near the pier."

"I still don't understand why we couldn't just go after her tonight," Kaden grumbled to herself.

"We need to have a plan. We need to know what exactly we are up against and that won't happen if we go in there blind. We wouldn't be helping anyone by doing that."

"And you figured all this out by yourself?" she wondered.

"Of course not," he snorted. "I had some help from a Seer friend of mine," Finley said as if it was something anyone would have done.

"Couldn't this Seer friend of yours just tell you where she was?" Kaden felt like there were so many easier ways of getting this done and didn't understand why it took Finley so long to use them.

"His gift doesn't work that way," he told her with his mouth full. "He can't see the future whenever he wants. He can only see what the gift allows him to see."

"And he knew about the number thing?"

Finley nodded, "He's a smart fellow. He was around when numbers first appeared. He knows." Finley went to the sink to rinse the pan out. He turned on the water, cleaning off his fork along with the pan. As soon as he was done, he turned the water off, but still he heard water running. Kaden hunched over on her stool as soon as she knew what the sound was. Finley opened the cabinet underneath the sink to find a large puddle of water and a missing pipe. "You are an annoying guest, aren't you?" he closed the cabinet shut.

Finley took Kaden's bag with him to the couch and slammed his body down as he rummaged through it. Instead of pulling out his book of beasts, he took out Kaden's cell phone and turned it on. Kaden remained on the stool but turned in her seat to watch what Finley was doing to her belongings. As the phone flashed to life, several alerts popped up within seconds of it turning on. Finley scrunched his face as he read the screen. "A bunch of missed calls from…Quinn." Kaden quickly jumped out of her seat and took the phone from him before he had time to do anything else. "Who is Quinn and why aren't you calling her back?"

"Quinn is my sister," Kaden slipped the phone into her back pocket and plopped down on the couch next to Finley.

Finley sighed quietly to himself, "About earlier tonight, I should have shown up." He removed his necklace and placed it on the end table.

"Actually, you were right. Despite the fact that I want her to know what we're doing, she can't know. I don't want her to be a part of this, she's my baby sister and I'm supposed to protect her. I was stupid to think it was a good idea in the first place. It's better she thinks I'm having a meltdown or abandoning her."

"Being abandoned is one of the cruelest pains we suffer from," Finley sunk back further into the couch, twirling the gold dagger he snatched off the counter in his hand. Kaden knew exactly what Finley meant. The agony of being left by her father hurt, but the pain Quinn caused earlier was crippling. Her best friend was missing. Her heart was shattered and pulled apart into a million little pieces. And she felt utterly alone.

"Yeah…" she agreed. "But sometimes that pain makes us stronger."

The night was peaceful. The moon floated in the endless dark blue sky. Flickering fireflies were the only other light source the night provided. Chirping crickets surrounded Kaden as prickly pine needles scraped her bare feet in the middle of a dense forest she did not recognize. No one was around her. There was nothing but the everlasting rows of trees.

She wore a torn spaghetti strap, plain white nightgown that she had never seen before with her flowing blonde hair falling down in curls. "Hello?" her voice echoed into the night. Kaden wasn't afraid of the darkness night had to offer, even as a little kid. What she feared was what was lurking in that darkness.

Her instincts kicked in and told her to walk. She wasn't sure where exactly it would lead her, but she knew she needed to do something. The pine needles pricked the soles of her feet with each step. They may have been bleeding, but she wasn't able to see.

In the distance, a faded light glowed bright yellow. It was the same color the fireflies glowed, yet this was the size of a human. "Hey!" she shouted to the moving silhouette. When the form didn't turn around and continued to walk away, Kaden ran after it. "Hey!" she shouted. "Wait!" She ignored the pain in her feet while her chest rose up and down as she breathed heavily, running faster toward the fading light. No matter how fast she ran, she didn't seem to get any closer to the mysterious person. Her feet slowed beneath her and she used a tree trunk to lean against when she realized she would never be able to catch up.

Kaden gasped for air, but watched the figure. As soon as she stopped moving, so did it. The figure was almost waiting for Kaden to catch it.

Before, she couldn't make out any features of the person. She couldn't tell how it was glowing. But now as both Kaden and the figure were stopped, the figure turned around, and it was Megan. She was holding a lantern with a burning white candle inside of it. Kaden recognized it was her from the beautiful, long black hair that fell past her shoulders. A spark lit within Kaden. Run. And fast. To keep running until she reached Megan, "Megan!" Her feet pounded against the forest floor. This time as she ran the light grew brighter, filling Kaden with hope that she would reach her friend.

Suddenly, the light faded completely with no warning, urging Kaden to get to where it had disappeared.

She ran into a grass clearing. An old two story house

stood in the center. It was Kaden's house.

Her lungs burned a fiery pain, but that didn't stop her from darting for the house with hopes that Megan had disappeared inside. She flung the front door open to a house with no furniture and plain white walls. The only colored thing in the room was the bright red hair of the siren who stood in the living room, "Where did Megan go?" Kaden furiously demanded the siren to answer her. The siren's mouth moved, but Kaden couldn't hear her answer. "Where is she?!" she shouted with tears streaming down her flushed cheek. "What happened on the boat?!" The words slipped off her tongue despite the fact that Kaden had no intention of asking them. "Why can't I remember?!" The siren's lips answered each of her questions but Kaden couldn't comprehend any of them. "Stop it! Just stop it!" She clenched her hair in her fists and fell to her knees with tears welling in her eyes. "Please just stop!" She sobbed, closing her eyes tight to make the image go away.

When she opened her eyes again everything she saw was gone. She was no longer in her home with the siren. She was no longer stranded in the middle of the forest chasing Megan.

She was in Finley's apartment on the couch panting in a cold sweat as Finley snored from his bed. *It was a dream. Just a dream.*

CHAPTER XVI

The sun peeked through gray clouds with the anticipation of rain, though none came. With each step Kaden took, she was brought back to her nightmare. Her bare feet against sticking pine needles, the siren's haunting red lips, and Megan. Kaden's boots followed along the gum stained sidewalk not far behind Finley who seemed less bothered by his experience.

Kaden wiped the crust from her eye as she leaned forward inhaling the delight of diner coffee to wake her. The sticky booth was the same one she had sat in when Finley told her about the fae world. She was in the dark then. Before the diner was nothing but a place that served bad coffee. With the darkness of the coffee swirling and blending with milk, the place felt more like a lifeline. One she wanted to hold on to.

Finley sat across from her in the same outfit she had met him in. He had dark circles under his eyes just as she did, only hers were more visible with her pale skin. She spun her spoon around and around so mesmerized by the swirl she could fall asleep. As exhausted as she felt, there was a part of her that thought she didn't deserve to sleep. Megan had been missing for two days. Two days of what, Kaden didn't want to think about.

She wondered quietly to herself if she should have waited for the cops' help or if the way she had chosen was getting more done, but she would never know that answer.

"What do you think—" she found herself asking Finley. Kaden kept her attention on her coffee and the few bits of egg that remained on her plate.

"Yes?" he asked her back. When she glanced up from her plate she found Finley waiting for her to finish her thought.

Kaden sighed, dropping her fork to her plate. She glanced out the window for a moment, trying to reach memories she couldn't find. "What do you think happened between you and the siren?" Finley shifted his attention quickly from the bite he was about to eat to her as he furrowed his eyebrows from the unusual question.

"I don't know," he shrugged. He popped a large sliver of pancake in his mouth, "Why?"

"Well," she shifted uneasily in her spot. "Before I blacked out, I saw you come out of the siren's bedroom."

Finley raised a brow, "I think the question you should be asking is: who *wouldn't* want to sleep with me?"

Kaden rolled her eyes, "That's not what I meant," she

said. "It doesn't bother you that you can't remember?"

"Nope," he replied easily, popping another bite of food into his mouth and grinning back at her. "Are you done?" Finley wondered.

She glanced down at her cold plate and the steaming coffee she only half drank. Kaden pushed it toward the center of the table, "How could you not care about the missing pieces?" she pressed.

Finley pulled out his wallet, which Kaden didn't think he had. "Well it clearly bothers you," he slapped the money on the table. "There are more important things to worry about," he added. "Like catching the bus for example."

The bus was filled more with body odor than people. When it slowed to a halt, both Finley and Kaden stepped out onto a curb with a sign that read Twenty Eighth Avenue.

As the fumes of the public transit forced a cough out of Kaden's lungs she asked, "I thought you said Thorndyke?" when she noticed the sign.

"It's only a block or two this way," Finley nodded his head in the direction. "You never know when someone is tailing you." Finley gestured his head for Kaden to follow, "Come on."

The blocks surrounding the ports were mostly warehouses and rows and rows of cargo crates. Most of the warehouses were manufacturing companies, some had signs that named the company, others' didn't. A majority of people walking the streets were workers from either the buildings or the pier. They strolled, studying any nook and cranny they could get a sneak peek at without being noticed. Among the many structures, they found nothing out of the ordinary.

Finley glanced down at Kaden, taking note that she hadn't brought her backpack with her, "You brought the knife, right?" he asked her.

Kaden lifted her sweatshirt up just enough to show him that her knife was hidden behind her belt.

"Good."

"What about you?" She didn't see him take any weapon from his apartment before they left. "What did you bring in case we run into trouble?"

"At first my plan was to use you as a distraction," he took her by the shoulders to place her in front of him as a shield. "But you're too short, you'd be a terrible shield."

Kaden let out a laugh, but was instantly hit with a wave of guilt. Her smile slid back to a frown, "Seriously though." She moved back to walking beside him.

"Don't you worry," he opened his jacket and lifted a part of his knife up from his pocket. It wasn't like the one Kaden had. His was a sai sword. A straight iron blade with a gold handle. The handle had two sharp points that curved in the same direction as the blade.

"Very nice," she said. "Where did you get all the blades?"

"The Seelie Court," he answered. Finley concealed his weapon back up in his jacket.

"You were a part of the Seelie Court," she recalled Theodore mentioning. "Right?"

"For a time," he told her. "I was the Commander of the Seelie Court. All of us got sai swords for weapons, sometimes real swords if needed," Finley eyed a worker eating his lunch on the curb.

"So you were in charge of other knights then? Seems like a high rank. Yet, you left…" Kaden was hoping to hear his answer to why he left, but he didn't say anything. "Where did you get the blade you gave me?" They were only two blocks away from the pier. Kaden could smell the seafood cooking from nearby restaurants. "It has more detail to it than the sai sword. Was it personalized?"

"It was handcrafted for me. A gift." Just as they were about to pass the next alley, Finley held his arm out to stop Kaden from walking past it. He pushed her back with his arm to put her up against the warehouse's wall. Both their backs pressed against the cold brick. The angle allowed them to see into the alley as a group of men waited in front of the adjacent warehouse's door. Kaden saw a familiar face that she recalled from the pub the night she and Megan had gone out. It was the tattooed man who had accompanied Riley. His stance expressed his lack of enthusiasm in the performance of the other men who were putting each other in head locks. A female fae stood on the sidelines egging them on to hit harder, punch more, and knock the other one out. "We found them," Finley whispered.

"I remember him," she whispered. "The tattooed guy, he was from the pub."

"His name is Gabriel," Finley said. The group was far enough down the alley that they wouldn't be able to notice the two of them peering around the corner.

"What do you think they're waiting for?" she asked him quietly. The warehouse they seemed to own, or at least use, was bigger than all the other warehouses. Most of the building's windows were blacked out or too foggy to get a good look at what was inside. Even the low to the ground windows had something on the inside covering them.

"We're about to find out," he said as a black, beat-up van pulled into the opposite side of the alley. The vehicle caught the attention of the faeries, causing them to stop their childish behavior.

When the van rolled to a stop next to the side door, Riley hopped out of the driver's seat. The others jumped into action to unload the back of the truck, but neither Kaden nor Finley could clearly see what was inside.

"How many are we expecting for tonight?" Riley asked Gabriel like they were best of friends, but Gabriel clearly had no interest in being friends of any sort with Riley.

"I estimate about fourteen hundred, maybe more." Gabriel's voice didn't match his appearance at all. He was a beefy guy, almost like a bouncer, yet his voice was so innocent and calm.

Each of the three fae carried brown sacks into the building where Riley and Gabriel stood. They unloaded them inside the building so they could go back out and get more. Kaden guessed they carried about twelve sacks inside before they only had one left. The female fae grabbed the last of the load and proceeded to head for the door again. Before she made it through the entrance, the sack she carried began to squirm. *It's a person,* Kaden thought. The girl in the bag tried to kick as much as possible. The fae struggled to keep her over her shoulder. Gabriel stepped in and threw the girl over his shoulder to finish the load without a problem.

"We have to do something," she put one step forward in an attempt to make her presence known to the fae in the alley. Finley clenched her arm and threw her back in her place against the wall. "What if one of them is Megan?" she half whispered and half yelled to him.

"It isn't Megan," he reassured her. "They must have just picked these girls up last night."

"Even if it isn't Megan," Kaden began, "they're still innocent girls. We have to do something."

"And we will—" Finley began to speak when footsteps came in their direction.

"Finley," Riley's accent rang out through the alley causing Kaden's arm hairs to stand on end. She slid further away from the edge of the building to hide her presence. "Come to join us, have you?" Finley instantaneously looked away from Kaden so Riley wouldn't know he wasn't alone.

"Just thought I'd stop by," he told him. "Have a chat." Finley disappeared down the alley to prevent Riley getting any closer to the end of the building.

"Is that so? It wouldn't have anything to do with you asking questions about us, would it? Because as you may be aware, you are no longer a part of the Seelie Court ergo you have zero say in the matter. Unless of course you are here to join us... Doyle will be thrilled."

"Actually," Finley's voice became distant as he stepped farther down the alley. "It's about a girl you took from the pub."

"Girl? What girl?" Kaden knew by the way Riley spoke with arrogance, that he had a smug smile written across his face.

"I'm sure you know I spend quite a lot of time at that pub. You've caused somewhat of a problem for me with cops asking questions and all. Wouldn't want them to catch on to what you've got going on here or any other fae for that matter."

"My apologies, lad. Perhaps you will join us as a peace offering tonight. We have been hosting some cage games and I'm sure Doyle would love your company," his invitation was a threat. Either Finley would go voluntarily or the small group would try to force him.

"No need to apologize to me," he said coolly. "Just the entire fae community as you put them at risk. And as for your offer, I'm afraid I will decline."

"Oh, but I must insist. Surely you're curious. You've been asking questions about us and you're here now, aren't you?" There was a pause between the two, then a punch. Kaden didn't know if Finley had punched Riley or vice versa. She was unsure if she should run out and help or if she was meant to stay hidden. She weighed her options. She could run out and help but she wouldn't be of much use. Kaden barely knew how to use a kitchen knife, let alone a fae dagger. But there were three others in the alley, not to mention a massive Gabriel who could return any minute from inside.

With scuffling feet and a few more punches, Kaden ran out from behind the building, dagger in hand. She saw

Riley had Finley on his knees, just about to punch Finley once again. Finley blocked the hit with his arm, he snatched Riley's arm and hit him with a right hook. Riley was cowered, rubbing his eye as the other three fae ran to defend him. The two men who had been fighting each other before went after Finley together. Finley had his sai sword handy, stabbing one of the men in the stomach as the other jumped on his back with a choke hold around his neck. The bloody, dead body of the first man fell to the asphalt. Finley rammed his back as hard as he could into the building's wall. The man's grip loosened and Finley flipped him over his head. The man's body hit the ground hard with a loud thump.

Kaden got to the scene just as the female fae went for Finley as well. She was planning on helping Finley with the two fae he was fighting off, but he seemed to have everything under control, swiftly moving like a dancer.

Riley grinned at her, "I remember you." Kaden charged him, pushing him to the ground. She climbed on top of him with her knife just inches away from his eye, his hand gripping her wrist tightly preventing any more damage to his rat-like face. She used her other hand, which was not dominant at all, to punch Riley in the other eye. It didn't affect him that much but it provided Kaden with enough time to get up and kick him forcefully in the ribs. With adrenaline coursing through her veins she was able to crack a few under her boot.

"How does that feel?" She kicked as much as she could, each blow with more force than the last. Kaden had never felt the energy that came with beating someone up.

She didn't like violence at all but right at that moment she liked it, and didn't care.

Two more fae bodies filled the alleyway that Finley had taken out while Kaden wasn't paying attention. Gabriel had appeared, getting a few good hits to Finley's face.

Just as Kaden was about to kick Riley directly in his face when she saw Megan standing next to the van. She looked the same as she did when Kaden last saw her, only her expression was plain with no emotion. "Megan?"

Kaden was about to go after her friend when she heard Finley yell, "It's not real!" Gabriel threw Finley into the wall.

Riley grabbed Kaden by the ankle pulling her down. He crawled on top of her with his hands tightening around her neck. She tried to kick him in the groin but he had her legs pinned down. She took two fingers and jabbed them into Riley's eyes and he shrieked like a little girl. He loosened his grip with the distraction of pain. Kaden coughed as she reached for her knife next to her. Once she had it in her hand she turned back to Riley. Instead of stabbing him, she ended up stabbing the asphalt. Kaden sat up quickly searching for him, but he was gone, and so was the hallucination of Megan.

Finley was surrounded by four bodies, the two men, the female fae, and to Kaden's surprise, Gabriel. He wiped his blade on his sleeve before placing it back in his coat.

"We have to go," he said and Kaden wasn't going to argue. They both ran down the alley away from the scene.

"Wait," Kaden said. She slowed to a stop at the opening of the alley's mouth. "What about Megan?"

"We have to come back," Finley explained with blood dripping down the side of his face. "Take my hand," he held it out for Kaden to take. She took one last glance over her shoulder before she gripped his hand and once she did they teleported somewhere unknown to Kaden.

CHAPTER XVII

"Brian," Megan warned as she watched her older brother plop more than enough food onto his plate. "Stop hogging the mashed potatoes." Across the dining room table he sat, matching her doe eyes and testing one another. He plopped another dollop onto his plate. Megan kicked him under the table not so discreetly. At the head of the table her mother and father sat as they always had. Beside her, just like every Sunday night dinner was Kaden, swallowing a laugh along with her chicken.

Megan's father cleared his throat, pulling the table away from his children's antics. "So," he said as he scooped up some peas for his plate. "Kaden, how's your mother?"

"Greg," her mother said suddenly. Megan didn't need to see her mother's expression to know she stared at her father with the same wide eyed look Megan was used to receiving. Her father was where she got the gift of bluntness.

"She's been better," Kaden shifted upright in her seat, feigning a smile. Megan kicked her foot as if to say 'you don't have to talk about it'. "How's work, Mr. Hanes?"

"Fine, just fine," he answered. Megan's dad wore thick framed glasses which without them would leave him almost blind.

"Have you decided on a college yet?" Brian asked her friend. Megan slumped back into her chair as she played with a piece of food on her plate.

"Not yet," she responded although Megan knew she wasn't planning on going.

Brian nodded his head politely and the table went silent for a moment. "Anyway," Megan shifted the direction of the conversation. She leaned over her plate to catch both her parents' attention. "Kaden and I were thinking of taking a road trip this summer since it's our first year out of school."

"What did you two have in mind?" her mother asked.

"We haven't decided yet," Megan looked at Kaden, "we were thinking somewhere along the lines of California."

"We'll see," her father said instead of flat out saying no.

"Maybe if you go with Brian the three of you can split the cost…" Megan's mother suggested.

Brian shot his mother a look, although she pretended she didn't notice. "John and I have plans this summer," he argued. "We have some gigs in a couple of local bars. I don't have time to babysit," he waved his fork at Megan who kicked him under the table harder than she had before.

"I am not a child," Megan insisted. "We don't need a babysitter," she turned to Brian. "When have you ever actually played a 'gig'?"

Brian threw a piece of biscuit at her, but she blocked it with her hand. "That's enough," their father chimed in.

Megan returned her focus to the meal that sat in front of her. She eyed her mothers' famous meatloaf that she spent two hours preparing. It was one of Megan's favorite meals since they only received it on special occasions, but Megan couldn't remember why her mother had made it that night. *Maybe Brian did something smart again.* She took a huge piece and drove it into her mouth.

As she chewed, she sensed something off she couldn't quite put her finger on. Perhaps a different spice her mother used. When her teeth were about to chomp down before she swallowed, she felt a slight tickle of movement. As she bit down on a piece of it, something squirted in her mouth. She instantaneously spit the piece out, revolted by its unusual texture.

Once the half chewed meatloaf was back on her plate, she saw that the unusual texture was not a new spice, but a squirming maggot. Megan gagged at the sight. She looked at the other food sitting on her plate. Buried within the meat and potatoes were more maggots and buzzing flies as if the meal had been sitting out for days. Bile rose from her stomach, but she managed to keep it down. "Something wrong, dear?" her mother asked innocently.

Megan's furrowed brow and pale face glanced over at her mother. She was seated upright with a blank stare, as was everyone else at the table. "Is there something wrong with *you*?" She said 'you' but she really meant 'all of you'. Each of them sat dazed staring at nothing, not even each other. "What's going on?" Her eyes shifted from one member of her family to the other.

"Nothing," Brian said. "What's wrong with you?" Her brother lifted up his steak knife and sliced a gash on each of his wrist without flinching.

"What the hell are you doing?!" Megan shot up and ran to her brother with a napkin to contain the blood seeping from his wound.

"It's okay," he told her. The crimson soaking up her dinner napkin said otherwise. She watched as the useless white changed color.

"Someone call 911 before he loses too much blood!" she barked at her family. No one moved.

"It's okay," her mother said as she mimicked the same act that her brother had just committed.

"What are you doing!? Are you insane!? Stop it!" She released the pressure from her brother's wrist and moved to her mother.

"Don't worry," Kaden said. "It's okay," she pressed her knife deep into her skin.

"Stop it!" Megan yelled.

"It's okay, sweetheart," her father said. "Just join us."

"You want to," both Brian and Kaden said in unison. "You know you do."

"Stop it!" She released her mother's wrist, staring with dread as blood leaked out of her loved ones. Megan fell back into the dining room wall with her hands over her ears as if it would help her.

"Join us," they all said. Their blood dripped down onto the floor, pooling into an ever growing red puddle.

"No! No!" Megan screamed at all of them. She squeezed her eyes tightly shut hoping it would disappear. She opened her eyes again to look for a way out when she noticed the room had no doors or windows for escape.

"It's easy" they continued to chant in a monotonous voice.

"Stop! Please! Stop it!" She slid down the wall and pressed her knees to her chest hiding her face. Her breath rose and fell into panic. She shook her head hoping it would all disappear. And it did. A wave of relief washed over her as she removed her hands from her ears and lifted her head up to see what happened. The chanting had stopped because each of them had their face pressed against their dinner plates. Their skin, deathly white. "No!"

When Megan woke up, she lay shivering in a cold sweat. The bare skin of her body drained of life, clenched together in the fetal position. Her once long black hair was nothing more than a buzz cut. More bile growled up her throat only this time she let it out and onto the rusted decay of her cage. For a moment, in the illusion, she was home. And then it was gone. Again. And Again. And Again.

Something drew pain to her right palm. Her shivers and chill were replaced with the thin piercing ache of a large paper cut. When she looked down at her hand where there was a steak knife. Her palm clasped it so tightly. She cut herself. With each hallucination she knew, she came closer and closer to death.

The cage she found herself in shrank in size with each hallucination or her own paranoia. Megan wasn't sure which it was. But she wasn't the only one in a cage. The stale room she was held captive in contained over two dozen other cages. Each cage enclosed a prisoner with her dignity stripped away. The only noise Megan had heard were the whimpers from the other girls and their sickness striping them away. Some called out for family too. Every night someone would come down to take another girl, and Megan never saw them again. When the girls were dragged up the stairs, a thunder of laughter and cheering would erupt from above. The only thing that scared Megan now was she knew she was next.

CHAPTER XVIII

Soaring evergreens surrounded Kaden as they stood on uneven terrain. The trees were tall enough to cover the sky above them, only allowing tiny puzzle pieces of light through. "We're just outside of Port Angeles," Finley told her before the question even became a thought in her mind. "Olympus Park," she said to herself. Standing in the center of nothing but forest reminded her of when they went to see Theodore except on a much larger scale. *If Theodore could go unnoticed in a small park*, Kaden wondered, *what could go unnoticed in a park this size?*

Unlike Discovery Park, Kaden and Finley were nowhere near a path or other people. The vast space was quiet, filling Kaden's ears with the sound of songbirds and running water. Being immersed in the woods after being in an alley moments before, Kaden silently took a moment to soak in the pleasant atmosphere, *Theodore would have a field day here.*

The air smelled of dew from the past few nights of rain. Although Kaden wore a sweatshirt, the mountain air came with a chilly breeze that caused the tiny hairs on her arm to stand on end. Finley suddenly dropped Kaden's hand from his. She had completely forgotten they were still holding each others' hands. "This way," he nodded his head toward the sound of the running stream.

Although Kaden lived two hours away from Olympus Park, she had only been there once with her parents before Quinn was born. She didn't remember the trip herself since she was only two, but she still held onto a picture the three of them had taken that day. The photo was taken on a bridge with Marymere Falls in the background. Her parents held her in a tight hug as they smiled on the bright summer day. Everytime Kaden looked at it, she felt her mother's smile was forced in the picture. It made it almost uncomfortable to look at. But still it was one of Kaden's favorites because it was the only one where her mother tried to be happy for the briefest moment.

"This place is incredible," Kaden said. She awed at the colors and scents to absorb the beauty. For a moment she had forgotten the reason they were there in the first place. Did that make her a bad person? For wanting to enjoy a moment even though her best friend wasn't here to enjoy it with her? Her guilt outweighed the moment, "How is this going to help Megan?"

"There are too many Dark faeries for just the two of us to fend off," Finley led the way, pulling branches to the side for Kaden to pass without being hit in the face.

"So whose help are we seeking this time?" she asked. "An army of gnomes?" she added to tease him, but Finley didn't laugh or smirk.

"The Seelie Court," he said with a flat tone. It took a second for Kaden to realize he wasn't joking. She wasn't sure how to respond. She didn't know whether this was a good thing or a bad thing. On one hand it was good because they would have a huge group of people to help them and, honestly, Kaden wondered why they hadn't gone to them in the first place if it was an option. However, Kaden got the feeling Finley really didn't want to be going to them for help. *Why would he do something he clearly doesn't want to do? All for Megan, someone he didn't even know?*

"How are we going to convince the Seelie Court to help us? Megan isn't a faerie or any other kind of fae for that matter. She means nothing to them."

"True," Finley said as the running water grew louder. "But this isn't just about Megan. There are other girls, too, and this has been going on for a while now. A lot longer than you've been involved. It just keeps getting worse. More girls go missing every year. Besides, someone kind of, sort of owes me."

The stream's current was strong, flowing slightly downhill. Some fallen trees lay trapped in the water along with a couple of boulders. It was at least four yards to the other side which had fewer trees but more rocks. Instead of going across, Finley headed upstream. Some of the rocks were moist and slippery, so Kaden took hold of a thick branch to help support her. "Why does the Seelie Court owe you? Aren't they just a bunch of royal snobs?"

"Is that what Theodore said?" Finley was more concerned with the gossip of the Seelie Court then answering the question of who owed him.

"No," Kaden shook her head trying to conceal the truth.

"I was with them for a very long time, was one of their best knights, until—" he began to say before he stopped himself.

"Until you left twenty or so years ago," she finished for him.

"Precisely. I fought many battles for them, trained their other knights, many of which wouldn't be alive if it weren't for me. The Seelie Court didn't want me to go, but things got…complicated. With the permission of the Queen, I hope she will grant us some of her army."

"Why didn't we just come here before?" Kaden thought out loud. It would have been so much easier than running around trying to fix the problem by themselves.

Finley stopped in his tracks and turned to Kaden, "One does not simply seek out help from the Seelie Court. One is granted it."

They slowly treaded up the hill which turned into more of a small mountain. The current to the stream grew faster as they got closer to its source. "The Seelie Court is just hidden in the middle of Olympus Park?"

"Not exactly. We have to get to Quinault Cascade. Then you'll see." Several levels of rocks guided the water down the mountain side. Despite the circumstances and the fear of arriving at the Seelie Court, Kaden felt alive and full of purpose. Like what she was doing was making a difference, and it was. Not only would she be saving Megan, but she would be saving a bunch of other girls too. It was something she hadn't felt in a long time.

"Can I ask you something?" She dodged mossy rocks to avoid slipping.

"You just did," he slightly turned back to look at her.

She laughed, half irritated. "You're so clever," Kaden mocked.

Though she couldn't see his face, she knew he smiled a little to himself, "Shoot."

"What happens when we get Megan? I mean…she's not going to be the same. Neither am I." Finley paused, half turning to her as he thought about what to say.

"Honestly," he sighed and waited until she was next to him. They walked side by side up the hill, "I don't know." The roaring of a waterfall grew noticeably louder, filling the silence.

"It's not like either of our families are going to believe us," Kaden's mind drifted to her sister again and how she reacted in the first place. Granted, she probably should have made sure Finley would come when she called, but then it's not something everyone is willing to believe.

"Even if I did show your family or her family, they wouldn't be the same. Everything they thought they knew would change. Plus, it's probably not safe for you or Megan to stay in Seattle."

"Why not?" she inquired.

"We *might* be able to get Megan back," he said. Kaden didn't like the emphasis he put on the word 'might'. "But if the Dark fae know who you are, they'll find you. They'll find your families. It's not likely we can manage to take out all of them. Especially Doyle," he spoke louder over the noise of the waterfall they still couldn't see.

"So, what? We just skip town with the money neither of us have?" Kaden questioned. He shrugged not knowing what to say. "What about you?"

"What about me?" he glanced over at her, unsure of what she meant.

"What happens to you once this is all over?" Kaden guessed he hadn't given it much thought as to what he'd do next since he didn't answer right away.

"Move. Head across the pond. See which country doesn't annoy me the most."

Kaden caught a glimpse of the waterfall as the water smacked down to the rushing waves of a small pool of water. "This whole time you've been away from the Seelie Court, you've never traveled?"

"I guess not," he admitted. "You could join me." Kaden's attention shifted from the gorgeous sight to Finley's surprising response. "And Megan, of course," he added quickly. Kaden half smiled at the thought of traveling around the world with Megan and Finley. She imagined how Megan and Finley would first meet in her mind before slipping on a mossy rock. She would have completely face planted if it weren't for her palms taking most of the blow.

Finley could not restrain from bursting out with laughter before he grabbed her elbow to help her back up. "It's not *that* funny," Kaden wiped her pants clean of dirt.

"Yes it is," he said through his laughter. "Come on, it's

up here." For Kaden's benefit, Finley directed them away from the waterfall further into the forest. The terrain grew steeper the more they went into the trees and bushes. Kaden grabbed onto anything she could in an attempt not to trip again. If she did, the fall would be much greater.

"Are there other things out here?" she asked Finley suddenly.

"What do you mean by 'things'?" he asked her back.

"You know…creatures." Part of her wasn't sure how to ask if there were man-eating monsters that secretly hunted them as they traveled far away from society.

"Of course," he told her casually. "A lot actually."

"Like…" she began for him.

"I courted a wood nymph from around here for a bit," Finley said. "Or maybe she was a water nymph?"

"How old *are* you exactly?" Kaden asked but quickly added, "And don't say old."

He frowned as though she was ruining all his fun, "Twenty." Kaden squinted at him. "Okay," he sighed, "a very youthful two hundred. Satisfied?"

"Two–," she found herself repeating. Kaden studied the age on his face only there was none to be found. "You're *old* old." He shot her a glare out of the corner of his eye.

At the peak of the cliff, Kaden and Finley stood a few yards away from the cascading water plummeting down. The water tumbled over the edge into the abyss below where the river flowed and beyond. "Which way now?" Kaden asked, her voice louder as the roaring water overpowered her.

Finley pointed further into the woods, "We have to go about a mile or so that way."

"Let's not waste any time," Kaden moved past him leading the way. As they put some distance between themselves and the waterfall, the ground grew less damp, making it easier to walk.

"We should be able to retrieve Megan," he said. "Tonight." Kaden sensed he was hesitant to finish his thought.

"We *are* going to retrieve her tonight," Kaden told him. What she didn't say was that she would do it with or without him. Especially knowing where she was. Even if she didn't know how. "So how come humans aren't concerned when they stumble upon a faerie?"

"The faeries don't just live in the middle of the forest," he answered the question like he thought it was obvious. "Have you ever heard of faerie rings?"

"Do I really need to answer that question?"

"Faerie rings are usually found in Europe and are much smaller, but we—" excitement was apparent in his voice. "I mean, the Seelie Courts have a much bigger one surrounding their land. It can go on for miles depending on how large the Court is."

"So what do faerie rings do?" she asked him.

"They're usually made from mushrooms and fungi, which form a circle. If you enter one it teleports you to the Other World," he explained. When he realized 'Other World' was a mystery to Kaden he added, "Which is a fancy way of saying not the mortal world."

"How big is their territory?" Kaden wondered.

"Big," Finley replied. Kaden noticed whenever he spoke about the Court, there was much excitement, but also, something she couldn't quite put her finger on. "There are old columns covered in mushrooms that form the circle."

Kaden pulled a leaf off a tree she passed. She twirled it in between her fingers, "How do they keep Dark fae out?"

"There's a protection spell that surrounds it to prevent other fae from getting in," he told her. "And they have guards."

She shot him a quick glance, "Guards?" A sudden added dread mingled uneasily with the rest of her. More faeries. More fighting. More time away from Megan.

"Statues actually," he tried to explain. "On top of each column are gargoyles. No fae can approach them without them noticing, and once they do, they attack. And they can be fierce."

"Then how do Light fae come and go?" Kaden flicked the leaf back to the ground.

"They don't leave," he said flatly. "The Queen controls who comes and goes. Only a handful, if any, are allowed to. The selected few have the power to dismiss the guards for a short amount of time."

"The Light faeries remain in a hidden fortress then?" Kaden wondered what it would be like to live in the forest, not able to ever leave or see what was beyond.

"Yes," he answered.

"How can they live like that?" she questioned. "They're just hiding?"

"Part of the reason I left."

"Back to the humans," she began as she thought about her questions carefully before asking them. "How does the protection spell work on them? If one happens to enter the faerie ring."

"A human may pass the faerie ring, but they can't see what truly lies there without a fae allowing them through."

"Oh, okay." Everything actually made sense to Kaden, which shocked her. "Wait," she paused as the wheels turned in her head. "How are we going to get to the Seelie Court if you can't go through?"

A Cheshire cat smile spread on Finley's face, "*We* aren't. You are."

Kaden pulled at his arm to stop him from walking, "What exactly, do I do?"

"When you pass the columns," he began to explain. "You won't notice anything changing. You will have a short window of time to speak to the faerie who appears to you before they erase your memory and send you away."

Kaden looked up the steep ridge, unable to see what lay beyond it. "And I tell them..." Her heart beat faster under her chest. She knew she had to get it right and probably only had one chance of doing so.

Finley thought about what Kaden should say to the faerie for a brief moment, "Sir Finley Treasach of Ballyshannon requests an audience with the Queen." He spoke with an elegance and grace Kaden hadn't heard before.

"Well that's a mouthful," she muttered under her breath. "Sir Finley of Ballyshannon," she sucked in a deep breath. "Got it."

"Go up this ridge," he pointed. "You'll see the columns with the gargoyles." Finley placed his hand on Kaden's shoulder as she looked up the ridge, "Don't worry."

Kaden held her breath for a long moment before letting it out. She glanced at Finley and back up the ridge. With each step she encouraged herself in her mind, *Megan needs you.*

As soon as she made it up the ridge, she found herself standing in a small clearing. A few feet away stood two towering columns forged of stone or marble, she wasn't sure. Perched on each one was a gargoyle, carved out of the same dark gray stone. Chipped with age and decorated in twirling overgrowth they loomed, casting shadows that left her uneasy. The gargoyle on the right column, stared down at her with a mischievous wry grin. The stone squatted down with its arms in between its legs, almost holding itself up. Its wings, along with most of his gray, humanlike body, were cracked stone, almost as if it were about to fall apart at any moment. The one to the left didn't help Kaden's fear of entering the Seelie Court. It had an open mouthed grin revealing sharp lion-like teeth. One of his hands was held up, as if it were waving or daring someone to try and pass him.

Their eyes followed Kaden as she neared the gap between the two columns. She couldn't tell if it was her own paranoia or if they were actually watching her like a vulture stalking its prey.

Just as her foot was about to pass the column to enter the Seelie Court, she heard stone rubbing against stone.

She froze.

With a lump in her throat, Kaden looked at the gargoyle to her right. Before its head faced forward and focused on the forest ahead, but had turned, looking down directly at Kaden like it was warning her if she took another step it would be the last thing she did.

Hesitant to make another move, she weighed her options. She could make a run for it and hopefully get to the faerie in time, which knowing her luck wouldn't end up working. Or she could wait outside the entrance like a coward while Megan remained locked up. She really didn't approve of either plan, especially with the way the gargoyles stalked her. But she went with her first option and darted forward.

Kaden ran forward without giving it much thought. Her feet carried her just outside the entrance. She smiled to herself, proud she was able to overcome her fear and run past the guards.

A gust of wind hit Kaden's neck, sending a chill down her spine. The flapping of heavy wings approached from behind her. She didn't need to turn around to know what it was.

Within seconds the gargoyle's talons clenched her shoulder, raising her feet off the ground she stood on. It sent her with a loud thump onto the ground past the columns. She rolled twice before finally coming to a stop with her back against the ground and her eyes looking up at two winged creatures circling her as they would circle their prey. Their wings spread to a much larger size when they were flying, larger than anything Kaden had ever seen.

The more aggressive gargoyle swooped down, his weight causing a hole in the ground he landed on. Despite having talons instead of finger nails and a ferocious face, his body was that of a human with a muscular torso and bulging arms complete with normal legs. On top of the columns they were cast in stone. But it walked towards her with a savage expression, it moved as easily as a human would.

Kaden used the heels of her feet and elbows to back away from the horrifying creature. The gargoyle spread its wings to their full length, casting her in shadow.

The second gargoyle landed behind Kaden just as the other one had, leaving a gaping hole where it landed. She stood to her feet as each of them closed in on her. A low, snarl escaped through their mouths.

A sound, like a horn, pierced through Kaden's ear drums. She clenched her hands to her ears, but the noise was barely muffled. At the sound of it, the gargoyles stopped abruptly in their place a mere inches away from Kaden's trembling face. The salivating creature with rage in its eyes watched her for a moment longer before a second horn echoed. Before he flew off, his upper lip quivered with anger as he clenched his fists at his sides. The third horn blast was what forced them to back away and retreat to their post.

"Well," Finley said as he came climbing up the hill. "I wasn't expecting that."

With the gargoyles on their posts Kaden was finally relieved to breathe again. She put her hands on her knees and leaned over to catch her breath, "They attacked me."

Her hands were shaking slightly but not enough where Finley would notice. "I thought you said they wouldn't attack me?"

"They shouldn't have," he watched her stand up straight again.

"Why didn't you blow the horn sooner? They were about to shred me alive."

Finley sighed with annoyance, "I didn't blow the horn. That is what I wanted to avoid."

"Then who did?" Kaden's question was shortly answered with the thunderous sound of hooves stomping on the forest's ground. She watched as three large white horses appeared out of thin air.

CHAPTER XIX

The white stallions corralled both Finley and Kaden with golden arrows aimed to kill. There was never a moment an arrow wasn't pointed directly at them. Dressed in golden armor that shone like freshly polished treasure with helmets to match and black riding pants the faeries harbored expressions of stone. The chest plates they wore all carved the same cross symbol as Finley's necklace, fitted perfectly to their bodies with the type of look like nothing could penetrate them. The riders didn't wear silver necklaces to disguise their true form. Pointed ears stuck out from their helmets.

After a few rounds of circling, the fae directed their horses to stand in a row in front of the two trespassers, still with their weapons aimed and ready. "Follow my lead and keep your mouth shut," Finley whispered to Kaden.

The stallion's white coat glowed almost unnaturally in the light. Still, their demeanor was threatening enough Kaden didn't risk moving a single foot out of place.

Finley didn't seem bothered by the fae or their steads. While Kaden could hardly keep her hand from shaking at her side. She didn't know if her fear was from the riders and their pointed arrows or if the gargoyles attacking her when they weren't supposed to was the cause for her tremor.

An invisible set of thundering hooves escaped the glamor of the Seelie Court, shaking the ground beneath Kaden's feet. The oversized black stallion emerged from the columns, frightening even the white horses. The black beauty carried a rider Kaden was not expecting. She wore a black chest armor unlike the other's gold ones with the warrior's cross engraved in it. She fashioned the same riding pants with no helmet or any shoes for that matter.

A strap across her chest held what resembled a ram's horn which had been hollowed out. Kaden assumed she was the one to call off the gargoyles. Her pin straight, silver-white hair fell to the small of her back with a single red feather. The shade of the feather matched the band of red paint she wore across her eyes.

The woman's stead reared up before slamming its hooves to the ground, taking its final stance. When she jumped down from her horse, the men finally lowered their weapons and dismounted just as she had. The man closest to her stood near her horse so it wouldn't try to get away. On each side of her hips were two shiny gold, sai swords identical to the ones Finley had.

Kaden thought about how perfect she always found

Finley to look, but the woman who walked forward was even more so. Her skin was fair and smooth with no wrinkles or dark circles under her eyes. She was practically angelic or close to it, "What is your business here, Finley?" The woman spoke directly to him, un-amused.

"Nice to see you too," he replied in a friendly way.

"I do not have time for child's play," she replied. She turned then, nodding for her men to mount their horses as she too headed back to her stallion.

"Because there is so much to do being hidden from the world," Finley stepped toward her. "We seek assistance from the Seelie Court," he said just as she mounted her horse.

She paused briefly, "The one you travel with is unknown to us. Why would I grant you entrance?" Finley looked at Kaden who was frozen in the same position.

"I have an obligation to her. I assure you she will cause no harm to the Seelie Court," his words were said with confidence.

"You are well aware of the Queen's rules. Permitting you is one thing, but your companion is another. I'm afraid I cannot."

"Keeley," he said, "we both know the Queen will see me. And as for my companion," he turned to Kaden who still seemed frozen in position. "I can assure you she is no threat."

The rider hesitated a moment before speaking again. Kaden watched as the muscles in her jaws tightened as her thoughts considered his request. "My fellowship with you pays for the entrance of the companion. If she threatens the

Court I will not hesitate to defend it. Do not make me regret my decision."

Her men guided their horses through the columns before Keeley followed behind them. Before Kaden and Finley went through, he removed his necklace from around his neck and slid it in his coat pocket. Kaden shot Finley a reluctant glance before they both followed behind the line of guards.

The moment Kaden's foot entered the realm of the Seelie Court, she watched with awe as the camouflage of foliage shifted to something more glorious. The sun shimmered through the treetops despite the day behind her having been painted in gray.

The forest ahead was covered in luscious shades of green. From dark to light the wilderness leaned more towards a botanical garden than anything else. A single dirt pathway trailed further into the depths of the Seelie Court, only big enough to support two horses and their riders at a time. Kaden and Finley held up the rear with Keeley and her black stead.

They passed exotic flowers and plants that could not possibly survive in the same climate together. There were flaming orange birds of paradise and blue dawn flower vines that climbed up a maple tree. Vibrant pinks, yellows, and turquoise flowers blossomed all around various trees Kaden had never seen before. Bees flew from flower to flower seeking their succulent juices. On one of the palm trees there was a heap of purple flowers with hues so brilliant Kaden couldn't comprehend. She reached out to feel the texture of it before they had completely moved on.

Under her finger tips, their velvety soft petals tickled. As soon as she let go of the petal, she was surprised to discover that they were not flowers but butterflies. All of the butterflies scattered away into the air around her. They lingered and floated gracefully. One landed on her shoulder. She looked over at its swirling lavender wings and placed a finger for it to crawl on. Its tiny legs walked up her index finger and fluttered its wings. Suddenly, the purple creature turned to a dull gray-brown shade. The wings shifted to something much smaller until it was nothing but a moth. "Kaden," Finley interrupted. The moth flew away, disappearing among the butterflies.

She lingered a moment longer before returning to the parade of fae. "Are we going to address the gargoyle situation?" Kaden whispered to Finley.

"Not now," he said. "We have a bigger issue at hand." She clung to the straps of her backpack as if they could somehow protect her for what lay ahead. Her nerves were overwhelmed and rigid with the idea of speaking to the Seelie Queen. She had never spoken to anyone with such power except maybe her principal in high school. Kaden couldn't understand why the gargoyles attacked her either. She glanced over her shoulder briefly to the butterflies which had settled back down on the palm tree.

"This place is...unusual," she said to herself as her eyes wandered from various plants and animals. The woman on the black horse whistled for her men to halt.

"Ride the boundary and secure the premises. I shall escort them personally," Keeley instructed the guards. Without question the riders galloped down the path, disappearing out of sight. Keeley directed her horse to turn towards the two of them, "What exactly is your plan of action?"

"I was hoping we could all join hands and save the world," Finley stroked her horse's mane. "But I doubt the Queen will appreciate the rude entrance we just made."

"And what is she?" Keeley gestured her head to Kaden. "The gargoyles could not detect anything from her." She spoke with strength and composure and a sharpness that frightened Kaden.

Finley pointed to Kaden, "That is a good question."

"What do you mean what am I?" Kaden asked shyly as if she was disturbing two teachers talking, but they both ignored her question. "Obviously," she started, "there's something wrong with your guards."

"Unknown," Finley said to Keeley, paying no attention to Kaden's poor excuse.

"What do you mean unknown? I'm not a fae, I'm hum-" Kaden was about to rant on about how there was no possible way she was a fae and how the gargoyles were probably just bored from lack of activity when Finley cut her off.

"Allow me to introduce Kaden Storm of Seattle Washington." The knight of the Seelie Court squinted her eyes as she scanned Kaden from top to bottom.

"Keeley Balin of Colchester England," she replied with skepticism.

"Here," Finley corrected, "she's the Knight of Bow and Feather."

A faint smile spread across Kaden's face. *The Knight of*

Bow and Feather, she repeated to herself. She wondered for the briefest moment, what Finley's title had been. "It's nice to meet you," she said.

"Pleasures all mine," Keeley replied as if saying the words were a chore. "I'm sure."

"Just to clarify, I'm not a fae," Kaden said to Keeley. "There's something wrong with your security system."

"Our guards are reliable," Keeley began. "You're the problem."

"I am not the problem. Tell her Finley," Kaden whacked Finley's arm but he didn't say anything. "Go on. Tell her I'm not a fae."

"I can't," he said.

"Why not?" she questioned.

"I can't tell her that since I don't know if it's true," he answered. Kaden stared at Finley. "The guards are never wrong. Never. Besides, it's not such a bad thing."

Kaden shook her head slightly, "I didn't say it was a bad thing, I'm saying it's not possible. Maybe you should get new guards to prevent something like this from happening again." There was a long moment where no one spoke. Kaden crossed her arms over her chest in an attempt to shake the growing irritation forming in her spine. "Why do all fae have European accents?" she asked to change the topic.

"Not all, just most of us," Finley walked next to the horse as they proceeded down the path. Kaden hung back a bit.

"She isn't going to be happy about any of this," Keeley butted in. She seemed to be in her own world, debating whether or not allowing them in the Seelie Court was the right choice. "And I can assure you she will *not* be happy about the girl."

"We'll just have to charm her, won't we, Shadow?" he said to the dark horse. Finley plucked a waxy green leaf off of a nearby plant. He held it in one hand and placed his other hand over it. When he lifted his hand the leaf had turned into a carrot, which he fed to Shadow.

"It is not *you* that I am worried about," Keeley argued. "What do you think will occur when I tell the Queen I let a former knight into the barrier along with an unknown fae? For all either of us know, she could be an informant for Doyle."

"I don't even know who Doyle is!" Kaden half-shouted in a hushed tone, which was ignored by Keeley.

"Do you trust me?" Finley asked Keeley.

"Of course I do. You know that," her voice shifted to be more sincere. The armor she wore around her men seemed to have dissipated once they were gone.

"Then trust that I would never betray you. If the Queen has a problem with your decision, then I will take the punishment." Keeley sighed, still unsure of her choice.

"My men were not happy with my choice. They still do not respect me as they did you." Keeley was more aggravated at herself then at Finley.

"They will come around," he encouraged her. "It has only been twenty years. Besides, I'm a hard act to follow." Finley winked at Keeley hoping it would make her feel better.

They reached a wooden bridge made from thick branches that bypassed a serene pond. Lavender lotus flowers floated among frogs, turtles, fish, and swans. "Even Shadow has not fully warmed up to me," she patted her horse's neck.

"She's a horse who has been through much suffering," Finley explained. "Trust does not come easily to her."

"She trusts *you*," Keeley noted.

"That's only because I rescued her from the pain she was forced to endure," Finley was the first to step foot off the old bridge.

"Shadow was your horse?" Kaden asked him.

"She's not just a 'horse'," he said as if it were undermining the glorious creature. Keeley chuckled quietly to herself at Finley's ridiculousness. "She's also a great companion."

"Cadell told me he spoke to you the other day," Keeley intervened.

"I needed answers. He seemed like the most logical person to go to." Kaden knew Finley had gone to see a friend for answers and she knew he was a Seer, but she wasn't sure that was who they were talking about. She didn't want to ask questions. After all, they seemed like they had been friends for a long time, so she refused to be the ignorant third wheel.

"He worries about you," she told him.

"He worries about everyone." The two continued back and forth while Kaden slowly trailed behind them, lost in her own rambling thoughts.

I wish Megan were here. Quinn would have a field day with her camera. I just don't understand why the gargoyles would come after me. Why me? I've lived my entire life completely normal or close enough to normal, Kaden's drifting thoughts were disturbed by something dropping in front of her. She picked it up, finding a ripe pear. She glanced up into the canopy to figure out where the pear had fallen from.

To her utter amazement, she looked up to the canopy and found dozens of tree houses. Real homes formed out of the trees and branches.

A wooden staircase twined around a tree trunk that led to the first story of a home. Then another staircase led to the second story and then the third. They were smaller than cabins but were built out of the same material with different shades of brown to camouflage them within the trees. The windows and doors on the houses had slightly crooked frames, but were crafted very nicely with black tracery. Some of the houses even had chimneys with smoke pouring out of them.

At the third story there were wooden plank bridges which connected each home to the other. A faerie, maybe in her mid-twenties, hung damp clothes off of the branch railing the bridge had. A young faerie boy carried a basket of fruit that was much larger than he was across the bridge above Kaden. He must not have noticed he dropped the pear.

The Seelie Court was beautiful in every way; it was its own place. A land kids dreamt about every night or read in fairytale books. A land they spent countless hours imagining existed in their own backyard.

Kaden followed as Finley and Keeley curved around a

corner revealing a small village. Fluted music carried over the humdrum of the villagers who were busy working. They passed by a muscular fae chopping up wood with an ax and another shaping a sword with hot metal. Some of the buildings were homes but most of them were workshops with carved wooden signs that stated their business. Kaden read, 'Blacksmith's', 'Delia's Pottery', and 'Meat shop'.

It was like stepping into a seventeenth century style village, with several lambs and sheep roaming around freely as children chased each other playing tag. The girls wore dresses made of mostly browns and greens, each of them had their hair down falling in curls.

The adults didn't pay much attention to Keeley on her monstrous horse. They made a clear path for her but they were too busy with their work. The children, however, went from running and laughing to silently waiting as they passed them.

In between two workshops was a small campfire with some children dancing around it. An older boy, younger than Kaden but older than the rest, played a pan pipe while another used a pot for a drum for the kids to dance to. The pipe player sat on top of one of several logs used as benches. His outfit was made of different shades of green patches sewn together with brown yarn, a brown belt around his waist, as well as green pants with brown boots. As soon as the boy spotted Finley he immediately stopped playing to dart toward him. The dancing kids froze as they watched the boy tackle Finley in a bear hug. Instead of waiting for the boy to return to playing their music, the children danced over to Finley as well, tugging on his coat.

Radiant young faces waited for the boy to release Finley out of his grip. Keeley ordered Shadow to stop to wait for Finley although she didn't seem too happy about it. "I thought you were a bloody hallucination!" The dirty blonde boy held Finley at arm's length to get a good look at him.

"It's me alright," Finley patted the boy on his shoulders with a big grin brightening his face.

"We thought we'd never see you again!" Two twin girls with brown curls said in unison from below Finley's eye level. Finley kneeled down to them, they looked about seven but who knew how old a faerie really was.

"Well, well, well, if it isn't Miss Julia and Miss Juliet. Last time I saw you two, you both were running from your mother with nothing but shoes on your little feet," he lifted them both, one in each arm like a football. "Jamie," he said as he spoke down to a young boy. "Catch any lightning bugs lately?"

"I have a whole jar!" the boy cheered. But his excitement turned into disappointment, "Mom makes me let them go, though."

One twin dangled in the air pretending to fly while the other watched Kaden, "Who's she?"

The other twin looked to where her sister was looking, "Is she a faerie? Or a lady friend?"

"Are you kidding? All the lady friends I need are right here," the girls giggled as he set them down on the ground again.

"How come she doesn't have pointy ears?" Jamie noticed. The kids grew silent, all noticing for the first time Kaden's ears. All at once they began to shout various guesses like 'Nymph', 'Witch', and even Jamie screamed 'Mermaid' at the top of his lungs then realized it made no sense.

"Is she a human?!" the pipe player shouted over all of them. The children went dead silent as if they would have never guessed that. Their innocent eyes widened with the possibility.

"Finley," Keeley urged for them to leave before the kids caused a bigger scene. She trotted forward for them to follow her.

"We have very important grown-up business to attend to," he tilted his head for Kaden to follow Keeley while he said his goodbyes. "Now I expect all of you to be on your very worst behavior."

"Are you coming back for good?" One of the twins tugged on the bottom of his coat.

"Don't you worry, Miss Julia," he patted her head before proceeding to follow after Kaden. The older boy chased after them while the rest remained where they were supposed to.

"You *are* human, aren't you?" A light in his eye shined with excitement. The boy had an English accent just like Keeley's but neither were as thick as Theodore's. "What's your name?"

She wasn't sure if she was allowed to answer the boy, but Keeley was ahead of her and Finley was behind her, "Kaden."

"Blaine..." Keeley said suddenly, "don't you have training?" She shouted over her shoulder.

Blaine ignored her as he walked backwards like he

wanted to watch Kaden. "I've never met a human before. What's it like?"

"What do you mean?" Kaden wondered. Being human was normal to her. If anything she should be asking what it's like to be fae.

"To live out in the Other World." Finley grabbed him and spun him around to face the normal direction.

"It's nice, I guess," Kaden glanced back at Finley for help on how to answer.

Finley took the hint and nodded to Kaden, "What's this about training, Blaine?"

Again, Blaine ignored the question that was directed toward him, "What do you do for fun?"

Kaden tried to pick basic answers, "Write, listen to music, watch T.V."

Blaine lifted his one eyebrow with curiosity, "What's T.V.?"

"A magical box that shows a moving picture," Finley stated.

"Well that sounds boring," Blaine stared at the ground trying to imagine a TV.

"What about this training?" Kaden asked him which made his face light up.

"Well, if you really want to know..." he watched her, really eager for her to ask.

"I really do," Kaden was sincere, she felt Finley roll his eyes behind her.

He stood up straight with his chest puffed out, "I'm training to become a knight, just like Finley was."

"That sounds like fun."

"Oh, it's not. It's extremely dangerous," Blaine exaggerated the details of what consisted of training. "Sword fighting, horseback riding, hand to hand combat, and how to use their power properly," he used his fingers to count off each element the training entailed. "Not to mention memorizing the Seelie Courts rules and regulations. I've tried three times, but you know what they say, the fourth time's the charm." He shrugged his shoulders.

"You had to try out four times?" Finley's voice was raised with a combination of both surprise and humor.

"Hey!" Blaine turned back to him, "It's not that easy."

"Especially when you don't pay attention," Keeley scoffed from upfront.

Blaine waved his hand to dismiss Keeley's comment. "How's life in the real world treating you, Finn?"

"It's fine," the answer was not very convincing.

"Just 'fine'? You can do whatever you want now."

"It's not as great as everyone around here makes it sound." There was a sorrow in Finley's voice, a real heart-wrenching sorrow. It had never occurred to Kaden that Finley was maybe forced to leave his home along with his friends, fellow warriors, and his horse.

"Maybe I'll come out there one day." He picked up a twig from the ground. "You can show me all the fun places—"

"Blaine, I think it's best you head back home. We are on our way to see the Queen," Keeley cut him off.

"Alright," he sighed and tossed the twig to the ground with an unnecessary roughness. He turned to run back to the village, but paused next to Finley. "Finley," he said with an innocent voice, "you're not staying, are you?"

"I'm afraid not," Finley avoided Blaine's puppy dog eyes. It even upset Kaden to hear Finley say those words.

Blaine glanced at the ground and nodded in disappointment. "It was lovely to meet such a nice human," Kaden stopped just before they were about to part ways. Blaine took her hand and kissed it gently, "I've always heard humans were spoiled imps. Glad everyone was wrong."

"It was nice to meet you too, Blaine."

"The pleasure's all mine, Kaden," he smiled lightly before he darted back to the campfire.

"If the Queen is anything like the rest of the faeries, I'm sure she'll be willing to help us," Kaden said with confidence.

It was cut short when Finley said, "She's not."

CHAPTER XX

The wildness of the Seelie Court's botanicals vanished as they grew closer to the residence of the Queen. Rows and rows of thick hedges cut with precision lined the once dirt pathway. Shrubs formed into shapes, flowers placed with perfectly separated space in between each one. The path of woodland ground turned to gray cobblestone under Kaden's feet. The lavish gardens surrounded a vine covered structure. Half castle and half fortress, the home stood in the center of the beauty, casting only a shadow on the entrance. "What happens when we get to the Seelie Court?" Kaden leaned closer to Finley with hopes Keeley would not be able to hear.

Finley looked over at her, "Keeley will escort me to the Queen while you wait in another part of the castle. Then when you are summoned by the Queen, Keeley will come get you." Kaden nodded as he spoke as if she understood. She nervously twirled the excess of the strap of her backpack in her finger.

"What if–?" she whispered even lower this time. "What if she won't help?"

A not-so-discrete scoff came from above as Keeley shook her head. "I doubt she will want to see you," she answered from atop her horse. "You were foolish to come here."

"Are your ears really that good at hearing?" Kaden asked with more volume to her words.

"No, you are just terrible at whispering," Keeley replied. Beside Kaden, Finley smiled and choked down a laugh.

"We can hear when our names are called," he explained. "It's almost like summoning us. There are other fae with much sharper hearing. And as for the Queen," he cleared his throat, "she's too egotistical not to at least show her face."

"How do you expect the Queen to help you with that demeanor?" Keeley doubled back, riding Shadow around Kaden and Finley as she scolded her friend, "You are the most stubborn fae I have ever known. If you would just show her an ounce of respect she *might* consider helping you."

"If I show her a glimpse of respect," Finley rebutted, "she will lose the respect she has for me."

"This is precisely why you lost everything—" Keeley said but cut her own words short when Finley's expression turned into a grimace.

"*This*," Finley began to say sharply, "is precisely why everyone here is a coward." Keeley tried to steady Shadow, who, at the sound of Finley's anger grew uneasy. "I may have lost everything," he paused for a split second on the word 'everything', "but everyone else lost their dignity."

Keeley glare and flared nostrils were enough for Kaden to know she disagreed with his stance. She turned the horse forward once more and trotted ahead.

A grand staircase from the gardens to the medieval relic that was the Seelie Court led Kaden and the others to a plateau of stone. The crunching of cobble under her boot reminded Kaden of the sound of horse drawn carriages. The noise was just how movies and television portrayed it. Looking over the vast railing, she was able to see the maze the hedges and shrubs had made. The design from above was symmetrical and in the center, had a fountain.

The castle itself was forged of stone as if each one had been placed manually. The surface of the outside was anything but smooth. Covered in aged spots, vines crawled up its towering walls. Keeley climbed down from her steed, handing the reins over to another.

They walked under the gatehouse where more fae knights stood eyeing the visitors. Once inside the courtyard, before the grand door was a magnificent fountain spewing water. In its center was the statue of victory. The sculpture Kaden had known was missing a head and its arms. But the one she saw before her a completed sculpture. Her clothes she wore clung to her skin from a rainstorm, illustrating a scene the viewer couldn't see. The woman's windblown hair and clothes flew behind her from an invisible gusting wind. Her raised wings indicated that she had just descended from heaven onto the prow of a ship.

Tree branches formed the railing of the balcony which was being patrolled by numerous guards. Standing only three stories high, the castle had tall pointed windows with various colors of stained glass. The one thing that stood out the most to Kaden was the large, solid gold doors which had two guards in front of them. The doors had eight different panels, each with their own high relief illustrating a story.

Kaden did not have enough time to analyze the doors before Keeley directed the two men to open them, "Oscail na doirse." With her words the doors swung open swiftly. Kaden took a single step inside the inner workings of the Seelie Court before Keeley grabbed her by the elbow. The pain that shot through Kaden's nerves made her wince. But Keeley didn't stop. She dragged Kaden down the cloister hall while Finley remained at the entrance behind her. Half of the wall to the left was made of solid stone while the other half was columns supporting the ceiling. The space between each column provided a view of a sizable garden which had a massive oak tree smack in the center, but it was too far away for Kaden to get a good view of it.

Motionless fae guards were posted at almost every door with hands on their hilts. A few handmaidens wearing midnight blue suede dresses roamed the halls averting their eyes as Keeley passed them. "Where are we going?" Kaden asked as they turned a tight corner. Keeley moved quickly hauling Kaden behind her as they passed a few curious faces.

"Stop talking," Keeley turned down an enclosed hall that was separate from the rest of the cloister. Unguarded dark wooden doors with black tracery lined the hall, "If the Queen finds out I brought an unknown fae into the Court, I will be chastened, or worse, for endangerment to the entire kingdom." She flung a door open, shoving Kaden inside before anyone else saw her. "Wait here," Keeley instructed. "Do not leave under any circumstances." Keeley shut the door immediately, so Kaden didn't have time to ask her any other questions.

The room Keeley left her in was a small sitting room attached to a bedroom. The walls were made of gray stone with stained glass windows across from the door. Two tapestries hung from either side of a dark wooden desk opposite a large fireplace. Archways on each side of the fireplace lead to the bedroom, which Kaden decided not to enter. Instead she sat on what she thought was a couch with a red cushion and gold patterns, but it was about as comfortable as sitting on a park bench. She closed her eyes and leaned back, focusing on the silence of the room. A gradual creek sounded from the door like someone was peeking in. When Kaden quickly glanced at the door no one was there, but it was slightly ajar. *It must have come unlatched,* she told herself as she went to re-latch it before anyone passed by the room. Once she sealed the door she glided across the room, examining the furniture's craftsmanship. She felt the wood's grain under her hands when she heard the pitter patter of footsteps. Kaden looked around the room half expecting to find someone had somehow snuck in without being seen. "Keeley?" Kaden called out, but there was no answer. She returned to her seat on the uncomfortable couch with her feet lifted off the ground as if it would somehow make her feel safer. Her eyes scanned the room back and forth, making sure no one was there. She let out a sigh of relief. Her shoulders relaxed from their tension when the fireplace she sat in front of suddenly lit itself.

Kaden jumped up, circling the room for somewhere to hide. She ended up backing her way through the archway of the bedroom, watching to see if anything else moved. An armchair next to the couch dragged out sideways, like someone pulled it out to sit in.

Nope, Kaden found a closet in the bedroom and she slid into it, holding the door shut behind her. *If anything's out there, it's not getting in here.* She waited, half expecting someone to tug on the other side of the door handle. "Boo!" a tiny voice tickled her ear sending Kaden to jump to the side. She scrambled to open the closet door and when she finally got it open, she fell out, turning to see who had whispered in her ear. A little girl with strawberry blonde hair popped out of the closet in a dark green satin dress. "Who," she asked politely, "are you?" Her hair waved down in curls passed her shoulders.

Kaden remained on the floor in awe of the little girl, "That was all you?"

"Maybe," she twirled side to side in her dress with a devilish smile. "I'm Gladys. What's your name?" Kaden went to answer the girls' questions but when she did she felt a large lump caught in her throat. Naturally, she tried to cough to make it go away, but it didn't work. It seemed to make it worse. The lump felt larger in her throat with each cough, like whatever it was, was crawling up. Her coughing intensified, becoming more frequent as the lump crawled its way up her throat she started gagging. The bulge formed in the back of her mouth which she proceeded to hack out onto the floor. A green, slimy ball with two eyes and four legs hopped away from Kaden. "What's the matter? Have a frog stuck in your throat?" Gladys giggled. Kaden wasn't sure who this evil child was, but she didn't want to stick around to find out what other things she would do.

She rose off the ground cautiously, "My name's Kaden."

"My name's Kaden," the girl mimicked. Kaden casually walked backwards at a slow pace.

"How old are you?" She asked to distract the girl from realizing she was making her way to the exit.

"How old are you?" The little girl followed Kaden to the sitting room swaying her dress playfully.

"Stop it," she asked Gladys. Kaden leaned against the door, her hand fiddling for the handle.

"Stop it." Kaden clicked the door handle down and was just about to open the door to make her great escape. "That's not a part of the game," Gladys sang. The little girl flung Kaden away from the door and onto the sofa with only the gesture of her hand. "Sit," she took a seat in an armchair next to Kaden who was being forced to stay seated. She had no control over any of her limbs as she attempted to run for the exit. Her entire body felt stitched to the couch, "Let's play another game."

"How can I play a game if I can't move?" Kaden tried to be coy to the little girl.

"You don't need to move," Gladys sat back in her chair which was too big for her small body. "Let's see what we can do."

CHAPTER XXI

The cloister hall remained the same as the day Finley left.

Draped in the natural light of the Seelie Court, the columns forged windows of great length. The view of the courtyard was no different from the wee hours of the summer nights he spent roaming the halls. Cool breezes passed through each column leaving a peaceful atmosphere he often sought during his spare time. The garden seemed to stretch endlessly as the courtyard was the main attraction for visitors to pass by despite it rarely being used. "Finley Treasach?" His name rang in his ear. Finley turned away from the view he missed most to find a plump woman in a dark purple dress with gold swirling patterns. "Is that you?" she asked. Her graying hair was tied back in a tight bun with three handmaidens in tow behind her.

"Your Grace," he said, bewildered by the familiar face.

"What are you doing here? Shouldn't you be at the Seelie Court in Wales?" The elder woman approached him with her maidens by her side. Finley took her hand, kissing the top of it as she bowed her head to him. The moment the proper greeting was finished she pulled him in for a tight hug.

"Please," she began, "you are like family." She released him, giving him a good look over from head to toe. "I'm here to visit my niece," she held his hands in hers as they exchanged words. "Forgive me, but I thought you were no longer a part of the Court?"

"I am afraid you are correct, your Grace," he admitted, although the words were vile on his tongue.

"It's Neala to you, not your Grace," Neala corrected him as her handmaidens patiently waited for them to be done with their conversation. "Why have you come back? Are you going to join again?"

"I am afraid not. My business here is more of a....favor of sorts." A group of several knights walked passed, sending silent glares that Neala didn't seem to notice.

She spoke softly, "May I ask what it concerns?"

He half smiled at her innocence, "Unfortunately, it's best that we don't discuss the matter which brought me back. Don't want to worry anyone," he winked at her.

"Well," she sighed as she squeezed his hands one last time. "I hope you retrieve the favor you seek. I must get to my chambers to change before supper," she hugged Finley once more. "It was lovely to see you."

"Always lovely to see you, your Grace," Finley

watched as she continued down the hall filled with an early evening glow gracing the walls.

"I summoned the Queen to her throne," Keeley said suddenly from behind Finley.

He spun to face her, "What did you tell her?" he wondered.

"That you had a favor to ask," Keeley nudged her head toward the garden. They followed a small path as they spoke. His steps trailed along with ease.

Finley's hands fell naturally behind his back, "How did she react when you told her it was me?" The garden's fresh flowers and dew dropped scents filled his nose. Earth and home.

"Surprised, actually." The sound of relief fell between them. Keeley had put her title on the line for him and for that he was grateful. "She'll be at her throne. The rest of the Court will appear in their chairs."

"Did she seem happy?" he asked her curiously. "Or perhaps angry?" The knight in him wanted to be prepared for any situation. Knowing the Queen as well as he did, he leaned toward the worst.

"She always appears... unsettled," Keeley scoffed. "And she will soon be extremely unsettled when she finds out about the unfamiliar fae I brought into the Court."

"She has a name Keeley," he corrected.

"I am well aware of her name," she assured him, "but here she will only be seen as a foreigner or a threat. You know as well as I that bringing her into our world is punishable by exile or imprisonment and I brought her into the heart of it. How do you suspect that will work out?"

Keeley sighed, preparing her posture for the Court. "I'm trusting you as I always have."

At the heart of the Seelie Court rested a bulky oak tree that stood taller than the castle itself. Atop a three stepped platform, carved into the base of the tree was the throne with elaborate patterns. Branches and vines aged over generations decorated the arms and legs. On either side of the throne were two seats designed with less elaborate patterns for the rest of the royals of the Court.

Council members made of dukes and duchesses from other Seelie Courts or distant relations to the Queen sat quietly in a semi circle facing the throne. Several guards lined next to each council member and two stationed by each side of the Queen's empty throne.

"Of course she's going to make a grand entrance," Finley said under his breath. Keeley slapped his gut but he didn't flinch.

"Her Majesty, the Queen," a guard announced. The council rose to their feet as the Queen gracefully glided down the oaks steps to her throne. Her sleeveless dress was a deep red that hugged her perfectly shaped body. The corset top had a puce pink under layer; the dress flowed down in layers with the same deep red color as the corset top. The texture of the dress resembled lovely soft red rose petals. Her chestnut hair was pulled back in an elegant loose bun with three black feathers clipped in it. Delicately placed at the top of her head was the gold leaf crown that had been passed down from her mother. A single strand of her hair fell in front of her pale face that made Finley want to brush it back.

Every faerie, excluding the guards, greeted the Queen with the proper regard by crossing one foot over the other and bending down to bow before her. Without acknowledging them, she took to her throne. "Sir Finley Treasach," her elegant voice said. His name fell soft against his ear. "It has been nearly two decades since you have stepped foot in my Court."

"Indeed it has, your Majesty," Finley answered with his most polite tone.

"My knight commander expressed to me that you request a favor," she said simply. "Although," the Queen's gaze shifted from Finley to Keeley, "I don't believe I owe you one."

"Surely you know that you do," Finley corrected. "Otherwise we would not be speaking. Your Majesty." She faintly smiled at his tone.

"Is that so?" The Queen was amused by his attitude.

"I have given my life aiding this Seelie Court. Training your warriors, fighting Dark fae off our lands, advising your mother—"

The Queen held her hand up to silence him, "Very well. You have made your point, but I will not grant you a favor or any aid, for that matter, until I am made aware of what it is."

"Your Majesty," he cleared his throat. Finley found himself glancing at the floor beneath his feet. He had one chance. Kaden had one chance. He sucked in his breath, "Over the last several years I have spent among the humans

I've noticed a grave increase of Dark fae."

"Treasach," she interrupted. "If this is an attempt to convince me to send my garrison to fight against the Dark fae you will not be pleased with my answer."

"I am requesting your assistance in a rescue mission. The Dark fae have been stealing people, particularly young women, for their own amusement," Finley held one hand behind his back as he walked in a circle. "Although I fear it could be something more."

"What you are asking is for me to pick a fight with our enemy, and this Seelie Court will not be a part of this nonsense."

"Your Majesty," a tiny man from the council coughed, "If I may." She nodded her approval to speak, although she did not seem to wish it. "Perhaps we should ponder his request. We are all well aware of the increase in Dark fae in the cities. It wouldn't hurt to consider it."

She sighed deeply with impatience, "I am curious. Who does the Dark King have in his possession that sends you to me?"

"Someone I know had her friend taken. I owe her my allegiance, for the abduction was partially my blunder," Finley spoke with his free hand gesturing as he paced the cobblestone. He was relieved that a member of the council spoke up to the Queen to consider the idea of aiding him. Finley caught a glimpse of her Grace Neala with her handmaidens beside the man. It was then that Finley was reminded that that was her husband, the Duke of the Seelie Court in Wales.

"A *girl*?" The Queen questioned with disgust. "You

come to me to save one girl? Surely this must be a joke," she rose from her throne. "Do not waste any more of my time with your nonsense. The Court has the utmost gratitude to you, Sir Finley Treasach. However, I will not start a war for you. Keeley," she shifted her attention off of Finely to her knight. "Have him escorted off the premises. I have said all there is to say."

"As you wish, your Majesty," Keeley took Finley's arm to guide him away, but he pulled away abruptly and moved as close as he could to the Queen without being killed.

"Your Majesty, wait," the guards pointed their golden spears at him to halt. She waved for her men to lower their weapons. "I cannot take 'no' for an answer. The girl is here," he said.

"The one you owe your allegiance to?" her voice grew firm and tense. Her brown eyes shot a glare to Keeley, "Why was I not made aware of this?" Keeley recoiled slightly but was about to answer the Queen.

"I just discovered myself that the girl is a fae," he said quickly. "I am not quite sure what kind of fae yet, but perhaps she could be of some use to your Court if she is in *your* debt." Finley cunningly made up a reason for the Queen to listen to him. He wasn't sure if it would work but decided to throw out the idea.

"I am still trying to grasp how my own knight allowed an unknown fae into *my* Court without *my* permission or knowledge. Keeley Balin," The Queen moved off of her platform and walked to face Keeley. "You have not been my knight for more than two decades. Just who do you think you are to make such a decision without my consent?"

"That was my doing your Majesty," Finley chimed in. The Queen sharply looked to Finley but remained in front of Keeley. "I forced Keeley's hand to allow both of us into the Court. Do not punish her for my actions."

"Finley Treasach," The Queen's voice became raspy with frustration. "This does not bode well for you. First, you seek my help, then you refuse the answer I give you, and now you tell me you brought an intruder into *my* Court. And Keeley," her eyes pierced her knight, "you do not answer to Treasach. I do not care if he has a knife clenched against your throat. You answer to me, and to me only, or die for this Court. Is that clear enough for you? Or do I need to be clearer?"

"No, your Majesty, I understand my actions were unforgivable and disrespectful. I only hope you will consider my apologies." The Queen did not respond to Keeley.

She stalked back to her throne, "Where is the girl now?"

"My chambers, your Majesty," Keeley replied sheepishly .

"Bring her to me," she held both hands behind her back, "and summon the Seer." Keeley darted off without so much as a word while two other guards went the opposite direction to gather the Seer. The Queen clenched her jaw as she turned to face Finley, "Quite the ordeal you've dug yourself into."

"You know me, I always enjoy pushing new boundaries," he said with a smug smile on his face even though he had no idea how he would convince the Queen to help.

Chapter XXII

Fingernails scratching against a chalkboard. The horrid noise echoed against Kaden's skull each time Gladys did not like the answer she was given. "Please," Kaden begged, "I'll do anything. Just make the pain stop." Gladys smiled gleefully as she forced Kaden to remain pinned down to the sofa, asking her various questions only she knew the answers to. Kaden felt like she was trapped in a game of jeopardy only all the answers were wrong and with each one the pain grew worse. With every question, Kaden cringed.

"Hmm…" Gladys tapped her index finger on her chin as she searched her devious mind for another question. "What's my favorite color?" She giggled and wiggled her feet which hung off the chair arm.

Kaden took a moment to think about it, she knew if she waited too long to answer Gladys would just create that sound to force her to answer. "Is it... green?" She swallowed hard awaiting the inevitable, agonizing pain to start. Gladys smiled, clapping her hands together like Kaden got a question correct. Unfortunately for Kaden her answer wasn't precise enough for the little demon. The screeching noise rattled Kaden's brain and her skull felt as if needles were scraping along it, which caused tears to well in the corners of her eyes. She couldn't scream. Not because she refused to, but because Gladys had somehow sealed her mouth shut with invisible glue.

"Evergreen was the correct answer. You should be more specific next time," Gladys taunted her. Suddenly the door swung open by Keeley who appeared confused by the pain and fear on Kaden's face.

"What," Keeley spat as she made her way halfway through the room, "on earth are you—" She froze. Her glare met the child seated in her armchair with wide eyes before she bowed. "Your Royal Highness," Keeley said. Kaden's gaze shifted back and forth between Gladys and Keeley.

Gladys jumped off the armchair, "We were just getting to know each other." Kaden's eyes widened as she tried to communicate to Keeley without speaking. Normally Megan or Quinn would be able to understand exactly what Kaden was trying to say but Keeley wrinkled her face.

"The Queen requests the presence of our guest," Keeley told the girl.

Gladys crossed her arms over her chest, "You can tell my mother she's *my* toy. And she can't have her until I'm done playing with her."

"Unfortunately," Keeley waved a hand over Kaden releasing her from the torment of Gladys. "Your Royal Highness, I must follow the Queen's orders."

"Fine," she huffed. "Mother always has to ruin my fun! When she's done with her I want her back. We have to finish our game. You were having fun weren't you?"

Kaden wiped the tears from the corners of her eyes, "Yes." She twisted her wrists and kicked her legs alive.

Gladys smiled brightly as she skipped merrily out of the room humming a tune to herself. "Your Royal Highness? She's…"

"The Princess, yes. Now hurry up," she lifted Kaden off the couch by her arm, "the Queen wants to see you and does not like to be kept waiting."

"What do I do when I meet her? What am I supposed to say?" Kaden questioned Keeley before she was faced with the unnerving experience. They made their way down the hall, Keeley leading the way forward with hurried steps. "I've never met a Queen before, how am I supposed to…"

Keeley spun to face Kaden, "Look, I worked extremely hard to be where I am now. Not many women attain a high rank here and I intend to keep mine. I betrayed the rules by letting you in here for Finley because I am loyal to my friends. But if you jeopardize him, or me, by messing up with the Queen, do not expect me to help you."

Kaden's brow furrowed at her threat. She didn't intend on causing anyone problems and certainly didn't expect anyone to understand where she was coming from. "I'm trying my best," she retorted. "Three days ago I had no idea any of this," she gestured to the walls, "existed. So I think I've been doing a pretty good job so far. And for your information, I'm not doing any of this for myself. I'm doing this because I'm loyal to *my* friend." Kaden pushed past Keeley down the hall they had first come to. Keeley remained standing in her spot. "Now," Kaden called back to her, "I don't know which way I'm supposed to go. Are you going to help me or not?" Keeley waited a moment before guiding her to where she needed to go.

"The Queen is as beautiful as a rose," she said. "But don't be fooled, she's as sharp as its thorns. Do not speak unless spoken to. Do not, under any circumstances, interrupt the Queen while she speaks." Keeley led Kaden into the garden following the cobblestone path. In the distance, Kaden saw the large oak tree she got a quick glimpse of when she first walked into the Seelie Court. She let out a sigh of relief.

"What am I supposed to tell her? What does she know about me?"

"She knows you are fae," Keeley explained.

"But I'm not—"

"Believe it or not," Keeley spoke before Kaden could finish her thought. "You are. And that's part of what's going to happen. The Queen has called on the Seer in order to see if he can tell what type of fae you are. How you masqueraded as human for so long, and so forth."

"How would that be possible?" Kaden rapidly searched through memories in her head to make sense of anything which could help her figure out how this could be possible.

But nothing. Both her parents were totally normal, her

sister was too. They never did anything out of the ordinary.

"The Queen is going to ask you several questions. Be sure to answer each one as completely as possible. And above all, do not make her mad," Keeley coached Kaden as they approached the massive oak tree.

"Any last advice?" Kaden asked.

Keeley paused, "Don't screw up."

Standing closer to the oak, with his hands placed behind his back, she saw Finley. Several guards surrounded the tree as if it was sacred. Kaden's curious eyes noticed the steps that spiraled down the tree leading to an empty throne. A young woman had one hand grasping the top of the throne facing away from everyone as if she were in deep thought. She stood formally, perfectly straight, and tilted her head to the side when she heard Keeley and Kaden arrive. Keeley gestured for Kaden to stop in the center of the cobblestone circle.

As soon as Kaden stopped, the Queen turned to face her. Acting in a panic Kaden crossed her legs and curtsied even though she did not wear a skirt. With the Queen's blank stare and lack of words, Kaden couldn't help but feel intimidated.

She squinted at Kaden. "What is your name?" The Queen stepped away from her throne to get a closer look at her, but she did not leave the platform.

"Kaden Storm," she answered right away as Keeley had instructed. "Your Majesty." The Queen sauntered along her platform with her eyes focused on the girl before her.

"Kaden Storm," The Queen repeated her name like she was trying to remember if she had ever heard of anyone with that name. "Where do you hail from?"

"Seattle, Washington." Kaden cringed back a bit as she was reminded of the game she played with Gladys.

"What are you?" she asked. Kaden snuck a glance to Finley who had one foot now on the steps leading to the Queen's throne. His body was half turned toward her, and the other half turned to the Queen. When Kaden didn't answer automatically he gently shifted his head to catch her eye. "Did you not hear the question? Or are you avoiding its answer?"

"Yes, your Majesty, I heard the question, I just...don't know the answer." Kaden's eyes fell to the floor as she wiggled her toes in her boots from uneasiness.

"Look at me," the Queen seethed. Kaden lifted her eyes to the Queen. "Do you come from a place where it is respectful to look to the ground rather than your superior?"

Kaden furrowed her eyebrows at the Queen's rude tone, "No, but I do come from a place where it is considered disrespectful to speak with such a tone." Kaden saw Finley shoot her a look out of the corner of her eye.

"As I told you before, your Majesty," Finley butted in. "We only just found out this afternoon."

"I am not talking to you, I am talking to *her*." She did not move her gaze off of Kaden, sending the hair on Kaden's arms to stand on end. "How have you lived your entire life not knowing what you are? The gargoyles, my guards," she glared at Keeley, "never make a mistake."

"I'm not sure, I didn't know any of this stuff was real," she knew the Queen was not pleased with any of her answers thus far, but she was only telling the truth.

"Why have you come here?" The Queen leaned forward intrigued to hear what her answer would be. "Are you aligned with the Dark fae?"

"No, your Majesty," she said. "My friend was taken along with numerous other girls. I was told by Finley that it would be nearly impossible to retrieve any of the girls without more manpower. That's why we came here, your Majesty."

"Why do you think this Court should assist you?"

"Because you're the Queen of the Light faeries, that's supposed to make you the good guys, right?"

"Just because we are the 'good guys' does not mean we have to be heroes," she snapped at Kaden as she abruptly made her way to her. The Queen walked down the platform to stand in front of Kaden. She was taller with perfect upright posture while Kaden slouched as she drew closer. "Do you question my leadership abilities, girl?" Kaden saw Finley roll his eyes as he took a seat on the wooden steps. Clearly the Queen caused overly dramatic scenes often.

Kaden looked directly in her eyes as she said, "Yes." The Queen was just about to lose her temper when one of her guards interrupted.

"Your Majesty, the Seer has arrived at your request." The Queen turned her head slightly, listening to the knight who announced the arrival of the Seer. She restrained herself, sharply turning back to her throne where Kaden thought she didn't belong.

"Bring him forth," she shouted and waved for the knight to bring the Seer into her view. A tall man with shoulder length red hair that had several gold leaves entangled in it entered the semicircle the Council made. He had a brown walking stick that stood taller than he did, the top of it shaped like a crescent moon. The dark blue, one shoulder toga he wore draped along the floor as he made his way in front of Kaden but still near the center of everyone. The Seer had gold cuffs on each of his wrists and on his forearms were swirling tattoos. The thing that drew everyone's attention to the Seer was the large ram's horns he had at the top of his forehead. They were twisted in one loop leaving the tip facing forward. His face wore no expression, or interest, for that matter, in the Queen. Even the Queen watched in awe as he entered the room. "Seer, can you enlighten us concerning," she flicked her hand at Kaden, "this?" The Seer silently turned to Kaden who was not too far behind him.

"I am unable to give you much knowledge of the girl," he turned his attention back to the throne, "my power does not work in such a way." His voice was soothing but monotone at the same time, mellow enough to fall asleep to.

"I understand you do not have control of what you foresee," she snapped. The Queen quickly relaxed her tone knowing the Seer had information she craved. "Is there anything you can tell me about helping her or what she is for that matter?" Without a word he closed his eyes taking in a deep breath.

The Seer opened his eye lids to reveal solely white eyes, "I have foreseen darkness on the horizon, followed by great destruction. Whether it involves the girl or not, I cannot say."

The Queen almost seemed frightened by what the Seer told her. She leaned forward with hesitation. "What will be the great destruction you see?"

"Many will fall victim, but it is unclear who those victims will be." The Seer closed his eyes again and this time when they opened they were back to normal looking green eyes.

"Have you a clue what the girl is?" He circled around Kaden, taking in every inch of her while she stood uncomfortably waiting for his response.

"There is something odd about her. Something that blocks out my abilities. A spell might help, perhaps."

"Maybe it's best if we take advantage of this, your Majesty," a council member said from beside her. "We know where the Dark fae will be. There will be plenty of them there to make an effective strike and send a message to the rest. Surely Doyle will be there as well. It's the perfect opportunity."

"Pardon me your Majesty," an older woman stepped closer to the circle. "If you don't mind my advice."

"Your Grace, Neala," the Queen glanced at her with furrowed eyebrows. "I was not aware you were invited to this meeting."

"Your Majesty, perhaps this would be a good thing. If there is a spell of some sort on this girl powerful enough to block out any indication of what exactly she is, maybe she could be useful to the Light fae if there is darkness on the rise."

The Queen pondered briefly, "What do you advise I do, Seer?"

"It is not my advice that will guide you to your destiny. It is the choices you make on your own," he watched Kaden, still curious about her.

"Perhaps the Seer's vision gives you all the more reason to assist us, your Majesty," Finley rose to his feet, the Queen merely glanced at him.

"How do you know she will not destroy my people?" She asked Finley, rubbing her chin with her thumb. "This great destruction could be the Light fae. Could it not, Seer?"

"It could be," he answered.

"Wouldn't you rather have someone with a powerful spell concealing their true form on your good side, your Majesty?" Finley added.

"Perhaps you are right. Or perhaps you are wrong and this girl will destroy my leadership. The choice is mine to make," she eyed Kaden up and down.

"You would let your own paranoia of being overthrown get in the way of having a powerful ally? Not to mention after years of hiding an opportunity to retaliate against the Dark fae," Finley ranted before the Queen who appeared to shut him out.

"Treasach, do not speak out of turn!" She yelled, her harsh voice echoed throughout the cloister garden. The Queen took a deep breath as she smoothed down her dress. "The best way to ensure she will not harm my Court is to keep her here. Imprisonment."

Kaden took a step forward, "What!?"

"Your Majesty," Finley broke in with an uproar, "we did not come here to be imprisoned! We came seeking aid.

You may refuse us your help but do not do this."

"Escort these three to the dungeons until further notice," she commanded the knights.

"Three? Your Majesty?" One of the knights asked as they took hold of Kaden and Finley.

"Yes, the Knight of Bow and Feather as well for letting them enter in the first place." Keeley's pupils were huge with shock. Some of the knights looked guilty for having to detain her, they gingerly took her elbow.

"Your Majesty, please, I beg your forgiveness," Keeley pleaded. The Queen did not answer as she headed back up her spiraling staircase.

"I don't have time for this! I have to get my friend! Please!" Kaden wrestled the two knights who held her as much as she could, though it would be no use since there were plenty more where they came from.

"Linette, this is ridiculous!" Finley had three knights holding him, one on each arm and the last blocking any view he had of the Queen. She did not pause or hesitate. The Seer along with four Councilmen and her Grace Neala were left in their silence as the three prisoners were dragged away.

CHAPTER XXIII

Down a damp stairwell the prisoners were escorted. Slippery stone covered in what Kaden didn't know, led to a level below the Court. With two knights grasping either side of their charge, they struggled in the cramped stairwell meant for one person to descend at a time. Kaden tugged and pulled any which way she could manage, but the grasp on her elbows only grew tighter. She fought against the restraint, unlike both Keeley and Finley. Kaden had half a mind to knock some sense into them. The closer they got to their destination the more the air around them grew thick with moisture and mold. It seeped into Kaden's nostrils as she took the final step off the narrow staircase.

Iron barred cells lined along on either side of the long corridor. Not one of them held prisoners. Before the prisoners quarters was a small wooden desk with the cell keeper standing post. Kaden wondered why on earth there was a cell keeper with no prisoners. Situated behind the cell keeper was a tall locked armoire, "Weapons," the cell keeper stated. The fae guards pulled Keeley up first, stripping her of all her hidden weapons. She stood stiffly as her own garrison removed her sai swords, an iron blade she had hidden along her lower back, the armor she wore along with the horn she carried. Finley nonchalantly cracked his neck but slipped a quick wink to Kaden. She looked at him bewildered by the gesture. If the guards weren't holding her tightly, she would have slapped him for getting her into such a mess.

When they were finished with Keeley, the knights took her to the first cell a few feet away from the table. One of the knights released his grip to unlock the cell's gate. He held the gate open for her to go in. When she didn't move, her other knight shoved her forward with his hand still on her elbow but she still didn't go into the cell. Instead, Keeley rapidly used all her body weight to fling the knight into the cell, sending him crashing against the back wall. She slammed the cell's gate shut on the other knight's hand which caused a loud crackling noise one could only assume were his bones breaking beneath his skin. One of Finley's knights quickly ran to detain her, but they ended up fighting each other. With all the knights distracted and debating whether or not they should release their prisoner to intervene, Finley used the chance to elbow the last of his knights in the face. He proceeded to quickly lurch for the cell keeper behind the desk while one of Kaden's knights let her go to avert a total disaster. Her other knight gripped her elbow tighter, but Kaden used her free hand to slip her blade out of her belt. She twisted her body quickly to stab him in the shoulder, but he grabbed her hand before she could pierce the skin. She lifted her knee to his groin which forced him to lean forward, not sending him to the ground like Kaden had anticipated. Kaden made a quick decision to head butt him which did result in him falling down completely but left her with distorted vision. Behind her, the roaring of a church bell sounded almost out of nowhere. She turned to see the cell keeper dangling on a large rope that was tucked away in the corner, leading out of the dungeon's ceiling. "Run!" Finley yelled. With three of the knights locked up and the rest knocked out, the three darted back up the narrow stairwell.

When Kaden swung the dungeons door open, they were greeted by two dozen knights with their swords pointed at them. The front man ordered for them to be restrained with iron shackles around their wrists and led back down to the dungeon. They removed all of their weapons, securely locking them away in the armoire, then escorted the injured knights out, and imprisoned them in separate cells. Kaden and Finley were next to one another while Keeley was across from Kaden.

Locked up, the Light fae left the prisoners without a cell keeper or guard of any kind watching them.

Kaden rattled, kicked, and threw herself against the cell bars. "It's no use," Keeley said as she leaned against the back of her cell. "The bars are made out of iron."

"So what?" Kaden tugged on each bar. "They could still be loose somewhere."

"They aren't," she slid down to sit on the cold ground. Kaden tried to twist a bolt on the hinge of the gate off, "What are you doing?"

"Trying to unhinge the gate. What does it look like I'm doing?" she answered harshly.

"It's not going to work," Keeley told her. Her comment only made Kaden try harder.

"At least I'm trying something."

"Finley and I can't try anything. The mere touch of the iron burns us and I know for a fact that we will not be able to get the gates open unless someone else opens them. Do you really think *you'll* be able to open the gate and release us? You can't even save your own friend." Kaden stopped fiddling with the bolt.

"Keeley…" Finley warned from his cell.

Kaden swallowed the lump in her throat, knowing Keeley was right. "We need to get out of here," she said mostly to herself as she analyzed the acoustics of her cell.

"These cells were meant to hold every kind of fae, iron bars with silver lining, the iron's even coated with salt," Finley leaned an arm on the cell bars that connected Kaden and Finley's cell. The sleeves from Finley's jacket protected his arms from the fiery burn of the iron.

"But I'm not a fae," she kicked the corner of her cell but the only thing that did was send shooting pain up her leg.

"Yes you are," Keeley closed her eyes and leaned her head back against the wall.

"No. I'm. Not."

"No fae can get past the gargoyles without being

noticed. They attacked you. They noticed you," Finley said. "The question is how."

Kaden kicked the bars harder as Finley spoke, "You promised me." Kaden hit the bars where Finley leaned against. "You promised you would help me save Megan. Now look where we are. Keeley's right, she is going to die because I couldn't get to her!"

"It's not Finley's fault," Keeley interrupted Kaden's angry ranting. "It's the Queen's paranoia and idiocy. She doesn't want to lose her power and is too scared to do anything that could jeopardize it."

"So that's it," Kaden raised her arms, then slapped them down to her sides. "We just sit in here until she decides to change her mind?" Kaden fell against the corner of her cell to a sitting position. "What about the Council or the Seer? He didn't seem to care at all for the Queen. Can he help us?"

"Cadell is not one to take sides. He's wise with a sympathetic point of view, but he can't act on it. His purpose is to advise the Queen but he doesn't make the decisions. Besides," Finley added, "he's a pacifist, so he wouldn't be much help in a fight."

"Don't speak ill of him, he's your only friend at the moment." Keeley crossed her legs over each other and relaxed in her place.

"And here I thought we were friends," Finley put his hand over his heart as if he were offended by her statement. "Just because he's my friend doesn't mean I don't think he needs to practice acting on his sympathies. You're just bitter because you fancy him and he won't save us from the Seelie

Court dungeon," Finley snorted while Keeley glared at his comment.

"He's just as much a prisoner to the Court as we are. The only difference is he's allowed visitation. Even if he managed to get us out, we would be wanted by the Seelie Court. All of us, including him, would be on the run, which wouldn't help any of us now that the Queen knows you both plan on saving her friend. She'll know precisely where to find you."

"I thought the Queen didn't know where the Dark fae were?" Kaden asked Keeley curiously.

"Of course she knows where they are. She knew as soon as Finley figured it out with Cadell. She forced him to tell her what he had been doing with Finley. You really think she lets him out of the Court without knowing exactly what he is doing?"

"So she controls who leaves and who stays? How?" Kaden wondered.

"The only person with that power besides the Queen is...was me," Keeley said with a hint of sadness. "There are only two, one for her and the other for her head Knight."

Keeley's gaze fell to the ground which made Kaden feel bad when she had to ask, "Two what?"

"Horns," Finley answered for Keeley. "The one Keeley used to call off the gargoyles. It isn't just to control them, it also controls the ability to leave the Seelie Court."

"They were taken from a deceased Seer, then hollowed out and consecrated by a powerful witch. I'm sure the Queen will send someone down soon to retrieve the one they have locked in that armoire."

"I'm actually surprised no one's down here watching us," Kaden mumbled.

"There's not much to watch," Finley said. "Behind these bars we are powerless, not to mention I severely injured the cell keeper."

"I just don't understand. If Cadell is powerful, why couldn't he see what kind of fae I am?" Kaden pressed her legs up against her chest so she was hugging them. "*If* I am one," she added.

"If someone powerful put a hex on you," Keeley answered, though Kaden didn't really want the question to be answered. "He wouldn't be able to tell. That's not his ability. He can see the future, but it changes with every decision we make."

"How long do you think the Queen will keep us down here?"

Finley did laps around his cell studying every nook and cranny, "For as long as she wants to. It could be days, months, maybe years."

Kaden couldn't imagine spending years in a dungeon, let alone five more minutes, not when Megan was still out there waiting to be rescued. Her memories brought her back to her first day of kindergarten when she met Megan for the first time. Kaden got lost looking for her classroom and Megan was the only one to help her find it. Ever since then, they were inseparable. Thirteen years later, Megan was the one who was lost and Kaden had to find her.

This whole thing was my fault. If we had chosen another place maybe we wouldn't be in this mess. It's because of me that she's going to die. I'm going to have to tell her parents that their daughter's life was cut too short because of me. I'm going to see everyone who loved her sobbing over an empty casket knowing it was all my fault. Kaden's jaw set. Her hands crumpled into fists. She hit the back of her head against the cold hard iron bars repeatedly for her punishment. She shouldn't have left Megan outside by herself. She knew better.

I'm a terrible friend, a terrible person. I don't deserve to survive this, she does. She wanted to keep smashing her head against the bars until her skull cracked open.

"Hey," Finley crouched down as close as he could to Kaden. He held his hands on the cell's bars despite the slight burning of his palms. "We're going to get out of here somehow. I just haven't figured out how…or when."

Kaden stopped hitting her head, "I don't care about me. I care about Megan." Her voice was barely above a whisper. Keeley didn't pay attention as she lounged on her cell floor getting comfortable with her surroundings. Finley took a seat against the cell bars as well so his back was up against Kaden's. He lifted his legs up just enough for him to place his elbow on his knees. "Do you still love her?" Kaden asked suddenly.

"Who?" he asked, though he knew exactly who Kaden was talking about.

"Linette."

He fiddled with a button on his coat, "Did Theodore tell you?"

As much as Kaden wished to put the blame on Theodore, she knew she wouldn't feel right about it. "I uh… may have read your letters. The ones from your gold book in your apartment."

Finley smiled weakly, "I should have known you would go through my stuff."

"I didn't go through all of it," Kaden started. "I didn't mean to anyway."

"To answer your question," he began, "I'm not in love. No. I used to think I would never stop loving her. Sometimes the person you're closest to, the one you always felt would be in your life forever, ends up turning into a stranger you can't recognize anymore."

"Then why did you keep her letters?" she asked him.

"To remind myself of the affection we once shared. The connection we once had. I was more dismayed at losing her as a friend than a lover, honestly. Her friendship meant more to me than anything else."

"That's a bit morbid, don't you think?" Kaden turned her body halfway to the side. "Feeling all that pain and heartache over and over again." Finley shrugged his shoulders.

"Feeling that pain is what makes us human. Well, like humans anyway. 'Everyone's heart is as fragile as glass. Some people can't help but lock theirs in an iron box for no one to see'," he chuckled to himself. "My mother told me that when I was twelve."

"What was she like?" Kaden asked. "Your mother."

"She was…strong, brave, kind. What about you?" he asked. "What is your mother like?"

Kaden waited to find the right word to describe her mother, "Complicated." Finley turned halfway just as Kaden did so they sat side by side.

"How so?"

"I don't really like to talk about it," she told him.

"Are you serious?" he raised his voice just above a whisper. "You read my personal love letters and you can't even tell me about your mother?"

"Fine," she sighed. "She's just...she spent a lot of time at a mental hospital, postpartum stress or something." Finley furrowed his eyebrows and was about to speak, but was thrown off by the pitter patter of small footsteps that echoed down the staircase bringing each of them to their feet to see who was coming down.

The hum of a sweet voice grew louder as the person came closer. They all held their breath as the person was about to appear from around the curve of the steps. A little girl with lush red hair in a green dress appeared wearing a smile, "I told you we would finish our game."

"Gladys!" Kaden found herself unexpectedly relieved to see the torturous little girl.

"A little birdie told me my mommy locked you up and that she was going to keep you here until she figured out what she wanted to do with you," she skipped to unlock Kaden's gate. "So I thought this would be more fun than continuing our game."

"You're just going to let me go?" Kaden hesitated before she exited the cell.

"No, her Grace Neala sent me to let Finley out too. I stole the keys from a knight in the medical wing." She used the huge ring of keys to unlock Finley's cell.

"What about Keeley?" he asked her.

"Don't worry about me," she gestured her head to the armoire. "You two go, take the horn with you."

"Keeley, we're not just going to leave you," he insisted.

"Yes you are. I don't want to leave Cadell here alone. And we don't have much time before someone comes down for that horn. So go." Finley took the keys from Gladys to unlock the armoire. He handed Kaden her dagger back which she tucked neatly under her sweatshirt and slung the horn over her shoulder. Finley took both his sai swords but left everything else there.

"Let's go," Finley started up the staircase followed by Gladys and Kaden.

"Her Grace Neala said there would be a horse waiting for you two outside the building," Gladys told them.

"What about the knights outside?" Kaden asked her as they hovered outside the dungeons exit.

"Don't worry about that," Finley said, waving his hand over Kaden. She felt nothing had changed, but when she looked down at her body, everything had changed. Instead of wearing her jeans and a sweatshirt she wore a suede dress that was identical to the dark blues ones the handmaidens wore. She saw long, straight brown hair hanging past her shoulders with a small braid pulled to the side. Kaden felt the features of her face had morphed to higher cheekbones with a button nose. The most unusual part was her ears. They were pointed like faeries. The horn Kaden slung over her shoulder was turned into a water jug and her knife appeared as a feather.

Finley morphed himself into a full armored knight with sandy blonde hair. His eyes were a shade lighter and he made himself the same height as Kaden, "We have to be quiet. We don't want to draw attention to ourselves."

Gladys crossed her arms over her chest and shifted her weight, "What about me? I want to be someone too!" Before, Gladys was a deviously twisted girl, now she was acting more like an attention seeking baby.

Finley cracked the door open to check if the coast was clear. "Just turn yourself into something."

"That's not fun, then I'll know what I am." Finley sighed and decided against arguing with the girl who was helping them escape. He waved his hand over her, and then stepped out into the hallway. When he saw no one was around, he signaled for them to follow after. Kaden glanced down at Gladys to make sure she was following. She was delightedly shocked to see Finley had turned Gladys into a chubby little boy dressed in a colorful court jester's outfit complete with a bell hat. Kaden couldn't resist smiling like an idiot to herself.

Finley stood tall as he walked down the hall with dignity and determination. Kaden mimicked the handmaid's she saw earlier and held her hands properly in front of her. Gladys skipped beside both of them, making the tiny bells on her hat jingle with each hop. They trailed Finley, who knew exactly where he was going. He made sharp turns to avoid passing other people in the halls and when they did have to pass people he nodded to them in acknowledgement.

When they got outside the building the evening sky had fallen into a starry night. Kaden assumed the time spent in the faeries' world somehow made time seem slower, but it actually moved at the same rate as the human world. A white horse rested just outside the front entrance with two knights standing watch from the balcony above and two next to the door. A man waited beside the horse holding onto its reins. "Her Grace Neala requested a horse for us," Finley said to the man.

He shifted his eyes from Finley to Kaden then down to Gladys, "Yes, this is the one."

"Your assistance is much appreciated," Finley said as he lifted himself onto the horse. He held his hand out for Kaden. Before she accepted his hand Kaden leaned over to Gladys. She was going to thank her for her help, but remembered Finley telling her faeries don't like to be thanked.

"Next time I see you," she told her, "I promise we'll play more games." Kaden slipped her hand gently inside Finley's who nearly pulled her arm out of her socket as he pulled her up behind him.

"What business do a handmaiden and a knight have at this time of night?" the man asked just as they were about to head off.

"That is our concern," Finley answered. Gladys waved goodbye to them as Finley commanded the horse to gallop down the cobblestone pathway.

It wasn't until they got to the village they heard the roaring sound of a church bell. Finley made the horse gallop faster as they went over the bridge.

When they made it to the entrance Finley stopped the horse and Kaden blew on the horn. It sounded like a trombone making a war call in the middle of a battle. Kaden felt empowered by it as if by using it she gained confidence and maybe even a little something more.

Control.

Kaden jumped off the horse's back as did Finley. She was reluctant to leave the horn behind, but placed it nicely on the back of the horse. "Maybe we should keep it," she said.

"No, the Queen will be after us for sure if she knows we have it. If we leave it behind there's a good chance she might not come looking for us. After all," he said, taking Kaden's hand as they ran past the columns. "She is afraid of her own shadow." And they teleported into the night.

CHAPTER XXIV

"A changeling?" Kaden repeated the unfamiliar word back to Finley. She watched from the door frame of the bathroom as he swept across his apartment with ease.

"It's a possibility," he said. "It's the only thing that makes sense to me. I mentioned it at the diner." He tossed his coat over the couch, tucking his sai swords into his belt. Kaden stared at him with her arms loosely crossed over her chest. Something about the posture felt safe. "A long time ago Dark fae used to switch their children with mortal children, although it's not very common now." He stuck his hand into his coat pocket. " Usually, they would switch them back." He shot Kaden a glance, "Don't know what went wrong with you."

"Let me get this straight," she paused to figure out her own thoughts. "You're telling me that not only am I a fae with some hex on me that makes me mortal, but my birth parents switched me for the mortal baby of the parents who raised me?" The words felt impossible falling off her tongue. More impossible than Megan being kidnapped.

"Yes," he said. He moved swiftly into the kitchen. Finley grabbed a jar from the back of one of his cabinets, "That's exactly what I'm saying to you."

"How could you know for sure?" she questioned. Kaden drew closer to the kitchen where Finley proceeded to place the jar and its mysterious red powder.

"I didn't say I was *sure* you were a changeling, it's more of an educated guess really."

"How–" Kaden found herself stuttering, "how did you get to that conclusion?" She used the island's counter top to steady herself. Everything was moving fast. Too fast.

"When you mentioned your mother being…ill," he answered delicately as he moved the jar away from Kaden.

"You got changeling from my mother being in a mental hospital?" she asked him.

Finley let out an exaggerated sigh as if her questions weren't the right ones or the right time to be asked. But she didn't care. "When the babies are switched," he began, "the mother knows. The Dark faeries enjoy watching as the mother slowly drives herself crazy. No one will believe her and there's nothing she can do about it until her real child is returned to her. Then her madness will cease to exist."

"That mea–" the words caught in Kaden's throat. "That means my mother was right the whole time." The world blurred around her. The bright lights of Finley's apartment suddenly seemed too bright. A knot pitted her stomach. The logical part of her brain knew there was no possible way anyone would know her mother was telling the truth the whole time. But it didn't matter. Kaden understood how her mother had felt. Her mother was angry, scared, and alone, knowing something was very wrong. No one listened to her. Her own husband turned his back on her. And she was right all along. "That means Quinn isn't related to me."

Finley stopped short of what he was doing. "Just because you aren't blood related doesn't mean she's not your family, Kaden. Blood relation isn't what's important. What matters is the connection you share with a person."

"So—so Quinn's real sister, my mother's real child, is out there somewhere," Kaden realized. She had always wanted there to be something more for her. Now that she had it, she wanted to take it all back.

"How should I know?" Finley returned to rummaging for weapons to see the sorrow that filled Kaden's eyes. It was only when Kaden didn't say anything that he heard his own words and what they must have sounded like to her. "I know this must be really hard," he turned to her glossened gaze. He lowered his head to catch her eyes but they were too far away, "but right now you need to be strong. For Megan."

She looked at him then. "I know," she said sullenly. "Just give me a minute." Kaden swallowed hard before leaving for the bathroom and sealing herself inside. She leaned her forehead against the back of the door. A tear trailed down her cheek but she swiped it away before it could get far. She went to the sink to splash cold water on her face with hope that it would prevent more tears. *Megan doesn't have the time for tears.* When she glanced up at the mirror, she caught a glimpse of her reflection. Her hair was tied back tightly into a ponytail but it was still long. Almost the same length as Megan's perfect black hair. *I can't be the same person I was three days ago. I can't be the same Kaden Storm.* She pulled her ponytail out. She opened the medicine cabinet and pulled out a small pair of trimming scissors. They were cold in her shaky hand. *I need to cut my ties.* Kaden took one last look at the girl staring back at her. She held a chunk of hair in her hand and watched as blonde locks fell into the sink.

Kaden didn't have Megan to console her. Quinn didn't believe her, her mother was fighting her own demons, and the only one Kaden could rely on was Finley: a loyal friend who was willing to die to help her. She watched as the girl she once was faded. The person in the mirror, with chopped hair and no more tears to shed, stared back. "You need to be strong."

Two solid knocks on the door pulled Kaden away from herself. "We need to get going," Finley's voice said from outside the door. "Cage games will start soon and we need to get there before they do so we can scope out where to break in." Kaden swung the door open and she adjusted her belt to ensure her dagger wouldn't fall out. Finley took one glance at her, "That's new."

"So we're going to shift into other people, right?"

"We don't need to, there aren't any guards. Besides, we're not looking for a fight. We're getting the girls and getting out." Finley handed Kaden the jar of red powder.

He looked Kaden up and down for a moment, "Here," he handed her his warrior necklace.

"What's this for?" Kaden asked as she hung it around her neck.

"Just a precaution, if someone sees you don't have pointed ears."

"What's the red powder for?" She began to twist the lid.

"Don't!" Finley clenched her hands over it to make sure it stayed closed. He twisted it back closed tightly, "It's an herb. Rowan is lethal to faeries." Finley put the jar inside Kaden's sweatshirt pocket. It stuck out like a sore thumb but it was the only place she could keep it besides her backpack, which would just get in the way. "Try not to kill me with it."

Finley teleported them into a damp, empty warehouse with boarded up windows. Across the street, was where the Dark faeries were piling in the side door of the other warehouse. Finley peeked through a crack in between two pieces of wood that boarded the windows. "It's just starting," he said lightly. "We'll wait until everyone's inside and they get started." He analyzed the scene for a few moments before letting Kaden take a look. "See the other side of the building? How no one's there?"

"Yeah," she said as her eyes fell to where he was talking about.

"That's where we're going. There should be a window to the basement there." Kaden pulled away from the window with a nod.

"There are a lot of them," she said under her breath.

"Probably over a thousand," he took his spot by the window again, "Easily."

"This is really dangerous," Kaden paced around a small circle.

"You're just acknowledging that now?" he scoffed. Every once in a while he would glance over at Kaden.

"No," she said, shaking her head. "I know, but… I know why I'm doing this. Why are you?"

Finley tilted his head with furrowed eyebrows, "I told you, it's my fault Megan was taken and I spent my last years at the Seelie Court trying to convince the Queen we needed to take action. This is me taking action."

"This is a suicide mission," she peered out of the window as the number of Dark fae outside decreased. "You know it and I know it. We'll be lucky if we get through five minutes of our plan." When Kaden looked back at Finley, his eyes were fixated on her.

"It's not like I have much going for me anyway," he shrugged his shoulders.

"What do you mean you have nothing going for you? You have a great life."

"No I don't. I have nothing to stop me from going in there. No one to mourn me," he answered as if he had already accepted his death.

"What about Keeley or Cadell or Blaine? You have all of them."

"When I left the Seelie Court I left all of them too. Seeing them today was the first time I've seen them in years.

I lost my family a long time ago," he answered flatly. He shifted his gaze back out the window.

"After all these years you've spent living with humans, you've never met anyone?" she argued.

"The only people I can truly be myself around are other fae, and if you've noticed there's only Dark fae running around."

"You were fine around me," she said.

He shot her a quick glance, "That's irrelevant," he said. "Your friend was taken and you needed help." Finley took one last glance out the dusty window, "Looks like we're up."

They landed outside, in the empty alley, ankle deep in a puddle. The overwhelming cheers and laughter that was inside the building seeped out. A small rectangular window for the basement was just above the pavement. Coated in dust with no light shining inside made it impossible to see through. "How do we know there are no guards?" Kaden worried.

"They're all busy with the cage game. Anyone willing to break into the Dark fae's place is an idiot." Finley used the back of his heel to shatter the glass of the window. "Except us of course," he added.

"What are you doing?" Kaden tried to yell in a whispered tone at the noise Finley had made.

"Relax," he replied. "They won't be able to hear anything."

"This would have been so much safer if the Queen

would have just sent a few knights," Kaden was filled with adrenaline. But the fear of getting caught made her jumpy. "Or just Keeley."

Finley climbed into the window first, checking the basement out before Kaden followed. He disappeared for a moment before he returned, waving for her to come in. "Watch the glass," he warned her. She avoided shards of glass as she climbed through but hung to the windowsill, her short legs searching for the ground beneath her. Finley grabbed her by the hips to place her on the ground safely.

When Kaden turned around she was greeted with a horrifying sight. Three dozen mini prison cages stood in rows filling the warehouse basement. They zigzagged all the way to a set of old metal steps. A single spotlight hovered above each cage, shining down on young girls, unclothed and shivering. Kaden took a step closer to find they were barely conscious, curled up in fetal positions. Mumbles and groans echoed sheepishly through the heavy air. And then, cheers from above.

All of the cages had locks, easy enough for Finley to snap his finger, removing each lock on the cages. "Locks are simple," he said in a whisper. "Hallucinations, however, are going to be hard. It'll take me some time to get the girls to walk on their own."

"Okay," Kaden scrambled to open each cage door for Finley to get to the girls. She examined each dehydrated face, waiting to see Megans.

Placing his hand against every girl's foreheads, Finley worked. Most of them whimpered or cried. Some of them were too afraid to come out of their cages. Kaden managed to guide the girls to the window and help them out while Finley hurried to remove each hallucination.

With fewer and fewer cages left, a large lump formed in Kaden's throat. She rushed to get through all the girls, and when she came to the last cage farthest from the window, she saw Megan was not in it.

An icy pain ran through Kaden's veins as she stood motionless before the last cage. The roaring sound from the crowd upstairs that once filled her ears faded into a distant silence. Finley's mouth was moving, speaking to Kaden, but the words were lost to her. He let the last girl lean against his body while he guided her to the window. She heard a muffled and distorted voice call her name over and over again, "Kaden!" Finley's hand clenched her upper arm leading her to their exit. His voice faded in and out, she could only manage to catch certain words he said as he pulled her to the window. "Megan," she heard him say, followed by 'not' and 'here'. Kaden felt like she couldn't manage to carry her own weight anymore. She wanted to fall to the ground in defeat, *Megan is not here.*

"We have to go, they'll be done upstairs any minute," Finley noticed the lifeless stare Kaden expressed. He knew she wouldn't be able to climb back out the window herself, "I'll pull you up okay?" He made it out the window then held his hand down for Kaden to grab, "Take my hand." But she just stood there. "Kaden," he snapped his finger in front of her face. "We have to get the girls to safety, come on," he shook his hand.

"She's upstairs," she said under her breath.

"Kaden we can't go up there," he told her firmly. "We

have to go right now." He watched her for a moment. "Listen to me, if you go upstairs neither you nor Megan will come back alive. Megan wouldn't want that. Take my hand." Without a second thought she decided she was leaving with Megan or she wasn't leaving at all.

CHAPTER XXV

Kaden was never much of a runner. Every year for her school's annual mile run, she always managed to lose her breath as she passed the finish line dead last. But that was then. She sprinted as if she had taken track for years toward the beat-up staircase. It could lead anywhere, but Kaden didn't care. She wasn't entirely sure if Megan *was* the girl upstairs. She had no way of knowing until she got up there. Behind her, she heard Finley's distant voice calling out to her. She didn't want him to follow her, she wanted him to get the rest of the girls to safety first. She didn't risk stopping the motion of her legs to have Finley convince her to leave with him.

Her momentum rushing to the stairs made her run full force into the brick wall. She patted her sweatshirt to make sure the jar of Rowan was still intact, and it was. She hurried up the stairs and used all her weight to force the door at the top of the open. The heavy metal opened into a hallway that was polluted with a thick purple smoke coming from cigarettes in a few fae hands.

The lighting in the hall was a dim red, mixing with the purple smoke to make it difficult to decipher which way she was supposed to go. To the right, through a red draped curtain, copious amounts of smoke seeped out along with an intoxicating smell. Forbidden delites wafted to her nostrils. In the haze that hit her, she was drawn to the red curtain room. But the roaring crowd to the left reminded her what she had to do.

Leaning against one side of the wall with a cigarette hanging out of her mouth was a Dark fae woman. Her hair was a sleek black, cut short and half shaved on one side. The woman like the others surrounding her were dressed in gothic style apparel with a cup in her hand. "Hey," she said as Kaden moved past her. Kaden didn't realize the girl was talking to her and frankly she could care less. "Blondie," she said as she pushed herself off the wall with her shoulder. She turned halfway to catch Kaden before she left the hallway.

Kaden didn't give her the time of day, so the girl grabbed her elbow. "Blondie, I'm talking to you," she snapped and pulled Kaden back toward her.

Kaden quickly looked down at the girl's grip on her elbow and tugged it away, "What?" she impatiently answered.

"What were you doing in the basement?" She put the cigarette into her cup to put it out.

Kaden didn't know what would be an acceptable reply that wouldn't get her exposed, so she said the first thing that came to mind. "Doyle asked me to check the basement. He thought someone was stupid enough to break in." The girl squinted an eye, hesitant to question an order made by Doyle.

"I don't recognize you," she scowled. "Have we met before?"

Both her anger and anxiety for Megan formed a wry smile across her face, "I think I would have remembered a hideous face like yours." The woman glared back at Kaden, her face twisted like she was about to punch her. The girl must have forced her anger down because she unclenched her fist and locked her jaw.

"You're lucky Doyle sent you on an errand or your blood would be spattered on this wall," she used a fist to hit the concrete wall next to her.

Kaden cocked another smile before she rounded the corner entering another hall filled with more fae than the last one. The hall opened up to a large room, half of the crowd was ecstatic while the other half booed angrily. Several white lights illuminated the space with one larger one hanging above a massive cage. Kaden couldn't see the bottom of the cage or who was in it. This was one of the times Kaden resented her height and the height of the biker-like men who surrounded the front of the cage. There were at least a thousand fae, maybe more, all squished and pressed up against the center cage.

Kaden squirmed her way in between yelling fae to get a closer look. Every one of them faced the center of the room, some of them held tiny pieces of paper in their hands like lottery tickets. "You son of a bitch!" A woman screamed from the back. A heavy push from behind shoved Kaden forward into the back of a muscular man who was twice her size. The man turned around to see who pushed him with a devilish look in his eyes. At first he looked at his eye level not realizing the one who pushed him was a small girl. He tilted his head down at her. The man cocked a half smile and swung his fist in the direction of her head. The thing about being small is it's very easy to shrink to the floor when needed, which is exactly what Kaden did. She got down on the ground letting a woman behind her take the punch instead. Kaden crawled away on her hands and knees as the misunderstanding turned into a massive fist fight between the two. The surrounding fae shifted their attention accordingly.

She got back to her feet slyly making her way away from the outbreak. As she rose, she noticed a set of stairs that led to the second level of the warehouse filled with more fae, but fewer on the main level. The people on the upper level leaned over the railing, waving tickets around like it was a parade. It was her best chance of seeing the center cage.

The amount of fae that lingered on the stairs was like a clogged artery; they were the people who desperately wanted to be on the ground level but were not as big as everyone else. From what Kaden was witnessing, cage games were the equivalent of underground wrestling matches, only it was a tormented soul they were betting on.

When she reached the top of the second level, her

attention was naturally drawn to one person. He was completely different from everyone else. He didn't seem to care at all for the shenanigans that were going on around him. The man sat in a chair with one of his legs dangling off its arm while his attention was on his fingernails. Kaden studied him, realizing the chair he sat in was made of skeletal bones. Two human skulls rested as the ears of the chair. What looked like a rib cage formed the chairs back with a spinal cord down the center. The man lounging in it had black, spiked hair with a purple tint to it. His patched jacket was purple as well and cut like a formal tuxedo, though it was old and beat-up. He wore dark brown patched pants with black leather and flat bottom boots.

It wasn't until Kaden saw Riley standing next to the young, unfamiliar man that she realized it was Doyle. She knew to avoid that name at any cost from what Finley had said about him, but she absolutely needed to steer clear of Riley. He would recognize her the moment he saw her.

She went in the opposite direction, still unable to get a visual of any kind. She didn't go that far away from the stairs before pushing a few fae out of the way so she could lean against the railing. When she was able to see the warehouse completely she immediately regretted her decision.

In the center of the room an oversized cage. Directly above it was a sign. A score board, almost. One that someone would expect to see at a football game only there were no points, but a timer. It read '2 days 3 hours 9 minutes 4 seconds'. The pieces of paper the fae carried were bets they had placed on her.

At first Kaden couldn't recognize the girl coiled in the cage. The lush locks she once had were nothing more than a buzz cut. Her body was frail, her skin sheet white. The Megan she knew was nowhere to be found.

Inside the cage with her was a jagged piece of glass. Frantically, Kaden studied the warehouse for her way to save her. Finley was right and Kaden knew it. There was no way of retrieving Megan without being caught. Every window, every door, every inch of the floor was covered with Dark fae. Even with the dagger she couldn't fight all of them. But, she still carried the red dust Finley gave her in her pocket. It might not kill all of them, but at least she could be beside Megan when they both died.

CHAPTER XXVI

Her demons whispered into her ear, into her soul. The body that carried her was nothing but an empty vessel, a hollow thing. The thread that she clung to frayed as her darkness swallowed her whole.

Megan's gaze fell to the shard of glass beside her. Light coming from somewhere and nowhere reflected off of it. The tips of her finger traced along the rigid edge, crimson slipping out of the tip of her finger. In the reflection, was the scared little girl she tried to hide behind.

Broken.

As she tilted the piece, the light revealed a familiar face with bleach blonde hair.

Kaden.

Now, she truly believed there was nothing.

CHAPTER XXVII

Kaden watched from the balcony as Megan lifted a piece of broken mirror. "No," Kaden whispered under her breath. Megan's pleading eyes fell to the jagged edges.

"No no no," Kaden shook her head desperately. The Dark fae leaned forward with anticipation around her. There were no windows, no doors for them to escape through. Just a sea of darkness. "Megan! Stop!" she shouted as loud as she could over the eagerness of the crowd.

Her voice fell on deaf ears. All she had to do was get Megan to snap out whatever hallucination she was trapped in. She would see Kaden and the monstrous creatures before her. All she needed to know was that she wasn't alone, "Megan!"

It was no use.

Megan slid the broken shard across her frail wrist with no hesitation. While the fae cheered more aggressively at the sight of oozing blood dripping down her arm, Kaden darted down the stairs pushing past anyone in her way, "I'm here, Megan! I'm right here!"

The dark red slithered down Megan's pale skin. No pain showed in her face as she turned for her second wrist.

It was too late.

By the time she reached the front of the cage the light in Megan's eyes was fading. She lay on her side in a growing pool of blood. Her eyelids barely flickered open. Kaden grasped the cage bars slipping one arm through to reach Megan's hand. "Stay with me, Megan! You can't leave me," she whimpered with her hand not able to reach far enough to get Megan's. "Please don't leave me."

Kaden forced her arm as far as she could through the cage to grab her hand when a buzzer sounded. The scoreboard flashed its final numbers, '2 days 3 hours 12 minutes 6 seconds'.

Cheers and groans echoed throughout.

I was right here and she didn't even know it, she thought.

Her hand was inches away from Megan's limp body, touching nothing but blood.

And they were all laughing.

They enjoyed it.

It was a rush. All of it.

Stealing.

Torturing.

Murder.

Fury Kaden had never known quickly churned her

despair to rage. Her blood boiled, her skin prickled with adrenaline.

When Kaden looked away from Megan to the monsters around her she found comradery, delight even from each of them. All but one person.

Doyle.

CHAPTER XXVIII

His eyes met hers as everyone around celebrated. Doyle watched her like she was the only interesting thing in the room. Up on his perch, he was well aware that Kaden did not belong among the rest of the crowd. That didn't prevent him from just waiting to see what she would do next.

With nothing left to lose, Kaden pulled her hand out of the cage, remnants of Megan's blood following her. She pulled the jar of Rowan out of her pocket, lifting it into the air. Kaden slammed the jar down with as much force as she could muster. The glass shattered into pieces and the red dust dispersed into the air, intoxicating the fae around her. At least a dozen fae fell heavily to their death from the fumes of the Rowan. Doyle cocked a smile and sat upright in his chair of skeletal bones.

Most of the Dark fae were backing away from the

remnants of the red dust that laid spread out at Kaden's feet. The room fell silent while everyone's eyes were on Kaden, yet hers were on Doyle. She held her clenched fists at her sides. Doyle began to slowly clap like he was finally entertained. "Leave us," his voice was deep with an underlying hint of a threat to the other fae. The Dark creatures listened to their leader and exited the warehouse quickly.

Kaden remained beside Megan as the room grew in size leaving only four people behind. Kaden, Megan, Doyle, and Riley by his side. "I was unaware of hosting the company of a mortal girl."

"You *had* dozens of mortal girls in the basement," she replied with hostility. Her tone echoed in the empty building.

Riley stood stupefied next to Doyle. "*Had?*" Doyle questioned with a dark chuckle. "I see. Am I to assume the one you've so heroically come for is that decaying corpse you stand beside?"

"Her name is Megan," her voice did not shake or sound at all weak. She never sounded more confident in her life.

"You mean her name *was* Megan," Riley added, crossing his arms over his chest. Kaden wanted nothing but to carve the smirk he wore right off his face.

"Tell me," Doyle stood up from his throne of bones and leaned over the railing, "who is it that guided you here?"

"I came alone," she lied, hoping Finley had gotten the girls to safety while she was upstairs.

"She was with Finley Treasach," Riley butted in like a kiss ass. "Her name is Kaden. Her rotting friend over there called her name out a few times." Doyle cocked his head to his minion. He raised his hand up to Riley, causing him to clench his ears and fall to his knees. Riley scratched at his skull like he heard an excruciating noise that only he could hear and he wanted to get rid of it.

"Silence is a virtue," Doyle lowered his hand and Riley tried to catch his breath once he was released from Doyle's power. "Now, fetch me young Treasach before I cut out your tongue." When Riley removed his hands from his ear Kaden caught a glimpse of some blood running out of his ear. He shot her a disgustingly irritated look before following his orders and exited the main part of the building.

"Finley isn't here anymore. You're wasting your time," she stepped over two dead fae to get closer to the balcony Doyle was on.

"But that is not the Treasach way. You see," he held both hands behind his back, "he was a brilliant warrior, the best of the West Coast if you ask me. But he always had one flaw."

"And what flaw would that be?" Kaden held her hand over her dagger, ready to make a quick move if she had to.

"His loyalty," he answered. "When he was head of the Light Court's army he remained with them no matter what obstacle they were against. It's that loyalty I wanted in my domain. Unfortunately for me he was too loyal to his morals. It's why he left the Seelie Court after all. Why he refused me on more than one occasion," Doyle made his way to the stairs. "I'm going to assume you share the same flaw as him."

"Why is that?" she asked, her eyes followed every move he made, anticipating him to attack.

"You still remain next to your newly deceased friend, do you not?" He almost hopped down the steps to the main floor where Kaden was. Her grip around her dagger grew tighter.

"Loyalty can get you killed," he stopped walking once he was on the main floor.

"If loyalty is my flaw, then what's yours?" It took all her strength to stay in her spot and not run towards him with her knife. She imagined herself jabbing it right into his jugular and watching as the blood poured out of his body.

"Darling," an amused smile crossed his face, "I'm flawless. Just look at me. I have subjects willing to do everything I ask of them. You can't buy that kind of power, you earn it." His dark purple eyes danced with delight as he took one step closer to her.

"So you just wave your hand and kill whoever you want? You just run around playing God?"

"Basically," he stepped to the side. Kaden mimicked his movement in the opposite direction. "It's frustrating to you, isn't it? Not knowing why your friend here has died."

"It's simple," Kaden's heart fluttered with rage under her chest. "She died for nothing. She died because you and your pathetic minions are sadistic bastards with nothing better to do than murder innocent people."

"Your friend took her own life. She didn't have to," he shrugged.

"She took her life because you forced her to! You pushed her too far!"

"My dear," he sighed, "that's life. It pushes you until you break. We take the weak and break them. What they do as a result is their choice."

"And if she didn't kill herself," her voice cracked with pain. "What would you have done?"

"Interesting," Doyle tapped his index finger on his chin, "it's never happened before."

"Well then go ahead, just kill me already," Kaden took a deep breath, just waiting for him to snap his fingers.

"Kill you?" he sounded confused, "my dear, that would be too simple. Especially since that's what you want, is it not? You want to die."

"No I don't," a tiny part of her knew he was right, while the other part of her ached for revenge she knew she probably wouldn't get.

"Look at you, all alone with nothing left. Ah but wait, there is someone. Mr. Treasach, he hasn't left you yet has he? Perhaps I should go see what's taking Riley so long," he twisted his body to leave the room. "I'll be back in a jiffy. And you might want to practice with that blade you have while you still can." With that, he disappeared from the room.

Kaden went back to the cage where Megan laid. She reached for her hand but couldn't grab it, she was too far away. Tears filled her eyes, two or three streamed down her soft cheek, "I'm so sorry, Megan. It's my fault you're gone." She soundlessly cried beside her friend.

A hand covered her mouth from behind her. She tried

to pull away from whoever held her when a familiar voice spoke into her ear. "Shsh. It's me," Finley whispered in her ear. When she nodded that she understood who it was, he removed his hand.

"What are you doing here? You were supposed to leave with the girls," she turned to face him. Her voice was a hushed tone with a hint of urgency. "Doyle and Riley went looking for you. They said you would come back, but I didn't think you would."

"I teleported the girls away and erased their memories of this," he glanced at each exit to make sure no one was coming. "Of course I came back. I wasn't about to leave you here to die by yourself. We need to go, take my hand." He held his hand out for her but she hesitated.

"How did you get past everyone? They would have noticed you right away," she took half a step back.

"What? That's not important," he shook his hand. "Come on."

"Not until you tell me how you got past them." She looked Finley up and down. He was the same as when she had last seen him. Nothing was different. He didn't have so much as a scrape or a scratch.

"We don't have time for this," he put his hands on her shoulders and shook her lightly. "I'm real, okay?"

Kaden was well aware of what the Dark fae were capable of. Any one of them could easily shape shift into Finley. Especially if Doyle had no intention of killing Kaden, it could be a twisted trick. "I don't believe you."

"You have to trust me. They're getting into your head. It's me!" Kaden moved backward, away from him. "Fine.

You don't believe me? Then kill me." He raised his arms up to signify his surrender. "I won't fight you, but then you'll have no way out of here."

"Kaden!" someone yelled from the top of the balcony. She turned quickly only to find Finley being held by two Dark fae. He was beaten half to death, face bruised and swollen. His clothes were torn with traces of blood. "Don't trust him!"

She flipped her knife out and pointed in the direction of the doppelganger. "Kaden, it's really me." Kaden wasn't sure who to trust, the bloody beaten up Finley or the one who stood before her. She looked into his eyes and for a split second, dark purple bled through his green irises.

Kaden swung a left hook into his face, he staggered back. "You're not Finley," she kicked his body against the cage. She went in for another kick, but Finley caught her ankle.

"I'm not going to fight you," he looked her right in the eye.

"I'm not an idiot. I know this is a trick." She pulled her leg away before punching him in the jaw again. Kaden stabbed him in the shoulder, then retracted the blade from his body. He held one hand over the fresh wound as it bled through his shirt. She went in for a second stab but he grabbed her wrist. He twisted her body so he held the knife with her hand to her neck.

"Listen to me," he said. "Focus." She gritted her teeth and elbowed him in the ribs. Before he let go of her, he took the knife and threw it away from her. "I don't want to hurt you." Kaden threw punches left and right until Finley fell to his knees. She kicked him with her boot right in the face. His nose bled profusely but he still didn't fight back. Finley fell to his side. Kaden kicked him in the ribs with so much force she felt his bones crack beneath her feet. She knew he would heal from his injuries soon. If she wanted to inflict real pain and make Doyle suffer she needed the knife.

She walked over to the knife and picked it up off the ground. She felt its weight in her hands. She had never truly hurt anyone before, but she looked at Megan's body and was reminded of the pain she suffered before she died. The death she had suffered for a simple game. She hovered over Finley's limp body, "Kaden, don't." With one last kick to his face, he was knocked unconscious.

She picked up the knife and with a fierce darkness in her voice said, "This is for my friend." Kaden bent down beside him, with both hands around the handle she plunged the iron knife through his heart. His blood seeped out from the deadly wound onto Kaden's once clean palms. She extracted the dagger from the body, waiting for it to transform from Finley to Doyle.

She looked over at the balcony where Finley was with the two guards. When she laid eyes on the three of them, they turned to purple smoke, disappearing into nothing. "No," she murmured. "No," she turned back to the dead body in front of her. Kaden lifted Finley's limp body onto her lap. "It was a trick, it had to be," she shook his shoulders rapidly, waiting for him to dissolve into purple smoke as the other three had. She hugged her arms around his body, gently rocking back and forth, "It was supposed to be a trick."

"Ah," Doyle glided into Kaden's peripheral view, "but it was a trick. Just not the one you thought it was." Finley's blood leaked onto her clothes as she held him tighter in her arms.

"His eyes turned purple," she barely raised her voice above a whisper. "It was supposed to be you. I saw your purple eyes."

"That's because that's what I wanted you to see. There is a darkness in your heart, Kaden," he kneeled down beside her. "That's the incredible thing about humans, each and every one of you contains a darkness that you lock away for no one to see. It brings me great joy to unleash that darkness to see what becomes of it when released." Doyle tucked a strand of Kaden's hair behind her ear, "Regrettably, Treasach had to pay the price for your darkness. But, I am going to do you a favor."

"What favor could you possibly do for me?" Kaden's tear filled eyes did not leave Finley's face.

"I am going to make all this," he gestured to both Megan and Finley, "go away."

"You can save them?" A light flicker of hope filled inside Kaden. She looked to Doyle, ignorant of what the cost of his favor might be.

"No, even better. I can make you forget," his soothing voice almost made forgetting everything sound appealing.

Riley, along with two more men came into the room. They hovered in the background while Doyle spoke to Kaden. Like the serpent tempting Eve in the garden of Eden.

"Forget?" she asked. "How would that be doing me a

favor? What I want is for them to be alive."

"Even if I could bring them back, I wouldn't," he waved his hand for the men to approach.

"Why would you want to make me forget?" She wanted to remember, she wanted to find out who she really was. She wanted to be able to claim revenge over her friends.

"As I've said only about a hundred times, your misery gives me pleasure," he slid a smile on his face as each man tugged her arms off Finley.

"Making me forget won't make me miserable," Kaden didn't try to fight her way out of the fae's grip. She was too broken inside to fight.

"I'm not just going to make you forget. I am going to send you back to your home, back to your incredibly boring life with the memory of your friend being taken. This way you will spend countless hours undergoing therapy sessions with no clue of what truly happened. There will be a hole in your heart, a pit in your stomach that can't be filled for the rest of your life." As the men lifted her to her feet, Doyle rose as well. He caressed his hand over her face, "I will leave bits and pieces with you, yet you will believe them to be dreams." Kaden's head felt as heavy as a rock, her eyes slowly shut like she was falling asleep. The last thing she saw before her eyes closed and she forgot everything were Doyle's dark, devious eyes staring back into hers.

EPILOGUE

An uproar of commotion woke Finley from his unconscious state. His eyes fluttered open to find iron chains wrapped around his bare skin. Flakes of rusted iron bore into his flesh. The burning sensation radiated throughout his body and in his veins. He was tethered to a chair that almost resembled an operating chair. The dull fluorescent lighting in the room was a mix of faded white and green. Mold clung to the crumbling walls. The stench of urine mingled with sweat permeated in the air. Jingling of keys brought Finley to his full alertness. To his left was a set of swinging double doors. On his right was a small kitchen table with several torture devices. There lay an iron knife, a saw covered in blood, a drill with a chunk of flesh or brain on its tip, Finley wasn't sure. The door swung open, letting in a massive gust of 'fresh air' into the room. For the brief moment the door was open Finley caught a glance of a dark hallway, "Good to see you're finally awake." Doyle entered the room wearing a rubber apron over his clothes, a splatter of blood in the center.

"Is this your plan?" Finley said. "Chain me down and have your way with me? If I knew things were going to get kinky I would have brought my hand cuffs." His voice was hoarse and dry from lack of water. Finley realized he wasn't aware of how long he had been knocked out.

"If I wanted to have my way with you, you would be chained to my bed." He strolled to the table and traced his fingers over the saw.

"Should I bother asking where I am?" Finley wiggled his wrist from the fiery burn of the chains.

"A sanctuary we keep," he lifted the saw and held it in the light to examine it. "We use it for those who would not obey."

"And Kaden?" he wondered. "Where is she? In another room?" Finley's eyes followed Doyle as he circled the back of the chair.

"Do not fret, for she has been handled," he imitated a formal English accent, straightening his posture. Finley's teeth gritted together. He tried to fight the rage boiling his blood by staring up at the ceiling. "I heard the girls you saved made it safely to the hospital. Too bad Kaden wasn't one of them."

Finley pushed himself to bite back the anger rising in his chest like he had been trained to. No use would come of it restrained the way he was.

"Why did you really capture those girls?" The words

fell out, harshly and bitter, too harshly and too bitter to get an honest reply. He imagined the fragile, broken girls safe from Doyle. Then, he imagined Kaden sitting across from him at the diner trying to hide a smile at one of his remarks. "There's no way it was purely entertainment," he noted, easing his words to a calmer tone. "Not with that many." Finley craned his neck to watch Doyle as he fiddled with the sharp edge.

"You always were sharper than the rest of the Seelie Court. I suppose that's what intrigues me about you." Doyle slapped the saw back down in its previous place. "The girls served their last judgment before their death. It's quite the opposite of what you would expect. Instead of looking for all the good they had done throughout their lives, I looked for the bad, the pathetic. I pulled all that out until they made their sacrifice to Him. After all, suicide is a sin."

"Him?" Finley mocked. "You are doing this for *Him*?" He didn't resist the urge to laugh even if it meant the possibility of getting his arm sawed off. "Are you really that insane? He left you on Earth for a reason."

"Laugh all you want," Doyle replied harshly. "But there are people in place, above me, who want this to happen quite desperately. We'll see who's laughing in the end. For now, you and I will be logging a lot of quality time together," he leaned over Finley. "You are going to tell me everything I want to know. For now, I'll leave you with Leila." Doyle snapped his fingers to indicate the woman outside the door to enter. "She will tend to your festering wounds and feed you. Then someone will escort you to your accommodations." As he stepped out of Finley's view, a young woman stepped in. Her light brown hair was braided to the side. The girl couldn't have been more than Finley's age, although her tired eyes and sunken face argued otherwise. As the door swung shut, she placed a wash bowl on the table and rinsed out a washcloth.

"I'm Finley," he introduced himself. She said nothing, only started to wash the gashes on his forehead. As long as the iron chains were on him, he knew he wouldn't be able to heal.

His intentions were to ask her questions about where they were, but for the time being he wanted to be kind. The off-white servant's dress she wore was ragged with huge dirt stains. Around her neck was a tight iron collar that irritated her tanned skin with bright red blisters, "That looks like it hurts." Without acknowledging him she proceeded to tend to his wounds. "Aren't you just a regular chatty Kathy," he needed to lighten up the mood if he wanted to ask her any questions, but that plan didn't seem to be going very well for him. The girl didn't look him in the eye or smile at his joke.

As soon as she finished, she left the room for two larger fae men to enter. One of them strapped an iron collar around his neck just like the one the girl wore. The other untied the chains that held him to the chair and replaced them with hand and ankle cuffs so Finley wouldn't be able to fight them.

They escorted Finley from the room and entered the dark hallway where loud angry voices filled the building. Once Finley realized just what type of place he was in, he wished he had been killed rather than captured.

The hallway turned into one large room, just like the warehouse. Only this had hundreds of cells. It was an old prison, three stories high with aggressive cell mates locked behind bars. Two to three fae occupied the small square spaces with a single bed and a bucket in the corner. The captives screamed and pounded on their cell bars. Guards strolled by with iron pipes to smash the fingers of the rowdy creatures. The place was overbearingly noisy with rage filling the air. The rotten smell was strong enough to make someone pass out, or at least, gag from its pungent stench. The lighting was the same greenish-white from the room Finley first awoke in, although the lights only hung outside the cells, not in them.

Finley was brought to a cell on the second level. The guards didn't remove any of his chains when they shoved him into the cell with a younger boy scrunched in the corner. They slammed the bars shut, "See you soon, Treasach." Both men laughed heartily at each other.

Finley plopped onto the mattress which resembled what sitting on a rock felt like. He lifted his feet to the bed, finagling the ankle chains which only ignited his skin with more pain. He pulled at them, tried to break them with his bare hands, "No use." Finley looked over to the voice huddled in the corner. He wore severely ripped clothing that revealed that his tanned skin was so dried and cracked that it made the Atacama Desert look saturated. "They leave for a while until you don't need anymore," he said in broken English. The latino accent the boy spoke with had yet to mature.

"Oh yeah?" Finley asked kindly. He dropped his

chains to the floor, eyeing the different prisoners ravaging in their own cells. Where are we anyway?"

The boy's deep brown, puppy eyes were wide when they met Finley's, "Hell."

FALLEN WARRIOR

And

LOST DAUGHTER

Anniversary Coming Soon

ACKNOWLEDGMENTS

A long time ago there was a girl who saw a picture of a faerie in a book and declared, one day, she would write a book about faeries. Little did I know that little girl was right. This book would not be possible if not for the people in my life who have supported me. When I was down, you picked me up. When I needed to talk, you answered the phone. When I had doubts, you encouraged me to continue. You know who you are. And I am forever grateful for each one of you.

Always,
Dylann

A Conversation with Dylann Rhea

What made you want to become a writer?

When I was young I came across these illustrations of fairies done by Amy Brown. I saw one of her works, pointed at it, and said, "I'm going to write a book about fairies". I was maybe nine. I don't think I knew what being a writer was. It wasn't until middle school that I learned what it was like to write your own story, have control over what happens, and play with characters. That experience, combined with my love for *The Outsiders,* shed light on writing and storytelling. I spent most of my eighth-grade year during class, recess, and even sleepovers dedicated to the first story I ever wrote. And I just fell in love with the freedom of it.

What inspires you to write?

There are a lot of little things that inspire me: verses from songs, lines of poetry, books and movies, friends and strangers. I pull different pieces of art that speak to me into this vortex that just kind of sits dormant in my brain until it's ready to explore. A lot of the time it's just a spark that flicks on the imagination and takes me to different worlds. Those stories and dreams keep me alive with curiosity until

I can't hold onto it anymore and it needs to explode on a page.

Can you share a moment from your personal life that inspired a scene or character in the book?

There is one small scene in this book that did happen to me and my friend - when Kaden and Megan are at the football game. My friend playfully pushed me while we were walking up a hill. I almost fell backward down that hill, and I yelled at her in a Southern accent. Because apparently, that's what you do when you fall suddenly.

Were there any themes or messages you consciously set out to explore in this book?

One of the biggest ones that came up was the idea that the good guys aren't always good. Our world is full of gray areas. It's not who you are, it's what you do. The gray area interests me and makes things so much more complex. And, of course, I am a sucker for found family stories. Finding people you connect with and who support you is such an essential part of human existence. I love having messy, broken characters find comfort in each other.

How do you approach world-building in your writing, particularly in genres like fantasy or science fiction?

I like to show the world gradually to the reader, where each book gets more and more in-depth and shows you parts of the world you didn't know were there. And of course, there are so many layers to it. As the readers are learning, so am I most of the time. I have yet to plan a world out before I write. As I work and research, pieces start to come together like a puzzle.

Are there any characters in the book that you relate to on a personal level?

Kaden is the character I relate to the most, especially at the time I was writing the story. A lot of her struggles were my struggles. But there are also parts of me in Finley. For him, it's like flipping a switch in my brain that also involves a lot of sugar. It's almost like I'm getting rid of the barrier in the brain that tells me not to say things. That's Finley.

What about the book surprised you the most?

There's a big plot point at the end of the book. When I started writing the story, I didn't know where it was headed, let alone how many books there would be. About halfway through I just knew there needed to be a big loss. It didn't shock me, but it shocked my friends and family.

Can you share a behind-the-scenes anecdote or interesting fact about the creation of this book?

The story is nothing like it was when I first started writing it. After high school, I spent a lot of time contemplating what interested me. The first thing that came to mind was how happy I was when I was writing in middle school. So, I started creating a story. That story revolved around hunters, witches, and werewolves. It was a bit of a mess. The only thing that connected them was Kaden. She was one of the main characters. After a while of trying to make it work, I knew it wasn't what I wanted, so I set it aside and didn't come back to it until about a year and a half later. Then it became Tormented Soul.

About the Author

Dylann Rhea is a writer and illustrator originally from Bergen County, New Jersey. Rhea writes books with magic, imagination, and on occasion creatures that don't speak. A *Reader's Favorite* recipient of a Five Star review, Rhea continues to doodle, daydream, and create with magic in her head and passion in her heart.